Dreams of an Orchid Flower

A novel by

Mahmoud Farra

It has become a burden

Table of Contents

Part One
A Man's Dreams

A thick, sucking swamp drags us under, slowing our steps and

tightening around our throats. History.

A monolith beneath whose weight we groan. We haul it behind us,

Shove it before us, bear it upon our backs.

Its iron chains bind our hands.

I am so very tired

I can no longer drag it. Each breath comes harder.

My life seeps away in the struggle to break it.

Who decreed that this stone defines us? Who claimed that without it,

Do we then have no future?

Today, I shattered a piece of my stone. I buried its hidden stories deep.

Now I laugh more freely,

and the sun spills brighter light upon me.

And still I am alive.

Chapter

ONE

"Looking for a woman in her thirties: beautiful, elegant, well-educated, cultured, and unattached."

Salah stopped typing. He thought for a moment, then glanced at his friend Hisham. They were the only two left in the office; everyone else had gone home. He read aloud what he had just written.

"Come on give me more details. What else should I put about the woman you're looking for in your dreams?"

Hisham smiled without lifting his head.
"Are you serious, Mr. Engineer? You're going to post this ad online?"

"Completely serious. I want to show you how incredible the internet is. It's not just a treasure trove of information it's a magic lamp! You make a wish, and it delivers. Now, tell me what qualities do you want in a woman?"

Hisham hesitated, then said quietly, "No, my friend. I'm married. I'm not playing this game."

"Coward."

"No—you're the crazy one. People will laugh at you."

"No one will know I posted the ad. I'll be nothing but an anonymous ghost. It's the idea that matters not the person."

"But in the end, you'll just be dealing with ghosts. Illusions. Nothing real."

"Except for the ideas. They're real, free, and unrestrained."

"I still don't understand the point. It sounds like a joke."

"Don't call it a joke. Finding the right woman is a serious matter. How else am I supposed to choose my life partner? It's always been a problem for me."

Hisham smirked. "And what exactly is the problem?"

"Simple I'm confused. There's no right way to choose. It's chaos. Everyone gives conflicting advice: 'Marry a tall woman so your kids won't be short.' 'Don't marry a very beautiful one too many admirers will cause trouble.' 'Pick someone moderately attractive but with good morals you'll be happy with her character.' 'Marry someone with average education so she won't boss you around.' 'Choose a poor girl she'll accept any life with you.' Or, 'Marry a rich one at least you won't have to worry about work and poverty.'"

"Why not just let love decide?" Hisham said with a laugh.

"My aunt always said: 'Never marry for love love blinds you to faults. Life's burdens will kill that love, and you'll see all the flaws you ignored. Then you'll regret it.' And that, my dear Hisham is the problem."

Hisham was only half-listening, still focused on his computer. "Are you even listening to me?" Salah asked, annoyed.

"Don't you have anything better to do than bother me with this nonsense?" Hisham replied.

"Nonsense? This is more important than anything you're doing. You just don't want to face the truth."

Hisham finally stopped working and turned his chair toward Salah, his eyes narrowing. "What? Why are you angry?" Salah teased. "Did I hit a nerve?"

"What truth am I avoiding? What are you implying?"

"Listen, I don't mean to offend you," Salah said, grinning, "but I don't think you're the happiest husband in the world."

Hisham replied angrily, "Arguing with my wife once doesn't mean I don't love her or that I'm unhappy."

"Stop dodging. It's me—Salah—your friend. Come on, tell me honestly: do you think you made the right choice when you married your wife?"

Hisham's face turned red. He shot Salah a reproachful look.

"Okay, let me rephrase: If you had the chance to choose again, would you still marry your wife or is there someone else you have in your mind you wish you had married?"

"You're wicked! I wish Amal were here to hear this!"

"You still don't get it. I'm not saying Amal is a bad woman God forbid. But maybe, just maybe, her life would have been happier with someone else. Or maybe your life would've been better with someone different. Do you understand the idea?"

"Why complicate things? Don't overthink it. Your job is to choose, and the rest is in God's hands."
Hisham went back to his work, but Salah wouldn't leave him alone.
"Tell me why did you choose *her* specifically, out of all the women in the world, to be your wife?"

Hisham replied with a sigh,
"She's my cousin."
"Then answer my question."

"What question?"

"Would you choose her again?"
"She's a good woman. I love her, and I'm satisfied with her. Don't make it too complicated."
"You mean she was simply available at the time. So, if she had been married, would you have married her sister, for example?"
"Maybe."
"You're depressing me."

"Why?"

"So, basically, any available, accessible woman you'd have married her? Don't you have any specific dreams? Personal desires? Particular traits in the woman you long for?"
"Of course I do. But where can I find her? And how long must I wait to meet her? And what if no such girl even exists?"
"Is it reasonable to throw ourselves at fate and the unknown and marry just anyone simply because the woman of our dreams isn't available at that moment? I think you should have waited and searched."
"Show us what you've got, genius. Go on wait and search for your superwoman."
"The problem is, I'm no genius with women, my friend. And you know that. That's why I came to you for help but you've let me down with your opinions."

Hisham sighed and said,
"If you don't like my opinions, then turn to the experiences of others around you."

He spun his chair and returned to his computer, irritated. But Salah circled around him from the other side of the office.

"Forget work for a moment. I'm honestly disappointed. I don't think a single person I know

actually *chose* their wife. All of them every single one had their wife forced upon them one way or another. Either she was a relative of theirs, or they met by coincidence. There's no scientific or civilized method to the process of choosing."

"Don't exhaust yourself. Whatever method you follow, the outcome is never guaranteed."

"I agree with you. Most of the time, the choice ends up being wrong for both parties, or at least for one of them."

"You have to be content with your choice. That's why they call it fate and destiny."

"So that's it? After centuries of scientific and technological advancement, do we return to fate and destiny? Isn't that disheartening?"

Hisham remained silent and did not comment. But Salah continued confidently, "As for me, I believe that my girl is definitely out there somewhere waiting for me. All I have to do is find the right path to her." Hisham said sarcastically, "I'm dying to know what she is like and what she looks like." And what do you want from her?"

"I also ask myself this question all the time. What do I want in the woman who will share my life? Her beauty? Her intelligence? Her sense of humor? Or her morals, culture, or perhaps her money?"

Salah thought for a moment, then turned to the screen, looked at the ad,

and typed: "Capable of establishing an intellectual and cultural

conversation."

Then he continued his discussion with Hisham:

"Then I wonder, what if all of these qualities were combined in one woman? What's the problem?"

"And do you think that if this woman were found, she would be satisfied with you? Would she agree to marry you?"
Salah laughed and said reproachfully:

"Today, I feel like you hate me and don't stand by me."

"Because you won't find a wife this way."

Salah smiled:
"But who said I want to get married? Who said I'm looking for a wife?"

Hisham turned around, surprised.

"And this ad?"
"I didn't write, 'I want a wife." I said, "I want a woman." That's different."

Hisham left his office and approached Salah angrily.

"And what about this pointless discussion all morning about the specifications of the ideal wife?"
"The problem, Salah, is that I don't want to commit myself to a wife. My problem is commitment."
"Commitment?"
"If I marry, I will stay faithful to my wife. But I love women all women. It's natural; it's who we, men, are. Loving women is in our nature. They're beautiful and captivating. I admit I'm weak and might not resist. I might cheat on my wife, even though I hate cheating."
"So, you want to be a womanizer."
"Me? No, no, I can't be a womanizer. You know me. I'm a coward and

clumsy with women." "Then there's nothing left for you but commitment

to your wife."

"But who am I to resist the charms of women? They say in France that the institution of marriage is based on three foundations: husband, wife, and lover or mistress. Cheating is a reality.
Statistics, sociologists. All historians agree." "Do you see me cheating on my

wife?" Salah smiled confidently and said:

"Every day."

"Me? You're a slanderer."

"Doesn't a beautiful woman on the street or in the market excite you?

Don't you imagine her in your arms?"

"So what? Is that cheating?"

"Yes, I think just thinking about a woman other than your wife is cheating."

"You're cruel. You can't stop yourself from thinking or imagining."

"That's what I've wanted to tell you since this morning. You're cheating on your wife involuntarily because you can't resist nature."

"So, what do you think the solution is? How do you intend to solve this problem?" "The solution is not to get married."

Hisham laughed, and his laughter grew louder. "What's wrong? What's making you laugh?"

"I thought you'd come up with a miraculous solution to marriage. Now you're running away from the problem, burying your head in the sand, and saying you won't get married."

"Of course, because I don't want to betray my partner's trust in me, and I won't hurt her feelings." "But that's not a solution. You can't live without a woman. Your hormones won't allow it."

"Here comes this ad. Look what I'm going to add:

"Capable of having an intimate sexual relationship without reservations."

"You're truly an idiot and a fool. Do you think you're in Paris? Do you think you'll find a woman in the Arab world who'll accept what you're offering her?"

"This is where the internet comes in, my dear. This is where the challenge of technology arises.
There must be a girl or woman who is searching for what I seek, sitting behind her computer, looking for me. A woman who yearns for freedom but is afraid to reveal what she truly wants. If Freud were alive today, he

might have recommended using the internet to address psychological issues. It's like a psychiatrist, before whom you're not ashamed to expose yourself and to whom you're not afraid to share your secrets, because your privacy is protected, your mask is on, and no one knows your identity."

Hisham looked at his watch and stood up.

"I'll let you search for the girl of your foolish dreams. As for me, there's a highly realistic girl. She's neither a ghost nor a fantasy. She's my wife, waiting for me at home for dinner. See you tomorrow at the office."

Hisham left the office, and Salah remained staring at the last sentence he'd written. He thought for a moment and decided to continue with this ad until the end. Then he smiled enthusiastically, determined to push it to its limits, so he typed:

'And without any obligations from either party.'

He felt relieved as he looked at what he'd typed in full:

Seeking a woman in her thirties who is beautiful, elegant, educated, and cultured. She should be single, able to engage in intellectual and cultural conversation, and open to establishing an intimate sexual relationship without reservations or obligations from either party.

He smiled as he placed his finger on the Enter button. The possible reactions crossed his mind, but he didn't hesitate; he pressed it with determination.

Chapter

Two

t'll be an amusing pastime, Salah thought as he sat back in his chair, his heart pounding. Minutes passed and nothing happened. Disappointed, his enthusiasm dimmed. He walked over to the fridge, grabbed something to eat, and returned to his desk to continue working on his engineering maps.

Then, the computer began announcing the arrival of responses from users in the chatroom:

Wounded Heart: "Make a reasonable request. "

Bint Al-Qamar: "Anything is possible except sex. Do you really think someone would just throw herself at you like that? "

Laila Al-Amriya: "Go look for a cultured prostitute. " Amwaj: "I support Laila Al-Amriya. "

Ahlam: "? "

Ibn Al-Jabal: "If you find this girl, give me her number. "

The Prince: "Where's the love? The emotion? The romance? You're a product of this materialistic era, where a man only thinks with his penis and only sees a woman's legs, breasts, and... "

Sweetheart: "Your dream girl? Not even in your dreams. "

Poet: "Blend Nancy Ajram, Huda Shaarawi, and Nelson Mandela and maybe you'll get what you want. "

Sami: "You're going to be waiting a long time. Grow up. " Ahlam: "?? "

Prisoner of Love: "You're bold, vulgar, and completely ill-mannered. "

The Prince: "I agree with Prisoner of Love and I'll add: you should be ashamed of yourself. " Ahlam: "?? "

Qamar Al-Layl: "The internet shouldn't be misused like this. "

The replies kept coming nonstop. He read them while working and chuckled to himself. Emails kept arriving in his inbox. Some were insulting, others mocking. But one caught his eye and stood out:

"Hello, Mr. Salah, I have the specifications you're looking for. "

He stopped working. He read the email carefully, then left it open. He turned away from it, trying not to give it too much thought. He went back to work, but found himself circling back to it. He couldn't help but return to it. He reread it and felt a sudden, unexpected thrill.

He noticed her name Ahlam among the other chat participants. But she hadn't written a comment just those two question marks.

He finished his work and rolled up the maps. Then he sat down again, staring at the open email for a long time. A dozen possibilities came to mind. The most likely one: it was a prank by some young guy. Deep down, he hadn't really expected a serious reply. He was almost sure everyone in that room had taken it as a joke.

He let the comments keep pouring in, said goodbye, and logged out of the chatroom. He paused at the email, closed it, deleted it, and emptied the trash.

Then he left the office and went home.

The next day, the first thing he did was open his inbox. There was another email from Ahlam:

"Hello, Mr. Salah, I have the specifications you requested. "

He felt elated, and his heart raced as he read it. But he didn't allow himself to be carried away by this feeling. He was a skeptical person, always cautious about such matters. He wasn't naive, nor was he easily deceived.

He stared at the email for a long time, wishing with all his heart that it was from a real girl. He carefully considered her words. The word *"Mr. "* caught his attention it conveyed politeness and tact. He noticed the extreme brevity of the message, which indicated great self-confidence. She had sent the message twice, clearly wanting to show determination, not fear or hesitation.

He hesitated before replying, then finally wrote:

"Thank you, Ahlam. Let me know when you're online so we can chat live. "

A minute passed before a reply came:

"I'm online now. "

Salah was confused; he hadn't expected such a quick response. He still had the feeling it might be a prank, but he was determined to play along. He could control the situation and had nothing to lose.

He opened the live chat program and saw Ahlam requesting to start a conversation. He clicked *"Accept. "*

"Hello, Mr. Salah. "
He felt a slight dread as he replied:
"Hello, Ahlam. "
He hesitated.

"Who are you? " "Ahlam. "

"I mean, do I know you? Have we met before? " "If I did, I wouldn't have agreed to contact you. " "Is Ahlam your real name? "

There was a delay in her response. "Does it matter? "

"No not right now, at least . "

"What do you do for a living, Mr. Salah? "

He liked the respectful tone, as well as her simple, concise questions. He hoped there was no trick, that the girl was real.

"My real job? "

"Of course—if you don't mind saying. "

"Why do you want to know? "

"To decide how I should interact with you. "

"She's no naive girl, " he thought. "She's intelligent and cultured. " He no longer minded being honest, as long as it didn't expose him.

"I work as an engineer for a company in Dubai. " "So I'm lucky. "

"Why? "

"Because I get to talk to someone like you. "

"She's good at charming men, " he thought. "Thank you. And what do you do? "

She didn't answer right away. Instead, she asked:

"Are you married? "

This irritated him and made him suspicious. He wondered if she might be one of the girls from the office, so he quickly reviewed each of them in his mind.

"No. And you? "

"I'll tell you everything about myself, Mr. Salah but not before I know more about you. Is that a problem? "

"Not at all. But could we drop the 'Mr.' title? " "I can't. Respect is essential, Mr. Salah. "

"Please? "

"Ok... Salah. "

Salah smiled. He liked her way of chatting it was delicate and feminine. "Are you handsome? "

Her sudden question surprised him. He laughed. "I don't know. But girls don't think I'm ugly. "

"I hope so. Do you have a clear picture of yourself? " "Yes. "

"Can you send it to me? "

"I'll look for it and send it to you later. " "I want it now. "

"Now? That isn't easy. I have to look through my files. " "Now. Please. "

"You're persistent. Okay, I'll try. Wait a moment. "

Salah quickly chose a photo of himself from his computer and sent it.

"You got it? "

"Yes. "

"What do you think? "

"I'm glad. Well, well, you are attractive. Girls must be falling in love with you. "

His heart pounded.

"I'm starting to like this girl. " "And you? Are you pretty? " "Yes. You'd like me. "

"Will you send me a picture? " "Not now. "

"Confident and self-assured. She wants to stay in control. " He admired that. She had every right to be cautious, but it also heightened his anxiety and unease. He felt like he was walking into a prank set up by his friends. While he hadn't told anyone in the office about the ad, Hisham knew about it he had been there the night it was published. Maybe he was behind this prank.

He paused and decided to test something. "How is Hisham? "

There was a delay. "Who's Hisham? "

 "Come on. I know this is a joke. I just want to know who you really are. Who's on the other side of this chat? Are you Hisham, aren't you? "

Another pause. He imagined his colleagues from the office were discussing what to reply.

 "It's clear you don't trust me. Did I say something that upset you? "

Salah didn't respond. Doubt had crept in, and he was no longer sure of anything. After all, what was he expecting?

 "I'm sorry, but it seems we won't continue. " Salah stared at the screen, uncertain and confused.
 "Well, it seems we won't be able to complete the introduction process. Unfortunately, I was starting to like you. Goodbye. "

The program announced Ahlam's exit from the chat.

Salah remained seated, staring at the final sentence. He felt sorry that the conversation had ended that way. But what else could he have done? What if it had all been a trick?

Damn the internet. You can never be sure who you're really dealing with.

He turned off his computer and convinced himself that he'd done the right thing.

Still, he was annoyed. He'd enjoyed the game, but regretted not discovering who was behind it.

That night, he couldn't get Ahlam out of his mind. Her ghost lingered with him. He felt torn between relief that he had avoided a trap and a lingering regret that he had let go of a rare and wonderful girl, someone hard to find.

The next day, Salah tried to act normally in the office. He watched Hisham from a distance, talked to him, and deliberately looked into his eyes. He didn't notice anything suspicious. Everything suggested that Hisham was innocent.

He also observed his other colleagues especially the girls but didn't detect anything odd in their behavior or their glances that might suggest they were part of a prank.

But Salah couldn't bear the suspicion for long. He had no choice but to confront Hisham openly. He told him everything that had happened.

 "A girl responded to your ad? "

"Tell me honestly are you behind this prank? "

Hisham laughed and denied any involvement, swearing several times that it wasn't him or anyone from the office. Salah believed him he had no other choice. Hisham was his friend, someone he trusted.

Was it a joke from one of his internet friends those "ghosts, " as he called them? Damn the internet! Was there truly no way to verify Ahlam's identity?

He spent most of the day at the construction site, distracted. Ahlam's ghost never left his mind, not for a moment. He couldn't forget her or her words. His heart pounded whenever he recalled them. He hid the reason for his anxiety and preoccupation from everyone.

Finally, his shift was over. He hurried home, eagerly checked his email, and examined it closely.

But to his disappointment, the message he was hoping for wasn't there. He stayed at his computer all evening, waiting. He didn't go out. A wave of depression washed over him.

He shouldn't have rushed to end the conversation he might have learned something about her... or whatever that was. If it were a game, he had to see it through to the end.

He opened her previous message and read it again and again. He thought about replying, asking her to come back to the chat room. But he held back. His pride wouldn't let him.

Still, her words echoed in his mind.

He weighed the risks and rewards and decided it was worth it. The unlikely gains he imagined were too tempting. He was willing to face the consequences.

He wrote:

"Ahlam, please return to the chatroom. I'm online now. "

He sent the message and sat at his desk, distracting himself by reviewing some designs. One eye was on the blueprints, the other on the screen. He waited a long time. Nothing appeared.

Should he send another message?

No. That would make him seem desperate, weak. It would diminish both her respect for him and his own. She might use it to her advantage, act coquettish and distant, and make him feel like a fool. No, he wouldn't message again. He hated people who said no when they meant yes.

Still, he wrote:

"Ahlam, I'm still online. If you can't log in tonight, please suggest a time that works for you. "

He regretted it the moment he hit send. It felt like begging. But he told himself the truth was worth it in the end.

He stayed up all night, depressed and disappointed, stung by wounded pride and a drop in self-confidence. He didn't even realize when he fell asleep on the couch beside his computer, the TV still on.

Suddenly, he woke up after midnight. Something startled him a flashing light on the screen and a familiar chime. The music announcing a new message. He sprang up.

There were several messages all from Ahlam. They had arrived one after the other. Each one said:

"I'm online now. "

He was confused. He checked the clock it was 2:00 a.m. The last message had come at 1:00. He was late.

He quickly opened the chat program. She wasn't there.

He waited. Still, she didn't appear. He cursed himself and sat fuming in front of the screen.

Suddenly, the screen flashed again, and the music played. Ahlam's name appeared in the chat window.

"Hello, Salah. "

A surge of joy swept through him at the sight of his name.

"Hello, Ahlam. "

"I'm so glad you wanted to talk again. I'm sorry I didn't respond to your first message I wasn't at the computer. "

He liked the warmth in her words. No teasing or hesitation. Still, he chose to be cautious.

"It's okay. I'm just glad you're still up. "

"I'm ready to stay up all night if it makes you happy. "

She's extraordinary, he thought. Can a woman be this gentle... this feminine?

"I'm sorry about last time. "

"Why? What happened last time? "

"For doubting you. Anyone in my place would've had doubts. "

"You're right, and I don't blame you. Tell me what can I do to erase the doubt? I don't want to lose you again. I'm pleased you reached out. "

"But you don't know me well enough. "

"I know you perfectly. "

"How? "

"From the ad. "

"What do you mean? The ad doesn't say anything about me. It just lists your supposed qualities. "

"The ad is also your mirror. "

"How so? "

"You're thoughtful, serious, full of life. You value freedom and independence. You hate restrictions. And you're disappointed in the girls around you. "

"How do you know all that? "

"If you'd found your dream girl, you wouldn't have turned to the internet. "

That's... scary.

"Are you married? " He asked after a pause.

"I was. "

"What happened? "

Another pause. The topic seemed to unsettle her. Fearing she might end the conversation, he quickly typed:

"I don't mean to pressure you. Don't answer if it's uncomfortable. But I'd love to know more about you. "

"It's okay. We got divorced. I have a five-year-old daughter. " "What caused the divorce? "

She was also late in replying. Perhaps he shouldn't have brought up that topic at least not now. He didn't want to drive her away. But then her answer came:

"Love. "

"I don't understand. "

"Love brings a man and a woman together. And love separates them. " "I still don't understand. Did he love another woman? "

"No, no. Not at all. He was very loyal. Why do you assume he hurt me?

Why not believe I was the one who broke him? You don't have to pity me. I'm not as weak as you might think. I'm made of steel, kneaded with hardness.
Salah laughed.

"You make me laugh. You really are a strange woman. " "Why? Because I'm trying to tell the truth? "

"I don't know if you're telling the truth or just saying something. But honestly, you're different. " "Your ad is just as strange and different. "

"I still don't understand why you left your husband. You say you loved him. " "Yes, very much. "

"Do you still love him? "

"Yes. "

"You're confusing me. "

"Why? Haven't I answered all your questions? "

"You have. But your clear answers have only made you more mysterious. " "Don't overthink it. Let time reveal the rest. "

"Do you have a job? " "Yes. "

"What do you do? " "I'll tell you later. " "When? "

"When we meet. "

His heart skipped a beat. "Do you want to meet? " "Don't you? "

 "Of course. Otherwise, what was the point of the ad? " "Set a time. "

His heart sank. He paused, hesitant, then typed:

"Will you abide by what I mentioned in the announcement? "

She didn't reply right away. "If you abide by it. "

Salah laughed at her boldness. He couldn't help but be impressed. She excited him, but he still feared it was all a prank. *Still, I'll take the risk,* he thought.

"What do you think of tomorrow night? " "Or what do you think of now? "

Salah was stunned. He glanced at his watch it was 3:00 a.m. "Are you crazy? "
"Yes. "

Salah laughed, but he sensed things were starting to take an unexpectedly serious turn. "But where could we meet now? Everything's closed in Dubai now. "

"The airport. In the cafeteria. "

Her answers came quickly and confidently. He felt a rush of excitement. He couldn't believe this was really happening.

"Why the airport? "
"A public place. A cafeteria that never closes. Travelers are coming and going. We can get lost among them. "
"Fine. I agree. "
"I'll meet you there in half an hour. " "How will I recognize you? "
"I'll recognize you. I have your photo. Now, hurry don't waste time. "

Salah jumped up, tore open his closet, and grabbed a special-occasion outfit. He dressed quickly. In the mirror, he saw that his beard had grown out. He hurried to the bathroom, shaved, splashed on his favorite cologne, and headed out of the house.

As I go to meet you, I walk in a dark tunnel, with only one direction and one end: you. In my heart, there is fear and longing. I've been searching for you since I was born, making my way toward the end of the tunnel, not knowing what lies beyond: heaven or hell?

Night had fully fallen over the city. The quiet, the glow of the streetlights, and the warm, humid air filled him with energy and joy. He got into his old car and looked around the inside, gathering scattered papers, discarding trash, and brushing off the seats. He checked the air conditioning. It was working. He wiped the windows clean, then sped away through the nearly empty streets.

For the first time, he unleashed his car.

But then a worrying thought slowed him down: *What if she's ugly?*

He tried to shake it off and focus on the road. Within minutes, he arrived at the airport. He parked, ready to step out but something made him hesitate.

His face grew hot.

What am I doing? This can't be true. How foolish I am. It must be a prank.

He grabbed a tissue and wiped the cold sweat from his brow and neck.

How did they manage to convince me to leave home at three in the morning to meet an unknown woman?

He rested his head on the steering wheel, worn out by the storm of thoughts in his mind.

How naïve. I've always considered myself thoughtful and cautious yet here I am, chasing an illusion called Ahlam.

He stayed in the car for several minutes, then finally stepped out and looked around, half- expecting to see a familiar face or vehicle.

What now? Should I go back?

He paced around the parking lot, then paused again.

It could be true. Maybe there is a girl waiting for me.

But what if she's ugly? Otherwise, why would she be so eager to meet? Beautiful women don't chase strangers online. Why would a gorgeous woman go out at this hour to meet someone she's never seen? And who is Salah, anyway, that a woman would leave her house at three in the morning for him?

Another, darker fear crept in:

What if this is a trap someone hiding, waiting to mock me?

A desperate idea struck him something to save face, just in case. He took out a piece of paper and wrote:

 "I've come to tell you that I've uncovered your plot. "

He slipped the paper into his pocket, feeling more reassured. This way, he made it clear to them that he had seen through their deception and wasn't fooled by their trick.

He glanced anxiously at his watch. He had to make a decision overthinking was draining him. Every thought and argument in his mind condemned the whole thing and urged him to go back home. Except for one: *"What if Ahlam is waiting for me inside? "* That single thought overpowered all the others. He stepped into the airport building.

He stood by the door, watching the arriving passengers and those waiting to greet them. There were only a few people, dragging their bags and moving in all directions. He walked cautiously toward the cafeteria, his eyes scanning every face. At any moment, he expected to recognize Someone perhaps one of his friends and the game would be over. But the unfamiliar faces reassured him. No one here knew him.

He continued walking, hesitant, his footsteps echoing in the nearly empty airport. The closer he got to the cafeteria, the faster his heart beat. He was walking toward the unknown.

The cafeteria was a large hall. Most of the tables were empty. A small family a man, a woman, and two children sat together, laughing as they ate cake and sipped tea. Two men occupied another table, drinking coffee. A man slept soundly in a leather chair, his head tilted back, his hand resting on his bag. A sense of calm and serenity filled the place.

In a remote, secluded corner, a young woman sat alone, holding a cup of coffee. He looked at her closely she was smiling at him. He walked toward her with confidence, then suddenly hesitated. A wave of nausea rose in his stomach. He paused, then slowly approached her table, stopping at the one next to hers. She was so beautiful that he didn't dare believe she could be the one waiting for him. He froze, his knees shaking.

But the woman stood up and smiled. More beautiful than a fashion model that was his first impression. She stepped closer and extended her hand.

"Hello, Salah. I'm Ahlam. "

He reached out and took her hand. It was soft, relaxed in his palm, completely surrendered to his touch. He was afraid to press too hard and hurt her. A wave of ecstasy swept over him as he inhaled her scent. She leaned in and kissed him on both cheeks. He nearly fainted when her warm lips touched his skin.

"Here, sit down, " she said reassuringly.

Salah slumped into his seat, asking himself what on earth he was doing there.

"This is your cup, " she said, pointing to another coffee cup on the table. "You like coffee, don't you? "

 "Yes, yes. Thank you. "

He held the cup while she gazed into his eyes. "How are you? "

"Fine. "

He didn't know where to look. He stole a glance at her, forcing a polite smile. She was still staring at him, her eyes bright and radiant.

He finally found the courage to look her directly in the eye. He still couldn't believe that this beautiful, elegant woman with soft chestnut hair and mesmerizing eyes was here for him.

Silently, he took a sip from the cup. She did the same. His nerves began to calm. He took another sip, and so did she. They were both silent, locked in each other's gaze. She smiled, and he smiled back. She tried to stifle a laugh. He smiled awkwardly, watching her cup tremble in her hand, almost slipping. He reached to help, but nearly spilled his own. She burst into laughter. He smiled, embarrassed, and her laughter infected him. She tried in vain to stop, covering her face, but she couldn't. Tears welled up in her eyes.

Eventually, she calmed down.

"Sorry… I don't know what came over me. "

Salah handed her a tissue. She wiped her tears. He felt relieved—his thoughts settled, and her tension faded.

"How are you now? " he asked, feeling his confidence return.
"Fine. Forgive me, Salah, that's never happened to me before. " "Don't worry. Laughing helped—it eased my tension. "
"Why do you have tension? Are you disappointed in me? " "Are you kidding? I'm disappointed in myself. "
"So now you're sure I wasn't deceiving you? "
"The truth is, I doubted it. until you held my hand. I'm ashamed of myself. "
 "Doubt is natural and necessary. Otherwise, you'd be naive. " "You're magnificent. I didn't expect that. "

She blushed and smiled. "Thank you. "

"Why did you come? "
 "What do you mean? "
"What made you respond to the ad? "

She smiled gently and said,

"Because I fit the criteria. "

"You don't need the internet to find a man. I'm sure if you pointed to that guy sitting over there, he'd come crawling to you. "

She laughed and glanced toward the man he'd mentioned, then looked back at him. "I liked your ad. That's all. "

"Where are you from? "

"Does it really matter where I'm from or what I do? "

 "You said you'd tell me later. "

"Okay... I'll tell you later. "

 " Can I guess? "

Ahlam smiled and leaned back in her chair. "Okay. Let's see how good you are at guessing. "

Salah smiled and examined her features her face, her hair, her clothes. "May I see your hands? "

"Are you going to read my palm? " she teased, laughing, and held out her hands. He hesitated, but she gently placed them in his. He felt their softness and warmth. Her openness and ease made him feel at peace. Still, he couldn't meet her eyes, afraid his gaze might reveal the desire she'd awakened in him.

His smile faded, and silence fell. He closed his eyes, feeling her warmth travel from her hands into his body. He could hear his own heartbeat racing. He felt a strong urge to cry. He quickly opened his eyes and looked at her. Her smile had vanished, too. She was staring at him, her gaze searching, and she squeezed his hands.

"Did you find anything? " she asked softly.

"I don't think you work. These hands. they can't belong to a working woman. " He tried to pull his hands away, but she held on tight.

"Keep them there, please. It gives me comfort and reassurance. "

He felt the heat in his hands and cheeks. He squeezed her hands and asked, "Are you real? "

She laughed, squeezing his hands back. "Why do you say that? "

"You can't be anything but a dream. " "Thank you. "

"Is your name really Ahlam? " "Does that matter? "

"No, what matters is you. "

Ahlam got up from her seat and picked up her purse. "May I go to the bathroom? "

He smiled and said, "No. "

She looked at him, laughing in surprise. "No? Why? "

"I don't want you to leave me. "

She sat back down, smiling. Salah looked at her in surprise. "I was joking, " he said

"I won't go if it bothers you. "

Salah laughed.

"You're amazing. Go ahead. "

Ahlam smiled, picked up her purse, and stood up again. She walked toward the bathrooms. He watched her as she walked away. Tall, with a beautifully proportioned body and stunning legs draped beneath a tight skirt that barely covered her knees. Her graceful walk conveyed sophistication, and her elegant attire exuded taste. Everything about her suggested he was dreaming.

She suddenly stopped, then turned around again.

"Will you walk with me to the bathroom? I'd be more comfortable if you came along. "

 "With pleasure, " he said, rising from his seat. Then he added, laughing, "Were you afraid I might run away? "

She paused and looked at him, surprised by the question. "Maybe, " she said.

She took his hand and intertwined her fingers with his. He didn't feel awkward walking beside her. He felt comfortable and free, as if he'd known her for a long time. He walked silently beside her. He didn't feel the need to speak or act a certain way.

She clung to his arm with both of hers like a child holding her father, or like a lover who didn't want to let go of her beloved. The scent of her perfume wafted through the air, and he felt an intense excitement.

They reached a long corridor leading to a door that concealed both the men's and women's bathrooms. They walked down the corridor until they reached the door at the end. He let go of her arm and opened it for her to pass, but she grabbed his hands and pulled him with her behind the door. She cupped his face with both hands and planted a long, passionate kiss on his lips as she pressed her body against his.

Her sudden movement startled him. His heartbeat raced as he wraps his arms around her tightly, his lips resting on her neck, enjoying the warmth of her breath on his chest. She pushes him against the bathroom door, pressing her whole body into him. He leans back, feeling trapped, and gives in to her advances. He allows her to unbutton his shirt and trace her fingers across his chest. He felt every part of her pressed against him, almost hearing her heartbeat in sync with his own. A wave of desire crashes over him, nearing climax until they hear footsteps outside in the corridor.

She quickly pulled away and slipped into the women's bathroom. He stood there for a few seconds, panting and sweating, then gathered himself and rushed into the men's bathroom. He stood in the middle of the room, breathing heavily. He looked at himself in the mirror—his face was red and tense. His clothes were disheveled, as if he'd just been in a fight. He straightened his clothes and hair, washed his face with cold water, dried it, and then took a deep breath to steady himself. He glanced one last time at the mirror and exited the bathroom.

She wasn't waiting by the door. He walked down the long corridor she wasn't there either. He went back to the cafeteria, but their table was empty. He stood there, confused, scanning the area in every direction. He hurried through the airport hallways, pushing through the crowd, looking everywhere.

Where did she go? Could she really have vanished? The idea unsettled him. He had to find her he might never get another chance.

He rushed back toward the bathrooms and found her standing at the entrance to the corridor. He felt life return to his body. He walked toward her, panting, trying to catch his breath.

"I'm sorry for what happened. I feel so embarrassed. "
Ahlam said.
He smiled and took her hand, still catching his breath.
"I'm the one who would've been sorry if I hadn't found you. I searched the whole airport for you. "
"I couldn't control myself when you held my hand. I feel so embarrassed. "

She looked around, as if scanning her surroundings. Then, as if reading his mind, she asked with a sly smile,

 "What are you thinking? "

He replied, carefully choosing his words,

"If only we could go somewhere more private. "

He watched the effect of his words on her face. Her eyes locked onto his, and without hesitation, she answered with enthusiasm,

"I agree. "

Her immediate response surprised him.

"Okay... let's set an appointment. How about the weekend? "

She interrupted him firmly,

 "Now. I want you now. "

In front of him stood a lioness, ready to devour him alive. She looked at him with hungry eyes. He glanced at his watch four in the morning. He thought about his work schedule for the next day and hesitated.

She approached him, kissed his cheek like a little girl, and whispered in his ear,

 "Now. "

He looked at his watch again, still unsure. "Now, please. "

He forgot about work and fear. A rush of adventure overcame him. He took her hand and led her toward the exit.

 "Okay... where would you like to go? "

he asked. "Jebel Ali Hotel, "

she replied without hesitation.

He stopped and looked at her, surprised, but she continued with a smile,

"I booked a room under your name. "

"When did that happen? "
he asked, shocked.
"While you were in the bathroom, I went to the front desk and made the reservation. "
"But how did you know I'd say yes? "
"I knew you wouldn't disappoint me. "

It was past four in the morning. Night still draped over the city. Salah got into the car, and Ahlam sat beside him.

Who would've thought that just an hour ago, a woman this beautiful would be sitting next to me? Who would believe we're going to a hotel to have sex?

He looked at her as she leaned her head back, eyes closed, hair fluttering in the breeze. Her dress had fallen. He stole glances at her, thinking,

"This can't be real. "

The car sped down the highway. Silence and stillness cloaked the city. It was still asleep.

Ahlam leaned toward him as he wrapped his arm around her shoulders. She pressed against him and rested her head on his shoulder. The scent of her perfume and hair filled his senses, making him feel high and refreshed. Her dress slipped lower, but she didn't care. She took his hand and placed it on her leg. Heat surged through his body. He slowed the car and tried to pull his hand away, but in a sudden move, she shifted and pounced on his lips, sucking them.

He clenched the steering wheel tightly, fearing he would lose control. She moved from his lips to his chest and neck, kissing him while trying to unbutton his shirt. He lost control of the wheel.

The car started to swerve. He yelled for her to stop her face was blocking his view but she ignored him. His efforts to calm her down failed. He slammed on the brakes. The car veered off the main road, onto the sand, and plunged into darkness. It rocked wildly before coming to a stop. A cloud of dust enveloped the car, hiding everything.

Darkness surrounded them. He couldn't see outside. He turned to her. She was still panting with excitement and intensity, looking at him intently, her lips wet.

"What's the matter with you? " he asked angrily. "Are you okay? "

She didn't answer but lunged at his lips again. She climbed over the console and wedged herself between him and the steering wheel. She wrapped her arms around his head, restraining his movements and making him completely captive.

His anger blended with desire. He threw back his head and closed his eyes, his nose pressed against her breasts, his tongue tasting the sweat on her neck. Overwhelmed by her passionate kisses, he gave in.

When she finally calmed down and her fervor subsided, she still sat astride him in the seat, his head resting on her chest, his body frozen. Minutes passed as they both panted, droplets of sweat falling from her brow onto his skin. At last, she moved back, rose from his lap, and calmly.

returned to her own seat. She straightened her clothes, then turned to him. In her eyes lingered the flutter of a child who knows she's done wrong and braces for the inevitable scolding.

Salah stared at her in disbelief, feeling a rush of fear and anger tighten his chest. He said nothing; instead, he yanked open the car door so forcefully that dust billowed in. He tumbled out and slammed the door shut behind him.

He paced around the car, inspecting the tires and underside for damage. Sand covered every surface, but the tires were intact, and there was no dent in the body. Leaning his back against the door, he tried to steady his breath, piece together what had just happened, and find a way out of this madness. The nearest streetlights glowed about a dozen meters away.

Ahlam climbed out of the car and strolled to his side. She leaned against the fender, wrapping herself coquettishly around him. He recoiled, scowling, and then turned to her, voice shaking, "Are you insane? You nearly got us killed! What were you thinking? "

She said nothing, tears brimming, her gaze fixed on him. He pressed on, anger rising, "What's wrong with you? You were calm, reasonable then suddenly you became a sexual maniac! "

In muffled sobs, she began to speak, but he could not catch her words. He moved closer, and at last her tears fell freely.

 "What are you saying? "

he demanded.

She dabbed her cheeks and found her voice.

 "I'm saying it's your fault, not mine, "

she whispered, a rueful smile tugging at her lips. "I wasn't the one driving recklessly you were. You nearly killed us both. Yet...I forgive you. "

Without another word, she climbed back in. He bellowed after her,

 "You are crazy! "

He slammed into the driver's seat and roared away, then skidded to a halt on the roadside, utterly bewildered. His thoughts swirled: terror at the unknown danger, and a heady thrill unlike anything he'd ever known.

Ahlam turned to him, voice soft,

"Look at us an hour ago we'd never met, and now we've done everything lovers do: made love...and fought. Isn't that beautiful? "

Her words only fueled his fury. He remained silent, head spinning, then finally started the engine without looking at her. "We'd better go back the way we came. "

She watched him drive in pensive silence. Minutes passed before she spoke again, as though picking up an earlier thread:

"This is why we broke up. "

He glared at her. "What? "

"You asked why my husband and I separated. Now I'm answering. "

He scoffed,

"Honestly, I excuse him and I don't blame him. "

Her voice trembled with tears and anger. "Why? "

He sneered,

"Who would've put up with you? "

She bit her lip. "You're cruel...But I forgive you, because I know you're angry. "

She wiped away her tears. "I'm not asking you to marry me. You're the one who placed the ad I only fulfilled its terms. "

He remained silent, steering through the deserted highway.

She leaned forward, reproach in her voice:

"You're evading your own ad. "

She glanced at him with a wry smile, tears still in her eyes:

"Now I demand that you fulfill it. "

He burst into laughter. "You're one of a kind. What are you made of? "

She feigned sternness. "A mixture of girls' mischief and tenderness. "

Salah continued laughing. There was something about her he couldn't resist. She continued, wiping her tears:

"As for you, you're made of men's coarseness and cruelty. "

He pulled over to the roadside, still laughing. He handed her a tissue, and she wiped her cheeks and nose.

When you cried, the world collapsed. The storms fell silent, the sun went out, the cosmos dimmed, the planets stopped their dance, and poems lost their souls.

Smile bring back the light to my skies, for the galaxies have not yet finished their waltz.

He turned to her, his voice gentle. "I felt terrified there. What you did took me entirely by surprise. I never expected it. It made me lose my temper. However, I apologize for what I said.

She smiled and looked down, like a child seeking forgiveness. "Okay. I accept your apology. "

"Your behavior…it's so unexpected. "

"That's me. "

"Do you still want to go to the hotel? "

"Of course! "

Her exclamation rang with joy.

He hesitated. "I'm still afraid of what you might drag me into. "

She leaned forward, eyes bright. "You won't regret it. I'll be gentle…and you won't even notice me. Come on, let's go. "

She hummed softly as he started the engine. He smiled at her, then eased the car back onto the road.

By the time they reached the Jebel Ali Hotel, dawn was painting the sky with pale light. A valet ran forward, stunned to see a car covered in dust even the windshield was nearly opaque, except for a triangle cleared on the driver's side.

His amazement deepened when he opened the door and Ahlam stepped out, her smile radiant.

Her hair was tousled into a glorious mess, her skirt slightly torn, her once-pristine clothes rumpled. Salah, for his part, was equally disheveled: his shirt's top buttons were undone, and a fine layer of sand coated his hair and face.

"Why is he staring at us like that? "

Ahlam asked innocently. Salah grinned,

"He's simply dazzled by your beauty. "

She nudged him playfully with her elbow, a soft laugh escaping her lips.

They entered the hotel lobby. It was empty even the reception desk was unmanned. Soft music drifted from the corners. Everything was calm and serene.

The receptionist appeared and looked at them in surprise. "Hello, are you okay? What happened? "

 "A tire burst, "

Salah replied, glancing at Ahlam and smiling. "But we're fine. "

She handed them the room key and directed them to the elevator. They remained silent the entire way to the room. Salah opened the door, and they stepped inside. Ahlam rushed to the window to look out at the sea. The room was beautiful, with a view overlooking the beach.

"It's not my habit to stay in hotels with a beauty like you, "
Salah said, standing beside her as they watched the sea and the dawn light.
"Let's take a shower, "
he said, brushing the dust from his clothes and hair. "What? "
she wondered, incredulous. "Now? "
She pushed him onto the bed. "You want me to wait until you take a shower? "

She pulled him toward her without giving him a chance to object not that he wanted to. He held her close and let her take the lead. He watched as she undressed and lay naked before him, inviting him with a finger to join her. They spent the entire morning in bed. Their strength was drained, their bodies breathless with exhaustion but she was insatiable. She gave him no time to rest or catch his breath until he was utterly spent, unable to move. He lay on his back, eyes closed. But she wasn't done.

"I'm not finished with you yet. " "Let me catch my breath. "   "You still want me, don't you? "
"Not now. Later. "

She shook him roughly.

"Get up, you lazy man. I'm right here in front of you. Look at me. Everything you see is yours take the opportunity. "

Her words stirred his desire once more. "You're merciless, "he said.

"I'm the opportunity that won't come again. I'll take you to distant horizons and help you discover new dimensions of pleasure. I'll immerse myself in your body and let you sail in mine. I love seeing you breathe your last in my arms. "

He looked at her, amazed by her words. She smiled.

"You'll see this will be the greatest adventure you've ever had. "

She didn't let him surrender. So, he gave himself to her. She played with his body, shaping it in strange and complex ways he hadn't known were possible, until he could no longer tell where his hands or feet were. She was like an engineer, mapping their positions with the precision of a master. He found himself entering a strange and magical world. By the time she was done, he lay like a corpse. They remained in each other's arms, panting and sweating. When their breathing calmed, she whispered in his ear. "Thank you. "

He laughed. "Did I meet the conditions of the ad? " "With distinction. "

She noticed the astonishment in his eyes.

"Why are you looking at me like that? You must be thinking this woman is a whore. " "No, no, I never thought that. "

She laughed, her face flushing with embarrassment, then said shyly, "Of course you did. I'm sometimes shocked by what I do myself. But compared to others, I'm without a doubt more daring, more experienced, and more professional. "

"Still, I wonder how you know all of this. "

She smiled and kissed him, "Now I need a hot shower. "

She jumped out of bed and went into the bathroom. He could hear her singing in the shower. He stayed in bed, reflecting in disbelief on the adventure of the past few hours.

He noticed her purse on the table by the bed. Curiosity got the better of him. He got out of bed and stood beside the table, hesitating. Should he open it and check her ID? He had to know who she was. The bathroom door was shut, and the sounds of running water and her singing were clearly audible.

He quietly unzipped the purse, eyes on the bathroom door. After a pause to make sure she was still occupied, he peeked inside. There was nothing significant just cosmetics, a bottle of perfume marked "999, "and a wad of cash. No identification. He was about to close the purse when he noticed something at the bottom. He reached out and saw that it was a solid object. He felt it without taking it out. It was a knife. He quickly pulled his hand out, zipped the purse closed, put it back in place, and returned to bed.

He tried hard to hide his unease as Ahlam emerged cheerfully, wearing a bathrobe, her hair wrapped in a towel. She lay beside him and began stroking his hair. He gently pushed her hand away.

"Aren't you tired? I wonder what you're made of. "
"Almond and honey. "
"I think you're made of cotton candy. "

Her cheeks flushed, and her smile widened. "I appreciate your sweetness. Thank you. "

"What about me? What am I made of? "

Her eyes examined his face, studying him intently. "I don't know. I haven't tasted all of you yet. "

 "Oh my God — you devoured me from head to toe. There's nothing left of me for you to taste! "

"We'll see. The day's still young. "

"You are a vampire. "

He jumped out of bed and went to the bathroom.

He sat in the tub and turned on the hot water, his mind preoccupied with the knife.

"It's only natural she'd carry something to defend herself. After all, she doesn't know me. "

The thought calmed him; he closed his eyes.

"Or maybe she's crazy... or a murderer. "

He didn't like that thought and pushed it away. But he concluded:

"I have to be careful. "

His whole body relaxed in the water. He no longer wanted to get out. But hunger forced him to open his eyes and finish his bath. He got out quickly to tell her he was hungry.

She was sitting there in her robe, her hair in a ponytail, with a table of breakfast in front of her.

"I was just about to ask you to order us some food. "
"I knew you would. " "You're amazing. "

She laughed, "I can always tell what's on your mind. "

They sat down to eat. He couldn't help but watch her. She looked at him questioningly: "Why are you looking at me like that? "

"You're much prettier without makeup. "

He continued to eat, but suddenly he reached out and softly brushed his hand over her face, feeling her skin and then her hair. She blushed and whispered, "Why did you do that? "

"I just wanted to be sure you're not a ghost. "

She kissed his hand. "Well, I'm not, I'm real, " she replied. She slowly ran her hand over his face.

"I'm afraid you might be the ghost. Tell me, what prompted you to publish the ad? " "Fun and curiosity. "

Ahlam laughed.

"No, it's not just for fun. It's much more than that, and don't tell me it was because you were bored. "

"Then what could it be? "

"It's honesty if you don't know. Transparency. You're not a deceiver and you're not good at deceiving. "

"What makes you think so? "

"Loneliness. It makes you think, meditate, and reflect. How long have you been in Dubai? " "I came for work two years ago. "

"See? It's loneliness and alienation. I've felt it too. "

"My friend Hisham also said the desert heat affects my balance. Honestly, I was just testing the internet's capabilities. "

"And what did you find? "

"It's really like Aladdin's lamp. I didn't expect a jinni to appear when I rubbed it but you did. " Ahlam didn't reply. She continued eating in silence. Salah looked at his watch.

"I'm supposed to be at work now. " He picked up his phone. "I have to call and tell them I'll be absent today. "

All his attempts to request a day off failed. Work was at a standstill, and he had to be at the construction sites because the workers were waiting for him.

"How will you go to work if you haven't slept all night? "

"Don't worry about me. You go to sleep. I'll try to show my face at work, then be back as soon as possible. "

"But you're exhausted. "

"It's because of you and your madness. "

He kissed her as he tucked her into bed. "I'll try not to be late. "

Then he left in a hurry.

Chapter

Three

Despite everything he'd been through the night before, Salah felt excited, happy, and energetic. His entire life stood on one side, and the past few hours on the other.

He got into the car and headed to work. He was eager to tell Hisham what had happened. Of course, he wouldn't tell him everything just enough to help him get a day off.

But he didn't expect Hisham's reaction. It was completely unexpected.

"Are you out of your mind? How did you get yourself tangled up with this stranger? What do you *really* know about her? Nothing! You don't know who she is or who might be pulling her strings. For all you know, she could drag you into something you'll never crawl out of. Are you that reckless? "

Salah opened his mouth, but Hisham didn't give him the chance.

"A woman like the one you've described wouldn't throw herself at a man unless she was hiding.

Something maybe she's part of a prostitution ring, human trafficking, drugs or something even worse. "

"She's not like that, Hisham. Believe me she's different. Sophisticated. Cultured. Sensitive. "

Hisham burst into loud, mocking laughter.

"Listen to yourself! She gave herself to you without knowing you. Does that sound like something a sane woman would do? "

Salah's silence was answer enough. The truth was, Hisham's words stung because they made sense. Too much sense. Even Salah couldn't fully convince himself that she was the balanced, dignified woman he wanted to believe in.

Hisham leaned forward, his voice dropping but his eyes sharp.

"This kind of woman is trouble. Either she's running from a problem, from her husband or she's something much darker a spy, a killer, a prostitute. Did that ever occur to you? Haven't you heard of escort girls online? Beautiful, educated, refined even with university degrees selling themselves for thousands a night. This woman fits that profile perfectly. And you know what's coming next? If you don't pay… God help you. "

The room felt smaller. Salah could hear his own breathing. Hisham's words wouldn't stop echoing in his head.

"Where is she now? " "In the hotel. "
"You left her alone in the hotel? Go and get rid of her immediately. "

He lowered his voice, serious and cold:

"Listen, Salah, I'm not joking. This is serious, and I don't know how you could've been so reckless. Don't worry about work today. Leave it to me. I'll cover your shift at the site, and I'll find someone to cover me in the office. As for you, go to that hotel right now. Don't wait. Give her what she wants, and send her away. End it. "

Salah left the office frustrated, disappointed, and confused. He felt a headache creeping in and was about to lose his balance. He didn't like what Hisham had said didn't want to believe it but the seeds of doubt had definitely been planted.

He stood in front of his car, frozen in hesitation.

Could it really be that Ahlam was doing this for money?

How could he even offer her money? Was it possible that all the laughter, the tears, the emotions everything had been nothing more than part of her job?

Is that why she never told me what she does?

Is that why she said, "I'll tell you later "? Why later?

Because later, she'd be sure I was too far in to walk away. How had he not seen it?

Now that he was already entangled, she could simply tell him she'd fulfilled the contract and then demand payment.

"But what if she's telling the truth?

What if everything she'd said was genuine? Then how would it look if he offered her money for her... "services'? "

He stood there, torn, time pressing in on him like a weight. He had to decide. And then, an idea came simple, elegant, and safe.

A gift.

A gift was the sophisticated solution. If she saw herself as a service provider, she could take it as payment. If she weren't, she might take it as a romantic gesture.

Either way, it would spare him the humiliation. He liked the idea.

Driving to a nearby market, he stepped into a small jewelry shop. "I'm looking for a gold ring, " he told the clerk. "It's a gift. "

The man pulled out a tray, displaying several rings at different prices. Salah hesitated, unsure how much to spend.

Sensing his uncertainty, the clerk offered a knowing smile. "Sometimes, the value of a gift depends on how close we are to the person and how much they mean to us. Is it for someone close? "

No, Salah thought. "Is she dear to you? "

She's just a stranger I met today.

The clerk picked up the cheapest ring. "This one should do. "

Salah held it, turning it between his fingers. Then a faint smile crossed his lips. "I'll take that one the more expensive one. "

He got into his car and drove toward the hotel, anxiety gnawing at him as conflicting thoughts battled in his mind. Over and over, he replayed the day's events, analyzing her every word and gesture, measuring them against Hisham's doubts. He felt utterly exhausted but the thought of getting rid of her, of ending this whole affair, brought him a sense of relief.

.When he arrived, he went straight to the room. He opened the door it was dark. She was still asleep, he guessed. He entered quietly and closed the door behind him. Feeling his way in the darkness, he moved toward the bed and waited for his eyes to adjust. Bumping into the mattress, he sat on the edge and ran his hand over the sheets, trying to find her. But the bed was empty. He quickly stood up and turned on the light. The room was empty. He hurried to the bathroom the tub was dry. Panic set in. His suspicions grew, echoing Hisham's. There was no sign of her. He picked up the phone and called the front desk. No one had seen her.

He searched the room under the bed, behind the curtains. Her bathrobe was on the bed. He opened the closet and saw her clothes still hanging, her purse untouched. Relief washed over him. She hadn't left. But the worry stayed where could she be? All her belongings were still there, even her underwear. She couldn't have gone far without clothes. Then he heard a faint voice coming from the bathroom. He listened closely singing? But there was no one in there. He moved toward the door, heart pounding. The sound grew clearer singing, soft and strange. He slowly opened the door and found her. Ahlam was sitting on the floor behind the door, naked, her head leaning against the wall, eyes closed, singing softly.

 "Tick, tick, tick... Um Suleiman. "

He froze. "Ahlam? Why are you here like this here? "She didn't open her eyes or acknowledge him. She kept singing, as if he didn't exist.

Water dripped from her soaked body. Her phone lay on the floor. She had her legs crossed, hands tucked between them, clutching something shiny.

"What's that in your hand? "

She crossed her legs tighter to hide it. He noticed red stains in the water around her. "Give it to me, Ahlam, "he said firmly.

She tightened her grip but continued singing.

Fearfully, he reached out and gently pried her legs apart. She didn't resist. He opened her hands. She was holding a knife.

He recoiled in shock.

"What are you doing?! "

She gave a weak, sarcastic smile. "Masturbating. "

He carefully pulled the knife from her hand. "Are you out of your mind? "

He lifted her off the floor and carried her in his arms. She wrapped her arms around his neck and rested her head on his chest.

"Are you angry with me? "
she asked.
"I'm not angry, Ahlam. I'm worried about you. "
"Why would you be? "

He laid her on the bed and covered her with the sheet. Then he sat beside her.

"Tell me what it is? What's wrong? "

She pulled the sheet over her head and didn't answer. "I want to help you. Tell me what can I do? "

She peeked out from under the covers. "We're sinning, aren't we? "

The question blindsided him. He froze, unsure how to answer.

"I can't help it, "she went on. "But I'm sure it's not my fault. There's something wrong with me how I'm made. You feel it, don't you? My body's not like other women's... but how would you know? You're too kind. I guess you've never been with anyone before me, so you have no one to compare to. "
"Calm down, "Salah said, brushing her hair back with his hand. "Hold me. Please. "

He leaned in to embrace her, but she bit his lip hard.

Salah shoved her away.

"What's wrong with you? Are you sick? You're crazy... obsessed. "

Ahlam slipped beneath the covers, pulling them over herself until she vanished completely.

He began pacing the room, anger and confusion churning inside him. He heard her crying, but it no longer touched him. His mind was made up he had to get rid of her.

Suddenly, her phone rang. The sound came from the bathroom.

Ahlam bolted out from under the covers like a wild animal and dashed inside, slamming the door.

Salah crept closer, straining to hear.

Her voice came through excited, loud, laughing and then that strange, lilting murmur again: "Tick, tick, tick... Um Suleiman. "

She flung the door open suddenly and caught him listening. Beaming, she pointed at the phone. "It's my daughter! "

She pressed the receiver to his ear and covered his mouth with her hand. On the other end, he heard a child singing. He handed her the phone and left the bathroom, sitting on the edge of the bed. His nerves began to calm. It seemed she'd snapped back to normal.

She came out a moment later still naked and climbed onto the bed, jumping up and down like a child. She was radiant, laughing, glowing with joy.

"What time is it? " she asked. "Twelve. "
"We still have time, " she chirped.

But Salah responded in a calm, flat voice without looking at her. "I think we should part ways. "

Ahlam froze mid-jump and looked at him carefully. His tone was calm, but his expression was serious and stern.

She approached him slowly, hugged him, and stroked his hair and neck.

"I'm sorry… for everything. Don't judge me too harshly. I know I scared you. But it was all just too much for me. "
"I'm tired of your surprises. "

She slid her fingers down his shirt and across his chest. He didn't stop her or perhaps, he didn't want to.

"I'll make it up to you. I promise. You won't regret it. "

He felt her lips on his neck, her hot breath tickling his skin.

"I can't see what connects us, " he said. "We have nothing in common, and we know nothing about each other. "
"We know everything, " she whispered in his ear. "I know that I enjoy myself with you, and I know that you enjoy yourself with me too—and that's enough. At least for me. "

He tried to recall Hisham's words and said, in a serious effort to dismiss her: "I think it's best for both of us to… "

He couldn't continue couldn't resist the lust of her lips, the teasing dance of her fingers, or the fiery breath blowing into his ear, burning away every one of Hisham's warnings.

"Should I continue, " she murmured, "or do you want me to stop? "

He swept her into his arms and carried her to the bed.

Damn Hisham and his warnings.

Hours later, Salah stood by the window, gazing out at the sea.

"You look bad-tempered, " she said. "Haven't you forgiven me yet? " "I'm angry with myself. "

She laughed. "I understand you being angry at me but why at yourself? "

"I can't stop myself from being swept away by your madness... your whims. And I can't understand you. You're a mystery to me. "
"I'm mysterious? " She tilted her head. "On the contrary, I've been honest with you from the start. "

She climbed onto the bed, standing tall and naked, arms raised high.

"See this? Naked on the outside, transparent on the inside. I'm not hiding anything from you. " He looked at her, smiled faintly, and said nothing.

She hopped down and headed for the bathroom. "Let's take a shower, then sleep. I'm exhausted. "

 "I'm sleepy too as if I haven't slept in a year. "

They slipped under the covers and soon drifted off. Salah felt a rare sense of peace as he closed his eyes content, reassured that this strange adventure had ended without disaster, and that by evening he would return to his everyday life.

He sank into a deep, heavy sleep until the shrill ring of the hotel's information line dragged him reluctantly awake.

"This is the hotel management. Do you want to extend your stay at the hotel one more day, Mr. Salah? " the clerk asked him.
"No. "
"Then you must leave before six o'clock, sir. " "What time is it now? "
"It's five. "

He got out of bed, still naked. Reaching for her beside him, he found only emptiness.

The room was dark. He flicked on the light. No Ahlam. Not in the bathroom, not behind the door. Where had she gone?

He rushed to the closet, yanking it open.

Empty.

Even his clothes were gone.

Oh my God—my wallet!

It had been in the pocket of those clothes.

The car keys? They'd been on the table by the bed. Gone.

He tore through the drawers and shelves—nothing.

Damn her. She took everything.

Trying to sound calm, he called the reception desk. "Yes, sir? How can I help you? "

 "I… uh… I'm looking for the lady who was staying here with me. " "Madam left in the car over an hour ago. "

Salah slammed his fists against the wall, then his head. Hisham had been right all along. She'd fooled him, stripped him bare, and fled in the car. She hadn't left him a single thing—not even underwear.

Only his shoes remained, half-hidden under the bed. Perhaps she'd overlooked them. He couldn't believe it. His blood boiled.

What now? What do I do? Call the police? And tell them what? That I was robbed by a woman whose real name I don't even know? A woman with no trace, no identity, no one who knows her? She's a ghost.

Or do I call Hisham? Ask him to bring me clothes?

He could already hear Hisham's laughter, the sneer in his voice, the sting of his gloating: *I warned you.*

He couldn't bear it.

Pacing the room, sweat sliding down his face, Salah felt trapped. Still, he had no choice. He lifted the receiver, started dialing And then he froze.

There was movement outside the door.

The handle turned. The door swung open.

And Ahlam walked in. Laughing, radiant, carrying shopping bags in her hands. She stopped short when she saw him.

"Are you finally awake? " Suddenly, his anger vanished.

She dropped the bags and rushed toward him. He embraced her joyfully, hugged her tightly, and kissed her.

"Where did you go? And where are my clothes? "

 "I wanted to apologize for the worries I caused you today — and to make up for the clothes I tore. "

She handed him a bag. "Look what I brought you. "

He opened it and took out a white linen suit and a white cotton shirt. "Is this for me? "

"Do you like it? "

"It's wonderful. " He felt ashamed of himself. *And I was the one who intended to give her money for her 'services.'*

"And my old clothes? "

"I didn't want to wake you, so I had to borrow your old clothes to get the right size. Look, I found your wallet and some of your personal belongings in the pockets. "

She placed the wallet on the table, along with the bag containing the gift box he had bought her.

He had wronged her and misjudged her. Once again, Ahlam had triumphed over Hisham's doubts.

"I was worried about you. I thought I'd never see you again. "
"Don't worry you won't get rid of me that easily. These are your old clothes. And these are new underwear. See? I didn't forget anything. I wanted it to be a surprise for you. "

He took out the clothes and examined them as she watched his reaction with a smile.

"This is exactly what I needed, " he said. "Especially the underwear. " "Still, you won't be needing it, " she whispered with playful charm.

He kept looking at her with a mix of affection and amazement.

"I told you, " she continued, "I'm always one step ahead. I know exactly what's going on in your head. "
"And what's in the other bag? "
"That one's mine. You're not allowed to see it. You'll see it later—at the party. " "What party? "
"Tonight, there's a special dinner at the hotel. There'll be a belly dancer. "

He walked toward her and said in a serious tone,
"Sorry, but we're leaving. I already told them we'd check out before six. "

She looked at him in surprise, disappointment clouding her face. "Leaving? "

She sat down on the bed, her voice dropping to a soft, sad tone. "But why? I thought we were having fun. "

 "I'm sorry, but I didn't plan for another night. There's work, commitments... life is waiting. "

Still holding the bag, she looked at it wistfully. "I was hoping to wear the new dress for you. "

He couldn't bring himself to say anything. Then she asked gently, "Do you really want to leave? Is that what you want? "

He hesitated. He was enjoying his stay with her more than he wanted to admit.

"Okay, okay, " he gave in. "Stop playing with my feelings. We'll stay another night. You're impossible to say no to. "

Ahlam let out a shriek of joy and hugged him tightly. "You won't regret it! It'll be an unforgettable night. "

He picked up the phone.

"I'll call the front desk to extend the reservation— " But she snatched the phone from his hand and set it back down. "No need. It's already done. "

He stared at her in disbelief.

"I told you, I'm always one step ahead of you. I knew you'd say yes. "

Chapter

Four

Salah got dressed in his new white linen suit while Ahlam remained under the covers, watching him. "Your taste in men's clothing is impeccable, " he said. "I love men in white. "

"Aren't you getting ready? "

"I need a little more time. You go ahead to the restaurant. "

"Don't be long. " Then, as he opened the door, she added playfully, "And don't run away. "

He went down to the hotel lobby, realizing he hadn't left his room since they arrived. He stepped onto the terrace overlooking the sea. Night had fallen. The sound of waves crashing below calmed him, but his mind was restless he kept replaying memories of Ahlam in his head: her wildness, her laughter, her unpredictability, but above all her tenderness. His imagination drifted in a sea of images of Ahlam in different poses. He could not stop his mind from replaying the scenes of her madness in bed.

Never in his life had he felt such satisfaction and fullness as he did now.

If he compared his entire past life with this single day, he would find that this day was richer in its outcome and achievements. It exceeded expectations. That thought filled him with a sense of bliss and contentment.

As he walked along the terrace, he noticed the admiring glances his new outfit drew. It gave him a quiet sense of pride. In every mirror he passed, he caught a glimpse he couldn't help but check himself again and again.

A waiter led him to a table Ahlam had reserved, near the dance floor. A Cuban band played energetic Latin music, and the restaurant buzzed with European tourists dancing and laughing. The atmosphere was vibrant, the energy infectious. He felt at ease, free and alive.

"If only you were here, Hisham, " he thought, "so I could show you how wrong you were. "

More than half an hour passed. The waiter came by a few times, reminding him that his companion's order would be brought once she arrived.

Then a hush fell over the crowd. People began whispering and looking toward the entrance. Salah followed their gaze, and his heart skipped a beat.

There she was.

Ahlam stood at the door, wearing a long black dress that exposed a generous portion of her chest. A high slit along one side revealed her entire leg. Every eye in the room turned toward her. She froze for a moment, scanning the room. When she spotted him, she began walking toward him, slow, graceful, magnetic—not paying attention to anyone else but him, as if there was no one else in the hall. Her hips swayed in rhythm with her steps, her hair cascading behind her.

He stood up to greet her. She reached him, smiling, her cheeks flushed with a touch of embarrassment.

"Am I late? " she asked. "Not at all. "

"What do you think? Do you like it? " "You look like a princess. "

"Is that really how you see me? "

"Just look around—see how everyone else is staring, stunned. "

"I don't care about them, " she said softly. "I only care what you think. " He raised an eyebrow. "Why me? "

"Because you're the one who placed the ad. "

Salah laughed.

"Any man would be proud to be seen with you. "

Ahlam sat across from him. He noticed how her bare back drew the attention of almost everyone—men and women alike.

He laughed and said,

"I can almost hear them wondering: What's a tramp like him doing with a goddess like her? "

"On the contrary, " she smiled, "I think women hate me for being with you; they are probably asking: What's this cheap woman doing with a handsome gentleman like him? "

"You still confuse me. I still wonder what I did to impress you so much? "

She whispered in his ear: "Because you are me. " "I don't understand. " "And because I am you. "

With the food came the Oriental dancer. She began to sway to the melodies of Umm Kulthum, moving gracefully from table to table. Her dance filled the air with excitement and passion, urging most of the audience to clap and join in the dancing.

Some of the revelers whispered in the dancer's ear and gestured toward Ahlam. The dancer approached her and started dancing beside her, but Ahlam ignored her, keeping her gaze fixed only on Salah.

The dancer took Ahlam's hand, inviting her to join the dance. Ahlam's face darkened as she gave her a look of refusal and apology. But the dancer persisted, tugging at her until she forced her to stand.

The crowd's clapping and enthusiasm grew louder, while Ahlam's embarrassment deepened.

Some of the revelers surrounded her, forming a circle, clapping and dancing around her. Her face soon disappeared among the dancers.

Salah grew restless and began searching for her. When she reappeared, her eyes were fixed on him. In them, he saw fear, a plea for rescue.

He leaped from his chair, pushed his way through the circle, and seized her hand. She collapsed into his arms, falling against his chest. He gathered her tightly to him, and he could almost hear the frantic beating of her heart against his chest.

"Are you okay? " he asked, concerned. "Please, don't let go of me. "

She buried her face in his chest so no one would see her tears. "What's wrong? "

"I'm scared. "
"There's nothing to be afraid of. " "Get me out of here. "

They left the restaurant and stepped onto the balcony. The sea air revived them. "Let's walk on the beach, " she said.

She took off her shoes and held them in her hand. "I love walking on the sand. "

The hotel lights shimmered on the waves. They walked in silence, listening to the crashing of the waves and feeling the cool water kiss their feet. They continued walking until they reached the farthest point of the hotel. Ahlam crossed the hotel fence, and Salah followed her. There was nothing but a deserted sandy beach. They kept walking away from the hotel until the lights disappeared, and darkness enveloped them.

Ahlam lay down on the sand, gazing up at the sky and stars. Salah walked toward the sea and stared into its dark expanse. Without turning, he asked,

"Look at the sea. What do you see? " "Darkness. "
"That's who you are—full of mystery and surprises. "

He heard her laugh.

 "Don't exaggerate. I'm not what you say. I'm just a simple woman who loves solitude. Crowds scare me. But I'm beautiful, and I love swimming. "

Salah laughed and stepped closer to the water.

"Do you know what I'm thinking about right now? Jumping into this sea. "

He turned toward her—she was gone. Only her clothes lay on the sand. He heard her voice from the water:

"I beat you to it, as usual. See? I'm always one step ahead of you. "

He stood at the edge, hesitant, listening to her voice. "The water's refreshing. Come. "

But he couldn't see her in the dark. "Where are you? I can't see you. "
"Come and catch me. "

He undressed and jumped into the water, swimming toward her voice. She was floating on her back, staring at the sky.

"The sky is beautiful. Do you see the stars? How lovely they are. "

He didn't reply. He just looked up and let the silence and waves wash over him. "The universe is beautiful. But still, it's a poor thing. "

"Poor thing? "
"Black holes will swallow it. Did you know that? The universe will consume

itself, dissolve, and return to nothing. "

"Where'd you get that idea? "

"All creatures carry the seeds of their demise. They harbor black holes inside them. I have one too. It will swallow me and destroy me. "

Salah laughed and splashed her.

"I know your black hole very well—it'll swallow me too and destroy me. "

Ahlam laughed and splashed him back.

"Idiot, " she said, throwing herself into his arms. "Didn't I tell you you'd breathe your last in my arms? " "Someone might see us. "

But she didn't care. She kissed his neck and whispered:

"Only fish can see us. "

Chapter
Five

They returned to the hotel at dawn. Their clothes were wet. They walked side by side, hand in hand. He wrapped his arm around her waist, and she rested her head against his chest. Her eyes were half-closed. At the entrance, he looked at her.

"Are you tired? "
"I'm exhausted. And sleepy. "

He stopped suddenly, turned to her, and his face grew thoughtful. After a pause, he said hesitantly,

"You and I... "

He trailed off. She tilted her head, curious. "You and I, what? "

"We make a good pair, don't we? "

Ahlam smiled, squeezing his arm with quiet delight. Salah continued:

"What do you think it is that binds us together like this? "

She burst out laughing. "The advertisement! "

He nudged her playfully with his elbow.

"Don't joke be serious. Don't you feel there's something deeper between us? " "What do you mean? "
 "I feel like I've known you forever. And when I'm with you… I'm truly happy. " "Me too, " she whispered.

He fell silent for a moment, as though weighing something. "There's something I've been carrying in my heart. "

Her eyes brightened. "What is it? "

He smiled, his gaze glowing with excitement. "Come with me. "

 "Where to? "
 "To the room. I have a surprise for you. "

He took her hand, and they hurried together to the room. At the bedside, he opened a drawer and pulled out a small gift box.

"I feel like I never want to be without you, " he said, opening it. Ahlam froze, her eyes widening as he revealed the ring.
"Will you marry me? "

Ahlam stood frozen, stunned by the surprise. She took the ring from him and sat down on the bed, staring at it in silence. For a long moment, she said nothing, while he stood beside her, smiling gently, waiting for her reaction.

At last, she lifted her face to him, a tear sliding down her cheek.

"Who wouldn't marry you? You're every girl's dream, " she whispered. Then, almost inaudibly, she added, "But you hardly know me. "

"I know you're made of honey and cream, " he said with a soft laugh.

Ahlam didn't reply. She remained still, her gaze fixed on the ring, lost in thought. He bent down and kissed her forehead tenderly. She stayed silent, stunned.

Taking her hand in his, he slipped the ring onto her finger. Then he kissed her lips and murmured, "Now it's time for bed. "

He began undressing, setting aside his evening clothes. "It's been such a full day one we'll remember for the rest of our lives. "

Sliding under the covers, he sighed, "I feel like I could sleep for a whole year. " Ahlam sat on the edge of the bed, watching him as his eyes grew heavy.

"Aren't you going to take off your clothes? You're tired too you should rest, " he said, his voice fading with drowsiness.

She brushed her fingers through his hair and whispered, "I love watching you sleep. " Then she bent close, kissed his eyelids, and began to sing softly:

"Tick, tick, tick... Um Suleiman... "

A faint smile touched his lips as he listened, eyes still closed. Within moments, he drifted into sleep.

When he woke up, it was midday. Ahlam wasn't in bed. Her side was made, as if it had been untouched. He called out for her, but no one answered. He checked the room and the bathroom nothing. The ring still lay beside the bed.

He opened the closet: only his clothes remained. Hers were gone. He called the receptionist.

"Madam paid the bill and left, " they said. "She asked us not to disturb you. "

The news hit him hard. He felt shaken by Ahlam's sudden and unexplained departure. He had no idea what she was thinking, what her intentions were.

He got dressed, gathered his belongings, and left the room. Then he waited in the hotel lobby. "Didn't she leave a message or say where she was going? " he asked.

 "No, " the clerk replied.

Frustrated and confused, Salah sat in silence. He had so much to say to her especially about the marriage proposal. But now, he didn't know if he'd ever get the chance.

How could he contact her? She hadn't left him an address.

His anger soon turned into fear. Fear that he might never see her again.

He stayed in the lobby for hours, trying to come up with explanations. Maybe she got lost? Maybe she had been delayed? He was afraid to leave in case she came back looking for him.

Then it hit him: maybe she went to the airport. He drove there, hoping she'd gone to retrieve her car. But he couldn't find her anywhere in the parking lot.

He went into the cafeteria and sat in the same spot where they'd been before. But she didn't appear. He asked the staff about her, but no one remembered her among the many travelers.

Was it possible that she'd just disappeared like that without a word, without goodbye? He returned home, checked his mailbox nothing. No letter, no message.

He sent her an email, waited all night in front of his computer for a reply.

But nothing came. The email bounced back: the address didn't exist.

"Did I upset her? " he wondered. "Did I say or do something wrong? " He tried to search for a reason, but found none. She had seemed happy… so happy she had sung him to sleep.

He couldn't sleep that night. The next morning, exhausted, he went to work and told Hisham everything. But Hisham's skeptical looks and sarcastic remarks were too much to bear.

Salah went back to the hotel. He kept asking about her, over and over. But nothing changed. Ahlam was gone.

She had vanished and he didn't know if she'd ever return.

The worst part? No one believed his story about Ahlam.

Still, he kept waiting. But for what? He didn't know anymore. Everyone doubted her existence even Hisham, who had never met or seen her, eventually started to believe Salah had made her up or dreamed her into being. All he ever heard was Salah talking about her.

Even the hotel staff cast doubt. They confirmed a reservation but only in Salah's name. There was no record of anyone named Ahlam.

Was it possible that he had imagined everything, as they all claimed? Had there ever truly been a woman named Ahlam?

Salah often went missing from work after that. But Hisham always knew where to find him on the same spot along Jebel Ali Road. His car was parked at the edge of the sand. Standing quietly.

Thinking. Remembering.

"This is where the car swerved. These are some of the tire marks in the sand. This is where Ahlam and I stood next to the car and argued. "

But he never concluded.

Is it possible he would never see her again? Never hear her laugh? Never watch her smile?

Days passed. Then months. Then years. Ahlam never returned.

But still, he couldn't stop longing for her.

Part Two
A Girl's Dreams

Chapter

Six

When I was born—when they said *"Congratulations "*—no one knew that you were born with me. That you would live inside me: in my eyes, in my heart, in the folds of my mind.

The air was fresh and cool on that autumn morning September 9, 1989 when the heavy wooden door of an old Damascene house creaked open in a narrow alley of the Qaymariyah neighborhood. A young man in his twenties stepped out. He walked briskly through the winding alleys, where the stones breathed history, mingling with the scent of orange leaves and the sweetness of jasmine.

That morning, he did not stop at the bakery, as he often did, to pick up a hot loaf of bread sprinkled with black seeds. He had a mission to carry out.

He reached the Nawfara Café, hurried past it, and bounded up its steps in three quick strides until he arrived at the door of the Umayyad Mosque. Turning left, he crossed the archway toward the Qaqabiyya Market, then continued along the mosque's wall until he reached the entrance of the Hamidiyya Souq.

Deliberately, he charged through the flocks of pigeons scattered across the square; they rose around him in a sudden cloud of wings. He gave no glances to the booksellers beneath the Roman arch, nor did he pause for his habit of sifting through their piles of old and new books. He didn't even greet his friend, the Shami berry seller. Today, he had an urgent mission.

He ran on through the market, dodging left and right to avoid colliding with shoppers and vendors' stalls. At last, he reached the intersection leading toward Al-Hariqa Street. He turned into it, his eyes scanning the distance ahead—until they locked on Abu Tawfiq, standing in the middle of the street.

The old man spotted him, rushed forward, and asked breathlessly:

"Has anything happened? "

The young man paused, catching his breath.

"No, nothing yet. But Umm Ibrahim has arrived. And they want you now. "
"Okay, I'll go. You stay in the shop. " "I want to go with you. "
"And the shop? Who will stand there? " "Please, I want to come with you. "
"Fine, fine close the shop and follow me. "

He handed the keys to his son and hurried toward the Hamidiyya Market, then veered right in the direction of the Umayyad Mosque. But before continuing toward Al-Qaymariyah, he stepped inside the mosque and prayed two rak'ahs, seeking blessings and Umm Tawfiq's safety.

After the prayer, he remained kneeling. Lifting his hands toward the sky, he supplicated:

"O God, Most Merciful of the merciful, have mercy on my wife, Umm Tawfiq, and envelop her in Your compassion. She is in Your hands now.

Protect her, and grant her a daughter who will be her companion in old age, a balm for her wounded heart, and a consolation for the child she lost in the prime of youth. O Lord, I ask nothing for myself I am content with what You have decreed. But fulfill her dream, O Lord. Grant her the daughter she has always longed for. Do not let her down, and do not forsake her. She is a righteous wife and a devoted mother. "

Here, Abu Tawfiq's voice cracked. Tears welled in his eyes, threatening to spill. For a moment, he nearly broke into sobs, but he steadied himself, wiped his cheeks with his palms, rose to his feet, and quickly exited the mosque.

Some of his children were playing near the door. He scolded them for leaving it open. He rang the bell announcing his arrival. Several women were gathered in the courtyard. As soon as they saw him, they began ululating. The midwife, Umm Ibrahim, rushed toward him: "Give me the treat, Abu Tawfiq, for the good news! God has answered your prayers you have a baby girl! May she grow up in your care! "

Abu Tawfiq could no longer hold back his tears. He entered the room to find Umm Tawfiq lying down with their daughter beside her.

"Here's Souad, " said Umm Tawfiq. "Look at her how beautiful she is. "
He glanced at the baby, then rested his head on his wife's chest and wept. "Thank God you're safe. "

He then picked up the baby girl, kissed her, brought his mouth close to her ear, and recited the call to prayer in her ear.

No one in the family had ever been pampered like Souad. Everyone loved her and wanted to carry and play with her. She became a living doll, the favorite pastime of all five of her brothers. The first thing they did after returning from school was rush to their mother's room, where Souad was. They brought her toys, carried her, sang to her, and competed to see who could make her laugh.

Even Farid, the youngest of the brothers ten years her senior loved her dearly. But he felt she was being spoiled with too many toys and constant carrying, which he believed was delaying her ability to walk. He resented that he hadn't received such attention and care when he was her age. So, in his mind, it was only fair to balance things out: when they pampered her excessively, he would be a little harsh. While they laughed at her, he yelled.

But his mother didn't appreciate these "favors, " and he received his share of beatings and scoldings. She wasn't convinced of his noble intentions. She kept saying he was jealous of her, while all he wanted was for her to receive a proper, strict upbringing. He disliked frivolity and pettiness.

Souad grew up in this house, surrounded by the utmost care from her mother, father, and older brothers. When Souad was five, Ahmed first caught her attention. She noticed how her entire family celebrated his visits and those of his family, though they didn't come often. Ahmed was ten years older than her, and she was still just a child too small to matter to him. He never paid her the slightest attention. He didn't even notice the little girl who hid shyly behind her mother, secretly watching and admiring him.

Later, she learned that they were relatives and that his family lived in Beirut, Lebanon. Ahmed shared a special bond with her brother, Farid. The two would spend long hours in Farid's room, talking about things that meant nothing to her. Souad would stand outside, listening to their laughter through the door, or peeking at them through the peephole. Every so often, Ahmed would courteously invite her inside, but she would blush, shake her head, and run away.

She adored his smile. Once, when she happened to sit beside him, he absentmindedly rested his hand on her head, his fingers gently stroking her hair while he went on speaking with Farid. She had never allowed anyone not even close relatives to touch her like that.

When she was six, Ahmed's family spent the summer in Damascus, staying in their suburban house. One day, Ahmed came to visit. As always, he ignored her presence. And as always, she hovered behind the door, eavesdropping.

That day, they were making plans to go to a party. Ahmed, catching a glimpse of her deliberately, turned and said jokingly:

"What do you say, Souad? Do you want to come with us to the party? "She couldn't believe her ears. Her heart leapt with joy.

But Farida threw her out of the room and locked the door behind her. Souad ran crying to her mother.

Shortly afterward, the two young men left the room and stood chatting at the door. She heard Ahmed mention her name, and she turned quickly to her mother:

 "I want to go with them to the party. Please, Mama let them take me. "But that was entirely out of the question for Farid.

"What are you going to do with us? This is a party for grown-ups. "

 "Take me with you. I want to go with you. "

 "God bless you, "her mother said. "Take her with you. She never leaves the house, never goes anywhere. She'll enjoy herself. "

Farid pushed Souad violently, so she hid behind her mother.

Where am I supposed to take her? Let someone else do it. The last thing I need is her.

Ahmed stood silently, observing the scene. Finally, he went over to Farid, pulled him toward the door, and whispered in his ear. Farid then turned to his sister, giving her a look of anger. He moved closer to her as she clung to her mother's dress. He nudged her head with his hand until she nearly lost her balance and fell.

"Come on, go and change your clothes. You're so annoying. Woe to you if I hear you fidgeting. "

Souad looked at Ahmed gratefully, and he winked at her with a smile. He said, laughing, "Come on, hurry. If you're late, we won't be able to take you. I want to see you looking beautiful. "

Souad's heart leaped with joy. She wanted to hug and kiss him. She wouldn't let him down she would be the most beautiful girl. She hurried to her room, pulling her mother by her dress. Her mother raised her hands in prayer for Ahmed. Meanwhile, Farid watched them, filled with anger and rage.

She was truly a beautiful girl. One would be proud to hold her hand, just as Ahmed did while walking with her down the street. Farid, on the other hand, walked beside her but avoided holding her hand. Ahmed led her to a party at one of the nearby houses, where a crowd of guests had gathered. She didn't know what the occasion was, but that hardly mattered. Everyone welcomed her warmly, celebrating her arrival as if she belonged. Ahmed seated her beside him at a table near the dance floor and brought her sweets, juice, and desserts. He gave her special attention, and she savored it. To Souad, there was no one in the world better than Ahmed, and she was ready to do whatever he asked.

Everything seemed perfect: the decorations, the lights, the music, the songs, the dancing, the dabkeh. The large, lively crowd amazed her, but she enjoyed watching them laugh, sing, and dance.

Farid and Ahmed were plotting something, whispering together at the edge of the table and exchanging glances toward a group of girls. Then Ahmed turned suddenly to her.

"Are you happy, Souad? "

She didn't answer, but smiled and nodded.

He pointed toward a distant table. "Do you see that girl in the blue dress? " She nodded again.

"What do you think of her? Is she as pretty as you? " Another nod.

"I want you to go to her and say: *'Uncle Ahmed is asking you—who's prettier, you or the moon?'*

Can you do that? "

Of course she could. Did he think she was stupid? She nodded firmly. "Good. Now repeat it back to me. "

She straightened herself with pride. "Uncle Ahmed asks you—who's prettier, you or the moon. "

 "Well done, " he said with a smile. "But don't let anyone else hear you. Just between you and her. Can you manage that? "

She nodded. He would trust her.

Souad walked over to the girl's table, holding up her dress slightly as she approached. The girl turned toward her, smiling in surprise at seeing her alone.

"What's your name? "the girl asked kindly.
"I'm Souad. "
"And who did you come with? "
"With my brother Farid and Uncle Ahmed. "

Then Souad leaned closer and whispered in her ear:

"Uncle Ahmed asks you who's prettier, you or the moon? "

The girl was confused, smiled, and shyly turned to look around. She saw Ahmed smiling at her from afar. She quickly turned back so as not to attract her family's attention. Ahmed approached the table and greeted the girl, her friends, and her family.

With extreme embarrassment, he said, "What are you doing here, Souad? Is this girl bothering you, miss? "

"No, no, on the contrary she's sweet and pretty. Is she your sister? "

He pointed to himself. "No, she's my cousin. She's Farid's sister. I'm Ahmed. "

Ahmed extended his hand and greeted the girl and her friends. He chatted with them, then called Farid over and introduced him.

Before the party ended, they returned to their table, and for the first time in a long while, Farid was pleased with her. He offered her pieces of candy, smiled at her, and asked if she was comfortable.

Souad instinctively knew that Ahmed and Farid had used her for some purpose she didn't fully understand. Still, she was proud of what she had done and even prouder of her success in delivering a small piece of paper to the girl in the blue dress and later, receiving a note from her, which made Ahmed so happy that he said to Farid:

 "We should take her with us to every party, right, Farid? " "Of course—if she listens and obeys. "

Souad was ready to listen and obey as long as Ahmed was pleased with her.

But that didn't happen. She never went to another party after that, because Ahmed had left.

Chapter

Seven

("Grow up fast, so I can bring you to our home. " – Fairuz)

She was eight years old. One day, her mother and aunt decided to travel to Beirut to shop for fabrics. Naturally, Souad went with them, and they were all to stay at Ahmed's family home.

Her joy was indescribable. How could it not be? They would be visiting Ahmed. That meant she would sleep under the same roof as him. The very thought set her imagination alight, filling her with dreams and secret hopes. She longed for him—his smile, his kindness, the way his hand had once stroked her hair.

But things did not unfold as she wished.

Ahmed wasn't there the day they arrived. She went to bed reluctantly, disappointed, without seeing him.

The next morning, when her family prepared to go to the market, Ahmed was still asleep.

His mother excused him: *"He came home late that night, that's his habit. He's always out with his friends ".*

Souad begged to stay behind. She wanted to wait until he woke, to stand before him so he could see how much she had grown. Surely, this time, he would notice her.

But her mother scolded her.

"How can you stay home alone? Did we come all this way just for you to sit inside? Come on you'll enjoy the markets of Beirut. "

Souad obeyed, though her heart wasn't in it. She wanted nothing from Beirut neither its sea, its markets, nor its cinemas if Ahmed wasn't there beside her.

But Ahmed was rarely home. He was always out with his circle of friends.

That evening, as usual, they returned weary from the market and went to bed early. Ahmed still had not come back. But Souad, stubborn in her hope, decided to wait for him.

The room where she slept with her family had a door that opened onto a balcony. She slipped outside, refusing to sleep, entertaining herself by watching the people passing in the street below, fighting off drowsiness.

Her wait did not last long.

At last, Ahmed arrived. She saw him get out of a taxi and enter the building. He opened the door quietly and went into his room without making a sound. He didn't notice Souad on the balcony, even though his room overlooked it.

She saw the light in his room turn on and heard him talking on the phone. She moved her chair deliberately, making a noise.

Ahmed poked his head out and saw her. He was surprised to see her, and a look of astonishment crossed his face. At first, he didn't recognize her. He studied her face for a moment, then broke into a wide smile. His eyes lit up with joy.

"Who? Souad? "

She smiled at him. He remembered her. He hadn't forgotten. Her heart swelled with happiness. "How are you? You've become a beautiful bride. Wait a minute "

He was still holding the receiver in his hand. "We have guests from Damascus. A beautiful girl

who'll blow your mind don't you believe it? She's here beside me, and she's prettier than you. Are you jealous? Talk to her. "

 "Come on, Souad, say hello to Wafaa. Don't be shy, just say hello and ask how she is. " "Hello, how are you? "

A young woman's voice came from the other end: "Hello, what's your name, sweetie? " "Souad. "

"How old are you? " "Eight years old. "
"Okay, my love, give me back Ahmed. "

Ahmed took the receiver.

"Did you hear yourself? Yes, you should be jealous of her she's charming. "

He kept talking and laughing as Souad followed him, happy about his repeated compliments on her beauty. She stood there, waiting for him to finish the call. But he kept talking, signaling for her to sit on a chair by the bed. He moved around the room holding the receiver. Every time he passed her, he would pat her on the head and play with her hair spontaneously. This was what she had always dreamed of.

Now Beirut has become more enjoyable with Ahmed's presence. She wondered about the secret of his sweet smile and why her body trembled and her temperature rose whenever he ran his fingers through her hair. He preferred her to his girlfriend. He had told her clearly: "She is gorgeous, and you should be jealous of her. "

This night was destined to be special in Souad's life a night to be remembered forever. When Ahmed ended the call, he asked her, "Are you hungry? "

She smiled but did not answer.

"As for me, I'm very hungry. What do you say we sneak into the kitchen and prepare something for ourselves? " He opened the door with a dramatic gesture, feigning fear and caution like a thief, and motioned for her to follow him.

In the kitchen, he asked, "What will you cook for us? " She laughed and said, "I don't know how to cook yet. "

He smiled in disappointment and said, "Then you'll make me a cheese sandwich. "

She nodded in agreement. He brought her bread and cheese and stood watching her as she prepared and wrapped the sandwich.

He took a bite and said, "What a wonderful sandwich the best one I've ever eaten in my life. " She knew he was exaggerating, but she was happy.

They returned to the room. He looked at her and studied her carefully, "How about I take some pictures of you? "

Souad smiled and nodded.

He took a camera from his closet, along with some cosmetics and a hairdryer. "Tonight we're going to make you a real princess, " he said.

He combed her hair and applied makeup to her face and lips. They spent the night taking pictures of her in various poses. They laughed a lot. She no longer felt shy around him. They grew closer, and their intimacy deepened.

It was the most beautiful night of Souad's life. It was a dream she would remember for the rest of her life.

The next morning, she was forced to wake up to her mother's voice urging her to get ready to travel back to Syria. She found her mother and aunt had prepared everything all their bags were ready by the door. She looked for Ahmed, but he was asleep. She knew he wouldn't wake up at this hour, especially after their late night together. She delayed getting dressed and passed by his room, making some noise in an attempt to wake him. But his door remained closed.

Souad left; she couldn't say goodbye to Ahmed. This pained her for a long time. She left Beirut, but her heart remained there.

Chapter
Eight

How long do I have to wait?

What do the fortune tellers say? What is this feeling in my chest?

It keeps me awake at night and won't let me sleep. She was twelve years old. She walked to school every day. Her school was nearby, but she chose a route that passed by Ahmed's family's house. The house was empty they only stayed there when they visited Damascus, and that was rare. However, she enjoyed passing by and gazing at the wall and the outer door. His house wasn't on the way to school, but she didn't mind the longer walk, as long as it reminded her of him. What good were all the roads if they didn't lead to Ahmed's house?

She didn't particularly like school, but she had come to love waking up in the morning because it meant passing by Ahmed's house. On holidays, she'd ride her bicycle and circle the house. During that time, she was a source of trouble for her brothers. Riding her bike in the public streets irritated them, especially Farid.

"I was with my friends on the bus when she passed us on her bike. They saw her, and the sarcastic comments started pouring in. I wished I could die at that moment. This is not appropriate for us. How could you allow her to ride a bike in the street like those street vagabonds like a tramp? "

But Abu Tawfiq, who had bought her the bike, told him firmly:

"You have nothing to do with her behavior. I am her father, and I am responsible for her. "

"Look at how permissive your upbringing has made her. You and my mother have spoiled her. She's not like other girls her age. Look at her face always pale, as if she's sick. She has no friends or social life. She's always in her room, not talking to or engaging with anyone. It's like there's something wrong with her. "

Umm Tawfiq interrupted him angrily:

"Don't you dare interfere in Souad's affairs. I won't allow you, or any of your brothers, to interfere in her life. If I ever hear that any of you have upset her, there will be consequences. "

Souad heard these conversations from her room. No one knew that her entire life revolved around Ahmed, and that nothing else mattered.

It was her greatest secret.

Contrary to what others might have imagined, her life was rich with emotions and full of love.

She was socially self-sufficient, needing no one outside of herself. She saw herself as a small planet in Ahmed's vast orbit, one among many that revolved around him. Yet, while the other planets slowly drifted away, she alone drew closer. She knew with absolute certainty that she was destined, one day, to fall fully into his gravity and merge with him. It was only a matter of time and patience and she had both in abundance.

By then, all her brothers had left home married and gone. All except Farid, who made her life miserable despite the wide gap in their ages. He was always a source of irritation. University hadn't changed him, despite his academic and social success. He had never forgiven her for being born, for pushing him out of first place. Her arrival had stripped him of the privileges he once enjoyed, robbing him of his favored status with their parents.

But everything shifted after the accident the accident that sent her to the hospital. At first, she thought Farid would show up only to gloat, to remind her that he had warned them all. Hadn't he begged the family to stop her from riding her bike? His prophecy had been fulfilled: Souad had been struck by a car while cycling. She was thrown to the ground, her hand broken, her body covered in bruises.

She had been anxiously awaiting his arrival. He hadn't come on the first day.

When she finally heard his voice in the hospital corridor outside her room, she turned to her mother, her terrified eyes silently pleading for protection.

"How many times have I told you not to ride that damned bike? " he barked. Then, softening, he added, "But it's not your fault it's your mother and father's. "

She looked at him, searching his eyes for a clue to his mood. He stepped closer, glanced at her bandaged hand, and with a sudden smile said:

"These are chocolate biscuits the best kind. The kind you steal from my room. They're all yours. "

He set them gently in her lap and sat on the bed beside her.

"If something happened to you God forbid who would sneak into my room and rummage through it? "

He smiled again. She couldn't believe her eyes.

"I still don't understand what you're always looking for in my things, " he teased.

How sweet his smile is, she thought. *Should I tell him I'm looking for a trace of his friend Ahmed?*

"From now on, I'll leave the room unlocked for you. I'll open all my drawers for you. "

Then he bent down and kissed her forehead. "The important thing is that you come home soon. "

Is it possible this is Farid saying these things?

Everyone asked her how the accident happened. She told them she had been speeding down the middle of the street, then suddenly switched lanes without signaling or noticing the car behind her, which led to the collision.

That was only part of the truth.

What she didn't tell anyone was that she had been chasing a taxi in which she had seen Ahmed. He was sitting in the back seat, by the window. The car was moving quickly. But the moment she spotted him, she didn't hesitate she raced after him with all her strength. She managed to come up on his left side, weaving through traffic, but he never noticed her. He was laughing and talking to the girl seated beside him.

The car picked up speed. Fear seized her, a sense of danger tightening her chest. But there was no turning back; she was already riding alongside him. He finally turned his head, saw the bike just as their eyes were about to meet, just as he was about to recognize her the taxi swerved sharply into a side street. Her bike, however, kept charging straight ahead.

Souad panicked, hesitated, and was unable to decide which way to turn. She slammed on the brakes with all her strength, but to her horror, they didn't respond. The bike was out of control. Disaster was coming. She tried to hold her line, but what she feared most happened the handlebars jerked sideways. She braced for the fall, already knowing what awaited her.

The bike veered right and slammed to the ground, skidding forward with her tangled in its momentum. Even as she tumbled, her eyes searched desperately to see if Ahmed had noticed her. Her head struck the asphalt. She rolled, crashing along with the bike for several meters. Unable to stop it, she kept her eyes shut tight, refusing to scream, clinging to her composure.

Pain tore through her knee her jeans must have ripped. She heard the screech of brakes, the cries of onlookers, but none of it frightened her as much as the thought of Ahmed being among them.

She lay face down in the middle of the street, cheek pressed to the pavement, unable to move. A shadow loomed over her, stretching long until it swallowed the sunlight. The roar of tires bore down on her then screeched to a stop, only centimeters from her face. The stench of burning rubber filled her nostrils.

She couldn't lift her head. From the corner of her eye, she saw people rushing toward her, voices rising. Someone shouted, "Are you okay? Can you move your hand? "

But she felt drained, as if her body had already given up. Two thoughts consumed her: Had Ahmed seen her fall? And what would Farid say when he found out?

She longed only to close her eyes and surrender to sleep, or perhaps to die. But she survived.

After the accident, Souad's life took a brighter turn. She gained a new friend perhaps her only true one: Farid. He became her guardian and protector. He chose her clothes, picked out her hairstyles, and helped her with her lessons and homework. He took her to restaurants and parties, introducing her to his friends and girlfriends. She told him everything her desires, her dreams, her fears and entrusted him with all her secrets. All but one: Ahmed.

A long time passed after the accident without her seeing him. But one day, she met him by chance while visiting relatives. She encountered him at the door, just as he was saying goodbye, about to leave. He greeted her casually as he hurried down the stairs, as though he hadn't recognized her. But halfway down, he paused, turned, studied her face carefully... then broke into a wide smile before continuing on his way.

Chapter

Nine

*Y*ou and I like the sun and the moon, Like night and day, Like summer and winter. I chase your shadow, Trace your steps, always a breath behind. We sit at the same table, yet never meet.

The most crucial encounter came when she turned fifteen. Her femininity had blossomed, and her beauty radiated with a new brilliance. She had become the focus of glances, the subject of whispers, the unspoken dream of young men and suitors alike. Farid was proud to parade her at parties, proud to introduce her as his sister. He had taught her the basics of manners and etiquette, yet her silence and shyness never left her and that very reserve gave her a rare, magnetic charm.

The party was held at a hotel, a gathering of medical students where Farid studied. He had bought her a special dress for the occasion.

 "You'll be the most beautiful girl tonight, " he told her. "Suitors will flock to you. What do you think? "

"I told you not to joke about this subject. Don't act as a matchmaker leave that to my mother. "

Dread tugged at her chest as she stepped into the hall, clinging tightly to Farid's arm. He guided her to a round table where some of his friends sat with their girlfriends.

"This is my sister, Souad. "
"Oh my God she's beautiful! " someone exclaimed.

Farid beamed at the compliment, prouder than she herself could ever be. She, meanwhile, felt out of place, sitting quietly while Farid mingled with his friends. Soft music drifted through the hall.

Then, suddenly, Farid's face lit up with joy. "Why are you late, man? I thought you weren't coming! "

A voice answered from behind her deep, familiar, unforgettable. At once her heart leapt, her cheeks flushed, and heat swept through her body. She didn't dare turn around.

Farid's words confirmed what her soul already knew:

"How are you, Ahmed? Thank God you're safe. When did you arrive? "

She stayed frozen, listening, while the two of them stood just behind her.

"I got in this morning, " Ahmed replied. "Honestly, I hesitated to come. I don't know many people here. I was afraid you wouldn't show, and I'd end up alone. "
"Who did you come with? "
"My cousin. What about you are you here alone? "
"No, " Farid said with a smile. "I have Souad with me. " Her heart skipped a beat.
"Souad? " Ahmed repeated.

She could feel his eyes searching her, settling on her, burning into her. Still, she didn't dare turn around.

"Hello, Souad. "

Finally, she turned to face him, smiling shyly. "Hello Ahmed, "

He stared at her, stunned. Then he sat on the chair beside her. "You're Souad? Is that really you? How are you? "

"I'm fine. "
"Do you remember me? "

She smiled and said softly, "Of course. "

"Oh my God, do you remember when you came to Beirut with your mother and aunt? " "Yes. "

"You were so young! Look at you now. Do you remember that night we spent together? I took pictures of you all evening. "

She smiled, blushing slightly, trying to stay composed. She didn't want to spoil the moment or appear foolish.

"Yes, I remember. I still have the photos you sent us. "
"Do you see that girl at the table across from us? That's my cousin, Rowaida. "

His cousin? His future wife? She wondered.

"She's beautiful, " she said hesitantly. "Is she your fiancée? "

Ahmed flinched. "No, of course not! Do you think I'd bring my fiancée to a party full of beautiful women? "

She laughed.

Well, maybe she's not his fiancée after all. Perhaps he did leave her at home.

But don't push too hard—he might get turned off. Still… I have to know.

"So… you left her at home? " "Who? "
"Your fiancée. "

He frowned, giving her a look of disapproval.

"Why are you so determined to make me have a fiancée? "

Then, firmly, he added, "Who's even thinking about marriage right now? "

He's upset. I should've kept my mouth shut. Say something—anything. Tell him you're sorry. Just don't let him walk away.

"Sorry… I didn't mean to upset you. "

He looked at her closely, his gaze deep and searching. Then he leaned toward her and said, "What would you say if I proposed to you? "

Souad was flustered. Her cheeks flushed, and her hand trembled so much she nearly dropped her glass.

"Leave Souad alone, " Farid interrupted. "Stop playing games with her. Go sit with your cousin. "
"My cousin doesn't even want me there. She brought me from Beirut just so her father would let her come to the party with me. "
"So now you're going to spend the whole night bothering poor Souad? Let her enjoy herself. " "And where should I go? I don't know anyone here except you two. "
"Then sit down and behave. " "Fine. I'll keep my mouth shut. "

He sat there, eyes scanning the room like a hunter stalking prey. His gaze finally settled on a beautiful girl with blonde hair and a sleek black dress. He whispered something to Farid, clearly trying not to let Souad overhear.

She watched him follow the girl's dancing clapping for her, locking eyes with her, trying to get her attention. But the girl completely ignored him.

Still, he didn't stop showering Souad with attention. He kept bringing her plates of food, drinks, and sweets, each time passing by the girl as if by accident. But none of his efforts worked.

Souad followed everything from the corner of her eye, saying nothing. She was relieved his flirting had failed.

Then suddenly, he turned and caught her staring at him. Confused, he realized she had uncovered his plan.

 "What? " he shouted over the music. "What do you mean? "
 "You're staring at me. "

She quickly looked away, trying to hide a smirk, his disappointment clear. "What? Why are you smiling like that? " he asked nervously.

She didn't answer, just burst into laughter when their eyes met. "Look at your sister, Farid. She's laughing at me! "

But Farid was too busy chatting with his friends to notice.

Ahmed waited for her to calm down, fidgeting, waiting for an explanation. She pointed discreetly toward the blonde girl. "It's that girl. "

"What about her? "
With calm precision, she said, "Should I go tell her: 'Uncle Ahmed is wondering who's prettier you or the moon?' "

"What? "

Ahmed's expression changed instantly. His reaction wasn't what she expected. He stared at her silently. Her face flushed with embarrassment. She looked away.

A heavy silence fell between them. Sweat gathered on her forehead.

Stupid. Stupid. Why did I say that?

She panicked, trying to think of a way to save the moment. She hadn't expected him to go quiet. Angry at herself, she fought back tears and lowered her head so he wouldn't see.

Not now, don't cry.

Quietly, he reached out and handed her a tissue.

She took it quickly, wiped away the tear, and dabbed her forehead. Then she raised her head, but still couldn't meet his gaze.

Why isn't he saying anything? Her lip quivered. *Please… say something, or I'll cry.*

"Your nose. " "What? "
"Your nose. I hadn't noticed it before. "

Souad was confused. She instinctively placed her hand over her nose, trying to hide it.

"Damn my nose. I hate it. It's big and pointy, like a witch's. I always told my mom my nose was big. "
"I love your nose. "

She smiled shyly, a little confused.

"You're making fun of me. It's big I know that. "
"Big? Who told you that? The most beautiful thing about your face is your nose. " "Really? "
"Pointy and upturned. It's a princess's nose. It has a pride that keeps young men at a distance. "

She didn't respond. She didn't know what to say.

I have to keep my mouth shut.

She distracted herself by watching Farid dance with one of his classmates.

"They must be circling you like flies. "

"Who? "
"The young men, of course. Tell me, is there a particular one? "

This is the right moment. I'll tell him my secret. What do I have to lose? Say it. This is your chance don't waste it. He loved your nose. What more do you want? He must know...

"Ahmed, come and meet my friend. "

It was Rowaida introducing her friend.

"This is Samar, and this is Ahmed my cousin. "

Samar was the one with the blonde hair and black dress. Ahmed jumped up to greet Samar warmly, leaving Souad consumed by anger and jealousy.

"Hello, how are you? What a happy coincidence! This is Souad, Farid's sister. She was impressed by your beauty and eager to meet you. Isn't that right, Souad? "

He looked at Souad and smiled slyly, almost maliciously. "Come on, tell her what we said about her. "

Hesitantly, in a low voice, Souad said

"He asked me who was prettier you or the moon. "

Samar laughed, her face flushing with embarrassment. She grabbed Rowaida's hand and pulled her away. They went to Rowaida's table, and before Ahmed could join them, he whispered to Souad:

"How can I repay you? You've done it again. You are my rifle, the one I hunt with. "

Souad surrendered to reality. What else could she do? This was her fate her destiny: that he would always abandon her for another girl. "

Timing never seemed to be on her side; it often worked against her. If Rowaida had been just a few seconds late, she might have confessed her love. She might have revealed her secret. But who knows what his reaction would have been? Maybe Rowaida's interruption had saved her. Maybe he just wasn't ready yet…

That evening, he completely forgot her. He spent the night talking with Rowaida and his new friend Samar, their laughter blending with the music, while she sat in silence. When he finally left with them, without even a goodbye, something inside her broke.

On the way home, Farid asked cheerfully,

 "How was your evening? Did you have a good time? "

She felt a lump in her throat. Tears threatened to spill, but she forced them back, lifting her chin as if nothing were wrong. "I had a lot of fun, " she said softly. "It was a wonderful evening. "

Chapter

Ten

Several months had passed since that party. Winter came. That afternoon was bitterly cold. She stepped out of the pharmacy into a downpour, the storm raging. Standing beneath the awning, she watched the sheets of rain, waiting for the torrent to ease before she dared cross the street.

Just then, she saw him at the door, about to go in. He smiled broadly, and her heart faltered.

"Hello, Souad. How are you? "

 "Hello. Are you in Damascus? "

"Yes, I've been here for a week. How's Farid? "

"He's fine. We don't see him much always at the hospital. "

 "And what are you doing here? "

"Waiting for the storm to ease a little. "

"Come on, I've got an umbrella. I'll take you home. "

He didn't give her a chance to refuse. She wasn't going to.

He slipped his arm around her, drawing her close under the umbrella. Their heads nearly touched. She felt as though they were lying together beneath a single blanket a small one. She caught the faint scent of shampoo in his hair, the brush of his coat sleeve against her cheek, the mingling of rain with wet wool. Then a sudden pang of embarrassment: she hadn't showered since yesterday. Her hair must be unkempt, her scent stale. But there was no escaping his arm. She didn't want to.

They crossed the street and walked several blocks until he stopped at the entrance of the building beside hers. From his pocket, he pulled a tissue and gently wiped the raindrops from her forehead and hair. Each time his fingers grazed her skin, she felt she might collapse.

He took her hand. Warmth flooded her face. "Your hands are cold. "

"Its okay home is close. "

Yet she didn't pull away. She let him hold her hand, wishing she could offer him the other one, too. Wishing the rain would never stop, that the storm would keep them stranded together under that umbrella forever.

Still holding her hand, she said shyly,

"Okay… goodbye. "But he didn't let go.

She tugged gently, reluctantly, and at last slipped her hand free. Turning toward her building, she whispered, almost pleading:

 "Don't forget to visit us. "Then she strolled to her door.

Oh God, what should I do? How can I allow him to go? I have to do something...

Suddenly, he grabbed her hand again.

"Do you think you'll get rid of me so easily? "

"No. I won't. Don't let me go. Please. "

"Do you know the Al-Qusour Cafeteria, in Al-Qusour Square? "

 "Yes, yes, I know it. "

"I'm going to meet some friends there for coffee. Come with me. They won't stay long. After they leave, we'll spend time together. You can tell me about yourself and Farid. I've missed you. "

Is that possible? Just the two of us? I can hardly believe it. I'll come!

"I don't know if I can. My mom is waiting for the medicine. "

"Don't believe that. I'll go with you. Just insist. I'll go with you, trust me. "

"Okay. You can go home first, then join us later. Take your time. I'll wait for you. "

Have some pride. Don't show your eagerness.

 "I don't know. I'm not sure I can. "

"No excuses. I'll wait for you. But don't be late. They won't stay more than an hour. "

She didn't answer, but smiled and quietly walked toward the entrance of her building. She looked behind her. He was still standing there, watching her.

When she disappeared inside, she flew up the stairs. Their apartment was on the fourth floor.

She had one hour.

"First thing, I'll take a shower. I hope it's hot. Then I'll dry and comb my hair—it looks like goat hair. And... oh yes, I'll trim the excess hair under my armpits. It won't take long. I'll be ready in time. I'll put on my new wool coat. And my leather boots. "

She reached the apartment door, opened it, and quickly entered. She tossed the medicine into her mother's lap and rushed to the bathroom.

"Why are you in such a hurry? What happened? "

"Is the water hot in the bathroom? "she asked urgently. Her mother followed after her.

"No, but I can heat it quickly. Did something happen? "

"No, but I ran into a friend who lives nearby. I have to go and copy some lessons from her. "

"Then postpone your shower until you get back. "

But Souad was already in the bathroom. She closed the door and turned on the tap. Oh my God, it's freezing.

"Are you going to take a cold shower? Are you crazy? " her mother called.

She answered from inside:

"Turn on the heater in my room quickly. " No one argued with Souad.

She gasped as she placed her head, then her body, under the icy water. She quickly applied shampoo and washed her hair.

"The important thing is to get the oil off. "

Then she soaped her body. Once was enough there wasn't time for more.

She rummaged through her mother's things and took a piece of sugar wax she had been hiding. She removed the hair under her armpits. Then she looked down.

Oh my God, how embarrassing.

She removed that too, enduring the pain with surprising patience and silence.

All of this took less than a quarter of an hour. She cleaned the bathroom thoroughly, ensuring that no hair was left behind. Then she dried off quickly, not caring that she was shivering from the cold. She left the bathroom, rushed into her room, and sat by the heater. She dressed quickly, then sat down to dry and comb her hair. Everything was calculated with care. In less than an hour, she was ready. She grabbed her umbrella, said goodbye to her mother, and left.

But halfway down the stairs, she remembered something. She quickly turned back, opened the door, and went into her mother's room. She sprayed perfume on her face, neck, and clothes, then left again.

Seconds later, she was outside. It was dark and cold. The storm was still raging. She walked briskly toward the cafeteria. It wasn't far.

I'll arrive earlier than expected.

The wind was strong, and the rain shower was relentless. "What if he's with a girl, as usual? "

"It doesn't matter. What matters is that I'm close to him, and he's trying to get close to me. "

The umbrella began to twist in her hand. The wind yanked and dragged it, and her weak hand couldn't control it. Suddenly, one of the metal rods snapped then another. It was useless now. She tried to close it, but it clamped down on her hand, and she cried out in pain. But she didn't complain she had to bear it.

Now exposed to the wind and rain, she pressed on. She was close now. She ran, protecting her head with her hand. It was no use the hairstyle was ruined. But that was fine. She would fix it when she arrived.

Water flowed like a river through the street. It was dark and deserted. Most shops were closed; their owners hiding indoors from the fury of the storm. Lightning lit up the sky, followed by thunder that shook the ground and sent shivers of fear down her spine.

Her coat was drenched. Rain ran down her face, blinding her. She wiped her eyes with the back of her hand. She looked miserable.

 "How am I going to meet him like this? I look ridiculous. But I won't turn back. He'll understand. I won't let the storm defeat me. "

The lights of the cafeteria appeared across the street. Ahmed and his friends were at the table by the window. His friends were getting ready to leave. He said goodbye to them.

Good. She wouldn't be embarrassed it would be just the two of them. Her heart leapt as his friends left and he returned alone to the table.

She began to carefully cross the stream of water flowing down the street, fighting the wind that pushed her back.

 "I won't give up. I've made it. "

He was looking towards her. She raised the broken umbrella and waved it. Suddenly, a car sped out of the darkness, splashing water all over her from head to toe. It got into her mouth and eyes.

She gasped, blinded, and wiped her eyes with both palms. As she stumbled back, she lost her balance and fell into a pool of muddy water.

Her new coat absorbed the filth like a sponge, and her feet swam in icy water inside her shoes. She scrambled to her feet.

 "What a disaster. Did Ahmed see me? "

She crossed back to the side of the street she had come from and hid in the shadow of a building entrance across from the cafeteria. There, she wiped the mud and water from her face and eyes. She looked down black mud covered her. Water streamed from her coat and down her legs like a waterfall.

She shivered. She brushed off what she could and tried to think of what could be fixed. She peeked through the iron gate. Ahmed was still inside, watching the storm, the swaying trees, and the occasional car navigating the flood.

 "There's no way I can't let him see me like this. "

She wiped her face and hair again with both hands. It was no use. She finally leaned back against the wall in defeat.

There was nothing more she could do. She couldn't face him like this. She had tried everything. She had fought nature itself and lost. But she didn't blame herself. She had resisted bravely.

Now, she squatted down, trembling and panting from emotion, trying to stay warm. She began to sneeze and then coughed hard.

She wanted to go home quickly but she couldn't move. He might see her from the window. He was surely watching, looking out for her. She stood only a few meters away, hiding her shame and disappointment.

Finally, he left the café, paused for a moment on the sidewalk, looked once more in the direction of her house… and walked away.

He disappeared.

That night, when Souad lay her head on the pillow and wrapped herself in thick blankets and wool covers, her anger and fear vanished. Her nerves calmed. A warmth spread through her body, and she felt a sense of peace.

Here, beneath the covers and in the safety of the dark, she always found her final refuge. Here, she felt safe and free to dream despite everything that had happened.

She didn't pity herself. She didn't let herself cry. On the contrary, she was proud. She had done everything she could.

It was true the storm had defeated her, but it was enough for her that Ahmed had waited until the very last moment. He had waited for her, despite the rain, cold, and storm.

She hugged her pillow, closed her eyes, and smiled.

Chapter
Eleven

am now the full moon—radiant and bright. I am the sun at its peak, ready for you.

Take me as yours. Accept me as an offering in your temple. Savor me with your morning coffee.

She turned seventeen, growing more beautiful and more desperate. The number of suitors increased by the day.

She hadn't heard from Ahmed since the night of the storm.

Now in high school, she had a close friend: Hanaa. Beautiful and blonde. The two girls were inseparable, attending the same school. Their classmates nicknamed them the "Baccara Girls, " after the famous blonde and brunette singers of the Baccara band. They both lived on the same street in the Tijara district.

The two were deeply in love, but Souad's love was more like a mirage, a beautiful illusion. Every morning, they would intentionally miss the school bus and walk from the Tijara district, located on the eastern edge of the city, to the Damascus Arabic School in Abu Rummaneh, situated on the western edge. Even that long walk wasn't enough to contain all the conversations they shared conversations they continued from their desks during class.

Hanaa was the only one who knew Souad's secret. And Souad was the only one who knew about Issam, whom Hanaa loved. Sometimes Hanaa met her lover secretly in the park, and Souad would accompany her, watching them from a distance. But Hanaa had never met Souad's lover. Souad herself wasn't sure if she would ever see him again. Sometimes she felt angry for tying her fate to him, leaving her heart at the mercy of chance and fate.

It was late winter, just before spring. The cold was sharp, but the skies were clear that day. As usual, school ended in the afternoon, and they left together.

 "Shall we walk? " "Of course. "

They took the road leading to Arnous Square, passing through al-Sibki Park. "There's a car following us, " Souad said.

"Ignore it. " "Is it Issam? "

"Maybe. But don't pay attention. "

"Would you get in the car if it were him? " "Of course not. Am I crazy? "

"Why not? Are you afraid of him? Doesn't he love you? "

"I know he does. But there are moral and social boundaries we shouldn't cross. What would he think of me if I got in his car? "

"Don't be so hard on him or yourself. "

"I won't allow myself to make that kind of mistake. If he truly loves me, let him propose to my family. "

"Don't you want him to kiss you? Don't you dream of drowning in his arms? " "Shut up, you idiot. There's the car, right next to us. Don't look! "

"He doesn't usually come by car. Should we go into the park? " "No. "

The car passed and stopped a few meters ahead. The door opened, and an elegant girl stepped out. Then, from the other side, a young man wearing a long coat and a wool scarf followed her. They both walked toward the park.

"It's not Issam, "Hanaa said.

Souad didn't respond. Her heart was pounding. She clutched Hanaa's hand and quickened her pace toward the young man and the girl.

"Wait, what's wrong with you? Let go of my hand! "Hanaa protested.

But Souad didn't answer. Instead, she marched forward and intentionally bumped into the young man.

"Sorry, I didn't see you, "Souad said.
"Souad? "
"Ahmed? "
"What a coincidence! How are you? "
"Fine. Sorry, I bumped into you. I didn't notice. "
"I'm glad you did. "

He turned to the girl beside him.

"This is Souad, one of our relatives from Damascus. "
"Hello, " said the girl, offering her hand. "This is my friend Hanaa, "

Souad said

The girl greeted them and stood waiting for Ahmed. "What are you doing here? " he asked.

"Our school is just over there, on the corner. We just finished for the day. "
"What a happy coincidence! How are you? How's Farid? "

The girl kept fidgeting, glancing around impatiently, clearly waiting for

Ahmed to finish talking. Souad noticed this and said,

"I won't bother you. Try to come visit us sometime. "

"Of course, I will. "

Then she turned to the girl, nodding politely. "Nice meeting you. " Hanaa took her hand, and they walked on.

"So that was Ahmed? I finally saw him. "

"Yes, that was him. My bad luck. Damn it I only ever run into him by chance, every few years. And he's always with some girl. "

"Why did you let him go? "

"What was I supposed to do? "

"I don't know… but you should've done something. At least apologize for missing the last time. "

"I think he forgot. "

Suddenly, she heard Ahmed calling her name from behind:

"Souad! "

She turned. Ahmed was hurrying toward them, smiling. Her heart pounded. "You two are quick! Why did you leave so fast? "

"I didn't want to interrupt you and your friend. " Ahmed laughed. "I left for you. "

"For me? "

"Of course. Come on, get in the car. I'll drive you. "

Souad couldn't believe her ears. But Hanaa quickly said, firmly,

"No, no, thank you. We want to walk. We missed the bus on purpose so that we could enjoy the weather. "

Souad didn't like Hanaa's response. She squeezed her hand, trying to get her to agree. But Ahmed cut in.

"Then I'll walk with you. "

Hanaa hesitated. Souad understood she was afraid of being seen, fearful of what her family would think.

Damn it, Hanaa, say yes just this once. Please.

Hanaa pulled her hand away from Souad's and said dryly, "You can go without me. I'll walk alone. "

Souad didn't argue. She looked at her friend apologetically, kissed her, and let her go. They waited a little while until she had walked away. Then they turned toward the car.

"Sorry about your friend. "
"Don't worry about her. We're used to walking home. "

Souad got into the car. It was a white, two-door vehicle with UAE license plates. Once inside, he looked at her for a long time, smiling. She was confused and didn't know what to say or do. He smiled and leaned in quietly until his face was just in front of hers. Her heart pounded, and she closed her eyes.

"Oh my God, he's going to kiss me? Here, on the street? Okay, fine, but I didn't brush my teeth. I must smell bad. Damn it. "

But he didn't kiss her. He only closed the car window, then turned back and started the engine. He didn't take off right away. He turned toward her, still smiling.

"So, how are you? "
"Fine. You shouldn't have sent your friend away. "
 "You're more important. Can you believe I was thinking about you today and planning to visit soon? How's Farid? "
"Still in France, as you know, completing his medical degree. " "And you? "
"I'm doing well in high school. "

His hair was shorter and thinner than before, and he looked stressed and tired.

 "I've been away a long time. I've been working in Dubai for a year now. I arrived yesterday. Are you hungry? "

 "I can't be late. My mom will be worried. " "Okay, whatever you want. "

Still, he didn't drive off. He kept looking at her, then suddenly said in a serious tone that frightened her:

"Don't move. "

He was looking at her chest. "What's wrong? "

"Don't be afraid. "

He reached toward her chest, brushing his fingers across it quickly, as if trying to shoo something away. She even felt his hand press against her breast.

"Okay, that's it. "
"What's wrong? "
"The fly flew away. "

Her face reddened, her heart pounded, and she froze in her seat in shock. As for him, he drove off, smiling calmly as if nothing had happened.

"Oh my God. He groped my breast. "

He turned to her and said, seeing how stunned she was:

"Sorry, but I had to shoo the fly away. Did that bother you? " *"Should I tell him there's another fly on the other breast?* " "No. No. But you surprised me. "

"Are you okay? You look agitated. " "I'm fine. "

"You don't talk much. Is that always how you are, or is it because of me? "

"Oh my God, where's the talking now? Where's the endless chatter with Hanaa? Say something, you idiot. "

"You must be upset. Listen, I was joking about the fly. I'm sorry. My jokes can be a bit much sometimes. I shouldn't have done that. "

"Never mind, I'm fine. "

"Say something. Don't sit there like a statue. Speak up. Show some of your femininity. It's Ahmed! "

"I want to go home. My mom will worry. "

"Damn it, what am I saying? I've ruined everything. He ditched that girl for me, you idiot. Stupid girl. Still a kid. Coward. "

"Okay, I get that. But I want to invite you to lunch tomorrow. What do you think? " *"Yes, yes. That's what I want. Don't ruin this. "*

"I don't think I can. Maybe another time. " *"You slut. "*

"I won't accept any excuses. Don't treat me like last time. " *"Oh my God, he remembers. He hasn't forgotten. "*

"What last time? "

"You made me wait in the storm. "

"Oh that!, I'm very sorry, my mom was sick that night. I couldn't leave her. I'm sorry. "

"It's okay. Luckily, you didn't come. It was freezing that day. The storm was rough, and the rain was unbearable. "

"Really? I didn't notice. "

"Then you'll accept my invitation tomorrow. "

"What more do you want? Don't make it hard for him. You won't get another chance. " "Okay. Tomorrow is halftime at school. They're letting us out early. "

"Great. "

"But we can't be late. "

"As you wish. I'll meet you at the school gate. " Before she got out of the car, he smiled and said:

"I can't believe you're Souad—the girl whom I combed her hair in Beirut. "

She smiled, turned away in embarrassment, and opened the door. Before she stepped out, he called to her:

"Listen. "

She leaned toward the window.

"I still love your nose. I still think it's a princess's nose. " "Thank you. "

She said it and walked away.

"Thank you? That's the best you can do? Oh my God, how does he stand your coldness? But he loves my nose. Do you know what that means? Oh, I don't even want to dream about it. "

He drove off. She hurried home, almost unable to believe what had just happened. As soon as she entered her room, she let out a squeal of joy and jumped on her bed.

"I have to prepare for tomorrow. There's so much to do. I have to look like a princess. "

Her evening was busy. For the first time, her mother saw her so active and energetic bathing, drying her hair, and ironing her clothes.

"There's an exhibition at school. I have to be ready. " "Will you be late? "
"No, no. But if I happen to be a little late, don't worry. Sometimes the officials arrive late. "

In the morning, the two girls met at the bus stop. Hanaa was ready to walk, as usual, but Souad wanted to take the bus.

"We're not walking today. I don't want to sweat or get my clothes dirty. Today, in particular, I want to keep my body clean. "

Hanaa looked at her in surprise. "Why all this? "

"He invited me to lunch. "

"Really? And you're going? " "Of course. "

"But someone may see you. "

"I don't care. We're going to a restaurant—a public place. " "Okay, but be careful. "

Souad looked at her and smiled, then suddenly burst into laughter, trying to stifle it. Hanaa whispered, "Calm down. What's wrong? "

"You know that lingerie store next to our house? " "Yes. What about it? " "Did you see the set displayed in the window? "

Hanaa looked at her, her mouth agape. Souad kept laughing and nodded. "Yes, yes. I'm wearing it right now. "

 "You slut! What are you planning? "

 "Nothing! I don't want to look like a child in front of him. " "Why? Are you going to take off your clothes in the restaurant? " "If necessary, " she said, laughing.

 "You're being crazy. You've lost your mind. " "It makes me feel more confident. "

"Since when has underwear ever boosted self-confidence? You're crazier than I thought. "At noon, the girls left school. Ahmed's car was waiting outside. A crowd of girls gathered behind the fence, staring and scrutinizing Ahmed's features. Souad walked out through the school gate and found the car door open. Behind her, she heard the girls' shouts and laughter. She ignored their sarcasm and got into the car.

"Are all the girls students as beautiful and charming as you? I should have been a teacher. " "You'd be a successful teacher. "

He looked surprised.

"That's the first time I've heard you say something nice about me. " "Why do you say that? "

"You made fun of me once at the hotel party have you forgotten? On another occasion, you left me waiting in the wind and rain. You never take me seriously. "

"I didn't mean to. I'm sorry. "

"Anyway, be careful. There's another fly on your chest. I'm going to shoo it away. " Reflexively, she covered her chest with both hands, and Ahmed burst out laughing. He drove off, heading toward Arnous Square, then continued to Shahbandar Square. "Where are we going? "

"I'm going to kidnap you. "

She smiled but didn't comment.

"Don't you want to know where I'm taking you? " "No. "

"I might detain you in an unknown location. " "I don't care. "

I'm just confident in the elegance of my underwear. "You're scary. "

Souad laughed. "Me? How? "

"You're so calm and confident. You make me nervous. "

"I'm not like that at all. I'm not as confident as you think. It's just that I often don't know what to say. Sorry. "

He took her hand.

"Your hands are cold. Are you feeling cold? Because we'll be staying out here in the open. " "I'm fine. The weather is nice. "

He looked at the clouds gathering in the sky. "It'll get colder soon. We'd better light a fire. "

From a small side room, he brought out a table, two chairs, and a charcoal stove. He placed them by the pond under the lemon tree. She sat in one of the chairs, watching him light the charcoal.

He suddenly stopped, looked up at her, and smiled.

"Why are you smiling? "

"Are you wearing lipstick? "

She touched her mouth with her fingers, her face reddening with embarrassment. "Yes. Why? "

"Close your mouth. " "Why? "
"Does it come in a certain flavor? "

Before she could reply, he leaned in and kissed her lips. Then he said, licking his lips, "It tastes like strawberry flavor. "

Her heart pounded so loudly, she felt it might stop.

She no longer knew what to say her thoughts froze by shock. Not because she was angry or scared, but because she was happy.

This was more than she had ever dreamed of.

 "Aren't we going to have the vodka now? " "No. "

"Why? "
"Because I'm reckless and unpredictable. "
"And what could you do… more than you already have? "

Ahmed laughed.

"You surprise me. You're more reckless than I am. " He carried the bags into the kitchen.

What are you doing? You fool! You've got what you wanted—you tasted his lips. What more do you want? Take it easy. Vodka? Don't rush things. What will he think of you?

She unbuttoned her shirt. The edge of her new bra was visible. She was sure he'd notice.

I bought it for him to see. He should see it.

Ahmed returned carrying two large glasses of orange juice. "Here. "

"Where's the vodka? "
"We'll drink the juice first. "

She took her glass and sipped a little.

They sat by the stove. Ahmed took out the sandwiches, heated one, and handed it to her. She noticed him staring at her exposed chest, so she deliberately bent down to take the sandwich.

You should see something other than my face, my hair, and my nose.

"What do you think of the juice? " "I like it. "

Everything around her was wonderful—the crackling of the coals and firewood in the stove, the water dripping from the trellis above them, the scent of the trees, the taste of the sausage, and oranges, and Ahmed's smile.

If only the world would end now.

She ate with a hunger she had never felt before. "I feel full, yet I still feel like I'm not satisfied. "

Ahmed watched her silently, gently turning the coals with a pair of tongs. Then he took the glass of juice from her hand.

"Try to stand up. " "Why? "

As soon as she rose from the chair, she felt dizzy and nearly lost her balance. He grabbed her hand, and she let herself fall into his grasp.

"What happened to me? I feel dizzy. " "That's because you're drunk. "
"Really? "

She closed her eyes and stood as if listening to something. "The world is spinning around me. Am I really drunk? " Ahmed laughed.

"Come on, try to walk in a straight line. "

She took a few steps and then began to stagger.

"It's a funny feeling. " Do you feel the same dizziness?

"No, I just enjoy seeing you drunk. "

"Oh my God, I see you here and then suddenly you're there. And I hear your voice from everywhere. "

"Come on, sit down. Close your coat well. The cold is harmful when you're in such a state. " The sun set behind a dark cloud. Ahmed looked up at the sky:

If it rains, we'll have to go inside.

Then he rubbed his hands together from the cold:

 "I'll put more coal. "

She left him busy laying the coal and firewood. She took off her coat and went down to the garden, walking among the trees, tangled branches, and wild plants. The universe around her transformed into a magical world where everything exuded poetry, music, and happiness. A strange euphoria coursed through her veins, making her see everything as beautiful. She glimpsed a beautiful plant hidden among the weeds. She sat on the ground next to it, held it, and took a whiff of it. Nature seemed different and cheerful to her today. She felt refreshed, and a chill ran through her body.

"Oh my God, what are you doing? " "Nothing. "

 "You're sitting on a puddle of mud. You're really drunk. Come here. " "No, I'm comfortable here. "

She felt his shadow over her, then his hands lifting her off the ground, her face against his chest. She smelled the scent of his perfume on his neck.

"I'm so happy. "

"No, you're so drunk. "

He sat her on the chair by the fireplace and brought her a blanket.

"There's no need for all this. I'm still fully conscious and in control of myself. " "Then stand by the fireplace to dry your pants. I don't want you to catch a cold. " Raindrops began to fall.
"I think we should go inside now. "

He led her by the hand, and they entered the house she had always dreamed of entering with him. To the living room. A large room with two large windows overlooking the garden and Illuminating the room. The floor was covered with several pieces of carpet. A large wooden closet sits at the top of the room, and on the floor were sofas, pillows, and sheepskin. Between the two windows stood a large diesel-powered fireplace.

"The room is cold. Sit on the rugs, lean on the pillows, and cover yourself with a blanket until I light the fireplace. "

Here she was, inside the house, with Ahmed. Many pictures covered the walls men and women of all ages in old photos.

"Where are you in these photos? "

Ahmed crouched at the fireplace, striking a flame to a tissue.

"Most of them are my family my grandfather and grandmother, my parents. My father grew up in this house with my aunt. "

He pointed to one frame. "That's me as a child, with my father and mother. "

As she studied the photographs, Ahmed turned his gaze from the fire to her. His voice softened: "I can hardly believe it that you're the same girl I used to tease, the one whose hair I messed up as a child. "

She smiled, leaning back against the wall.

He moved closer, bent over her, and kissed her lips. For the first time, she tasted him. The kiss deepened, long and lingering.

Hanaa will never believe this, she thought. Her head spun.

"I don't feel well. I feel nauseous. "

"I expected that. Your stomach must have caught a cold. But don't worry, we'll fix it. " "How? "

"Are you brave? "

"What do you mean? " "Come on. "

"He led her to the bathroom.

"The procedure is simple. Put your finger in your mouth and you'll vomit. " Souad was upset at the idea, but Ahmed pushed her into the bathroom.

"Do what I tell you. You'll feel better. Take your time. I'll wait for you in the room. "

"Isn't there another way? "

"This is the surest way. You'll quickly return to normal. "

"Who told you I want to return to normal? I want to stay drunk. "

She entered the bathroom, looked at herself in the mirror, and smiled. She hesitated before putting her finger in her mouth, but eventually she did. She didn't want to ruin the day. The nausea subsided, and she felt a sense of relief. She cleaned the bathroom and looked at herself again. Then she unbuttoned another button on her shirt and smiled. "You damned thing. "

Ahmed had brought the coal stove into the center of the room. "How are you now? "

"Can't you see me walking in a straight line? "

He held her hand, and she felt the warmth of his.

"You're still cold, and your socks are wet. Stand by the stove. Let them dry a little. "

But she wasn't thinking about the stove. She wanted to be hugged, to feel the warmth in his arms. "Why are you looking at me like that? "

She tried to remain silent, but she couldn't help but say:

"There's another fly on my chest. Don't you want to shoo it away? "

She placed his hand on her chest and left it there. Then she surrendered to his lips and arms.

She felt his warmth and sank into his arms, letting him carry her and stretch her out on a fur rug by the fireplace.

Reassured by the neatness of her underwear.

"Aren't you afraid of me? "
"No, I'm still the little girl who once had her hair combed by you. "

He brought a blanket, covered her, and sat by the fireplace. "We must behave. "

She began to remove her socks under the blanket. "What are you doing? "

"My socks are wet. "
"Give them to me, I'll put them near the fireplace. "

She handed him the socks and all her clothes. He looked at them and laughed. "Wrap yourself tightly in the blanket. "

There was silence, and Souad watched Ahmed stir the glowing coals in the fireplace. Outside, the rain was still falling.

"I'm cold. I wish you would take me in your arms. " "We don't want to do anything rash. "

But she lifted the blanket, inviting him to come under it. He couldn't resist and snuggled in beside her. He took her in his arms, and she clung to him, resting her head on his chest. "This is better, " she whispered.

After a few minutes of stillness and silence, she said, "Don't you want to dry your clothes? "

He laughed, "No. I don't trust myself with you in my arms. " "I don't care what you do to me. I'm happy with you. "

He pulled her close to his chest. They lay side by side, wrapped in each other's arms, with only the glow of the coals and the flickering fire lighting the room. The quiet crackle of chestnuts and corn kernels filled the silence between them.

After a while, he asked softly.

"How are you feeling now? "
"I'm good. I wish we could stay like this forever. " "But it's time to go. "

Souad clung to him, her arms tightening around his body. "Can't we wait a little longer? "

"No, " he said gently. "Your mother will worry. "

He sat in silence, watching as she dressed. They left the room exactly as it was, the warmth and scent of their closeness lingering in the air. At the door, before closing the house, he pulled her into his arms again and kissed her deeply.

"Your lips taste better than lipstick, " he whispered. She blushed but said nothing.
"Can I see you tomorrow? " She nodded.
"Then I'll wait for you at the school gate same time. " But he never came.

It had been a month since Ahmed left. He hadn't returned, hadn't appeared at the school, hadn't left so much as a message or a single word of farewell.

She thought endlessly about the reasons. Had she said something wrong? Behaved in a way that pushed him away? All she remembered was his gentleness, his tenderness, and the fact that he was the one who had asked to see her again. What had changed his mind? What had stopped him from coming back? Time went on. The suitors kept coming, but she refused to see anyone or let anyone talk to her about marriage. Her excuse was that she wanted to finish her studies, but it was a weak excuse. Her mind was distracted and distant from her studies, and her grades didn't show that she wanted to keep her education going.

Her cousin Jamil had loved her for a long time. More than once, he had sent his mother to propose, but Souad always refused—leaving both families in an awkward position. Her father never argued; he believed it was her right to choose.

Her mother, however, longed to see her only daughter happy. Jamil was handsome, educated, and well-mannered. He ran a successful tent and awning factory, had an excellent job, and could even provide Souad with her own car. By all accounts, he was an ideal match. Even Souad could find no real fault in him.

But what could she do? Her heart belonged to Ahmed. She could never belong to anyone else.

She withdrew into herself, spending her days locked in her room, leaving only for university and speaking to no one. Her brothers in Damascus tried to reason with her, but none succeeded.

Tawfiq, who lived in Kuwait, sided with their father: "Leave her alone. "

Farid, however, saw things differently. One day, he surprised the family by suddenly appearing from France. Souad could hardly believe her eyes when he walked into her room with his familiar smile. He was still her favorite brother. She rushed into his arms and burst into tears.

"You're the reason I came, " he told her gently. "I'm worried about you. "
"Don't worry, I'm fine. I just don't want to marry Jamil. "
"I know Jamil well, " Farid said, "and I know you, too. I know your character as well as his. I truly believe he's the right man for you and you

won't find anyone like him. But the choice is yours. Think carefully. "
"I don't want him. "
"Then that's enough. If you don't want him, you won't marry him. "

He fell silent for a moment, then added:

"I'll speak to Jamil. I'll explain. Leave it to me. " Her eyes filled with tears.
"Thank you. "

Farid brushed them away with his hand.

"You're precious to me. My sister, my friend. Do you remember the bike
accident? When I saw you unconscious in the hospital, I stayed beside you
all night. I cried that night. I was terrified of losing you. I blamed myself for
pushing you away. I realized how selfish I'd been—leaving you.

To loneliness when I should have been your companion. I promised myself
then that I would take responsibility for you, for your happiness. Do you
think I'd let you go so easily? "

"I wish you were here in Damascus with me, " she said. "I'm always with
you, " he replied, stroking her hair.
"Then why aren't you happy? What's keeping you from it? " She looked at
him cautiously. "What makes you say that? "
"A girl who rejects a man like Jamil is either crazy, or... " He paused. "Or in
love with someone else. "

She fell silent, lowering her gaze.

Farid gently turned her face toward him. "Is there another man? "

She hesitated, then gave a small nod. "Someone I know? "

She said nothing.

"Should I take your silence as a yes? " She kept her eyes on the ground.
"What's his name? " She shook her head.

There was no point in telling him. Ahmed had made no promises. She wasn't even sure he loved her. Perhaps it had all been a fleeting adventure for him. If she revealed his name, she might embarrass him—or worse, push him away. If he truly wanted her, he would have spoken, declared his intentions. But he hadn't.

"I won't pressure you to tell me, " Farid said at last. "Just know that I'm here—whenever you need me. "

And so Souad kept her secret. And Farid left.

A year had passed since the last encounter with Ahmed.

Souad was now attending university. She has grown more mature and more beautiful.

To this day, she still walks past her old school in Abu Rummaneh at noon. And every time a white car drives by, her heart sinks.

Part Three
Dreams of an Orchid Flower

Chapter
Twelve

ove, life, and existence.

Sex, childhood, and parenthood. Youth, old age, and death.

It's a long journey—a futile one. A relentless and frantic pursuit,

But toward what?

Will we ever reach the answer?

Souad approached me and cautiously turned her face toward me. In a low, whispering voice, she said, "There's someone following us. "

I turned around nervously. "Where? "

She glanced around cautiously, scanning in all directions.

"I don't know. He disappeared. But I sensed him walking behind me for a long time. "

I looked around again, searching for someone who might be watching us, but saw no one unusual.

"It must be the crowd, " I said. "Maybe he was just behind us by coincidence. "

"No, " she said. "I could smell his perfume behind me. He followed us for a long while. " "It's just the crowd, believe me. "

 "Maybe, " Souad replied, troubled and clearly unconvinced.

I didn't give it much thought. I asked her to ignore it, to calm down, and focus on her shopping. The new clothes, the gifts, and the extravagant items were more than enough to keep her busy all day, and soon, we forgot the whole thing.

This evening, the crowds were unlike any other day, and that was expected. Today was the ninth of September, 2009. This evening marked the launch of the Dubai Metro. People had flocked from all the emirates and from various Arab and international cities to witness the train's first run, scheduled to start at the previously announced hour.

We sat down to rest at a café located in the central lobby of the mall. A waiter came and placed two cups of coffee before us. The café was situated at the corner of the plaza in the center of the mall, giving us a clear view of the three levels, the escalators, and the bustling crowd.

I was tired, but Souad was the opposite full of energy and enthusiasm. She sipped her coffee, chatting excitedly about all that she'd seen, her face glowing with happiness as she awaited the grand event that was now about an hour away.

But then, her smile suddenly vanished. Her face darkened, and she fell silent. Her gaze froze upward toward one of the escalators. Then she quickly turned, as if trying to hide herself.

"What's wrong? " I asked, already anticipating the answer. She replied in a fearful, angry whisper, "He's over there. " "Where? "

"At the top of the escalator, on the second floor. On the balcony overlooking us. "

I turned to look at the balcony, but it was too high and crowded with people. It was impossible to distinguish anyone in particular.

"Do you still see him? "

"I don't know. I turned away quickly when I noticed him staring at me. "

"Okay, look again and show me where he is. "

Souad turned toward the balcony again, scanning the crowd nervously. "I don't see him anymore. "

"What does he look like? " I asked, still peering upward. "He's tall and thin… wearing white clothes. "

"You might be imagining it. Are you sure? "

She didn't answer. We kept staring upward, searching in vain. The balcony was crowded, as were the nearby shops, making it hard to see clearly.

"Maybe he went into one of the stores, " I said. "He's probably gone. "

"It's better to ignore it, " I added gently. "Let's go to the metro it's time. "

I tried hard not to let Souad's fear spoil the joy of witnessing this major event. We quickened our steps, moving with the crowd toward the station. I noticed that Souad had lost her excitement.

She seemed anxious, weighed down by worry.

"Are you still thinking about that man? " I asked. "Do you want us to go back and look for him? " "No need, " she replied. "We'll only ruin our evening. "

The sounds of the countdown began to rise over the loudspeakers, and excitement surged around us. The pace of the crowd quickened, and we moved with it. Souad muttered restlessly, "I'm starting to feel tired and hungry. "

"If you like, we can eat first and board the train after. "

"We'll be too late. There are long lines of people waiting for their turn on the metro. "

We stood in a long queue for more than an hour, waiting for our turn. It was nearly midnight, but the atmosphere was electric. The crowd was vibrant and patient couples, families, children playing, joking, and chatting as they waited.

Souad and I stood silently most of the time, simply observing. At last, our turn came. We reached the platform. A train arrived and its doors opened. To our surprise, it was already packed with passengers. Still, people rushed to board, and we were pushed along with them. We entered with difficulty.

There were only a few occupied seats along the walls of the train, with the central space left for standing. Like most, we remained standing. Despite the crowding, joy filled the faces of the passengers. Everyone seemed eager to be part of this historic moment.

Souad stood beside me, clearly uneasy. She couldn't find anything to hold onto for balance, so she clung tightly to my arm. I could tell she was scared, which was unusual she was always strong and confident. But here, inside the train, she seemed afraid. She wouldn't meet my eyes, and her smile had vanished.

The train departed amidst cheers, whistles, and laughter. I smiled at her. "Come on, cheer up. We're finally on the Dubai Metro. "

But she didn't respond. She kept her eyes fixed on the floor.

I noticed one of the seated passengers watching me. When our eyes met, he smiled warmly and nodded toward my wife. His gesture made it clear he was offering her his seat.

I smiled back in gratitude and tried to decline, but he stood and insisted.

Turning to Souad, I urged her to take it. To my surprise, she refused. I couldn't understand why, but there was no time to linger. The crowd was too dense, and she needed the rest. I guided her gently, and at last she sat, reluctant.

The man remained standing near me, smiling politely.

"Thank you, " I said. "She's not feeling well—indeed, she really needs the seat. "

He gave a courteous nod but said nothing. Tall and thin, with gray hair and dressed in a white linen shirt and trousers, he looked refined. The trace of expensive cologne lingered in the air. He shifted a few steps away, trying to blend into the crowd, yet I noticed his eyes flicking toward us from time to time.

Souad kept her gaze fixed on the floor. I leaned close and whispered, "Are you okay? "

She murmured something too faint to catch. Then, hesitantly, she lifted her head and whispered, "It's him. "

I turned, but the man was gone vanished into the press of passengers. "The same one who was following you? " I asked.

"Yes. It's him. " "You're certain? "
"Yes. I recognized him by his hair, his clothes… and his perfume. "

I scanned the train, and there by the door I spotted him again, waiting for the stop. I was about to move toward him when Souad gripped my hand.

"Please, leave him. We don't want trouble. He'll get off at the next station. "
"We need to know why he's been following you. "
"I don't know… " Her voice faltered. "Maybe it's only a coincidence. He was already on board before us he must have boarded at the previous station. "

I couldn't think of anything to say, especially now that he had distanced himself from her. But Souad remained uneasy, watching him anxiously.

The train stopped, and he was the first to exit. I felt a moment of relief but it didn't last. To our surprise, he remained standing outside, staring at Souad.

Souad blushed and looked away.

"Did you see the way he looked at me? " "How rude. Have you seen him before? "

She studied his face, searching her memory. "I don't think I've ever seen him before. "

The man stood motionless outside the train door, his eyes fixed on Souad, unaware of the jostling crowd around him. He looked like someone lost in a dream detached from the world, oblivious even to my presence.

Finally, the doors closed, and the stranger's face vanished behind them. The train continued on its journey. The crowding remained the same, but now it felt more amusing than tiring.

I asked her, "Are you relieved now? He's gone. " "Do you finally believe he was following me? "

"He's weird, I'll admit. But my instinct says he didn't mean any harm. " Then I tried to lighten the mood: "Don't forget, you owe him your seat. "

She stood, moved to my side, and slipped her hand into mine while gripping the overhead handle with the other.

"I'd rather stand by your side. "

I whispered, "Don't be ungrateful. All he did was try to be nice. " "Nice? That's what you call someone who's harassing me? " "Don't exaggerate. He hasn't done anything inappropriate. "

"What do you consider the bounds of decency? Should I wait until he puts his hands on me before you act? "

"If I fought every man who admired your beauty, I'd spend half my life in police stations and the other half in hospitals. "

Souad blushed and turned away, smiling despite herself.

We rode on until Al-Mushrif Station, then headed back to the Mall of the Emirates, where our car was parked. By the time we arrived, it was past midnight.

Most shops were closing, and the rooftop parking lot lay nearly deserted, with only a handful of cars scattered in the dim light.

I unlocked the car and started the engine.

Suddenly, I saw him standing in front of the car, staring at us as usual.

I turned to Souad, who was still outside the car, frozen and staring at him. I asked her to get in, but instead, she started walking toward him with determination.

I jumped out, rushed to her, and grabbed her arm. "Come back to the car. "

She didn't stop. She kept going until we stood only two steps away from him face-to-face. I tried to keep my voice steady. "You were on the train earlier, weren't you? "

He smiled without answering.

"Are you following us? " I pressed.
"Yes, " he replied calmly, his eyes fixed only on Souad. She stared back at him, pale with shock. "What do you want? " I demanded.
"The perfume. "
"What? What perfume? "
"The perfume Madame wears. " "Are you insane? "
"I'm sorry, " he said quietly. "But I won't leave until I know where she got it. "

I reached for my phone to call the police, but Souad stopped me with a touch on my hand. Then, with surprising composure, she opened her purse, took out a bottle of perfume, and handed it to him.

He hesitated, eyeing the bottle suspiciously. Then he took it and raised it slowly to his nose, closed his eyes, and inhaled deeply.

"Yes. That's it. "

He returned the bottle to Souad. "Thank you, madam. I only wanted to know where you found it. I've searched for it for years, without success. "

"Do you want it that badly? " she asked softly."It reminds me of a woman. "
"She must have meant a lot to you? " "More than you can imagine. "
"Then take it. Keep the bottle. "
"You are too generous. But I can't accept it. Whoever wears this perfume must be someone very special. "

His words and the odd solemnity in his tone only deepened my irritation.

Souad blushed.

"I insist you keep it, " she said. "You probably won't find it in the market again. "
The man bent and kissed her hand.
"You are wonderful, a true lady. But I cannot take something so precious from you. "
"I insist, " she pressed. "I won't deprive you of a memory so dear. Please accept it from me. " My jaw tightened at her words.
"You are very generous, " he replied, "but I must give you something in return. " "Don't be silly. "
"I insist. Ask for something. "

I muttered under my breath, impatient, "Just let him take it and let's go. "

But Souad ignored me completely. "All right, " she said softly. "Then I'll accept the perfume you're wearing. "

Fury rose in me, but I forced myself to stay silent.

He nodded, calm as ever. "I'll take that as a compliment but only if you agree to my one condition. "

Souad laughed lightly, her voice warm, feminine. "And what is that? "
"Thank you for accepting my invitation to dinner tonight. "

Before she could answer, I cut in, sharp and final. "I don't think so. It's too late. Maybe some other time. But thank you. "

He took out a business card and handed it to me. *Ahlam Engineering Consulting Office*, it read. "I insist on the invitation. Please accept. It's an opportunity to talk more about the perfume. "

Souad looked at me. "We were going to get dinner anyway, but I doubt any restaurants are open this late. "

"Leave it to me, madam, " he said. "I'm staying at the Jebel Ali Hotel. They'll definitely arrange a lovely dinner for us on the terrace, overlooking the beach. What do you say? "

I was distraught, searching for an excuse to decline, but Souad quickly whispered warmly, "Okay, as you wish. We'd be delighted to accept your invitation. "

"Thank you both. It's a pleasure and an honor to have you join me. Let's go—you can follow me. "

Chapter

Thirteen

I am not just one man. I am hundreds of men, lusting after thousands of women. Every day, I am reborn—a new man, desiring a new woman.

I am not a man of the present. I carry within me thousands of years of lust and hunger.

Anger and humiliation gnawed at me as I followed his taillights. "Why are you silent? " Souad asked. "You look upset. "

 "I don't understand your behavior. "
 "He looked miserable. I felt sorry for him, that's all. "

I didn't respond. I continued driving, staring straight ahead. Souad tried again to break my silence:

"Look at his car so luxurious. "
"Would you rather ride with him? "

"You're outraged... There's no need, " she said gently, resting her head on my shoulder. "You don't even like my perfume anymore. He has become nicer. "

Souad laughed softly.

"Why are you making such a fuss? I was just being polite. "

"Your behavior was unacceptable. You should have consulted me before accepting his invitation. We don't even know who he is. And yet... You looked thrilled when he kissed your hand. "

"No, I wasn't. I was embarrassed. "

"No, you were happy. If I hadn't been standing next to you, you might have offered him your other hand. "

She smiled and didn't respond.

"Would you rather I weren't with you? " I growled.

"You know, I was scared of him. If you hadn't been there, I wouldn't have spoken to him at all. "

I didn't really mean what I was saying. I was just trying to tease and provoke her. I knew she loved me, and I trusted her completely. But something that happened the night before still bothered me. Her behavior then was even stranger than today.

Yesterday afternoon, she'd called me at the office, "Please, come right away. "

She didn't provide any explanation. Her tone was calm, neither fearful nor anxious. The call didn't worry me, but it sparked my interest. She simply said, "You have to hurry, " and then ended the call.

When I left her that morning, she was still asleep. That made me wonder what could have happened?

I arrived quickly, as she asked. When I entered the apartment, it was dark and filled with a strange yet beautiful scent of perfume. Soft music floated through the air. Her voice came from the bedroom, quiet and whispering.

"I'm here. Don't turn on the light. " "Are you okay? "
"Come in. "

She stood before me, wearing the gold necklace I'd left for her on the bedside table my birthday gift to her. Her smile felt unfamiliar; her gaze seemed strange. Something sparkled in her eyes. She approached silently, took my hand, and led me like a child. I didn't recognize this woman. I walked toward the bed. She was new, different. The shy Souad was gone, replaced by a woman I didn't recognize one whose breath carried the scent of desire.

She pushed me onto the bed and straddled me like a fierce tigress, studying me and deciding where to start her feast. I surrendered completely to her touch. I didn't care who she had become or where her modesty had gone. I was mesmerized, eyes closed, drunk on the pleasure she was giving me. Occasionally, I opened my eyes and saw her staring at me, sweat glistening, moaning, and gasping. I had never seen her like this before. She was no longer the same Souad. But I wasn't upset I was captivated. This wasn't the time to ask questions. Enjoy now, ask later.

When I woke up in the morning, Souad lay beside me, lost in thought, staring at the ceiling. I greeted her, and she replied distantly, without turning her head. As I leaned in to kiss her, she quickly got out of bed, went into the bathroom, and locked the door. She dressed in silence,

absentmindedly. She barely touched her coffee. Her thoughts were elsewhere, or maybe she was trying to remember something.

On the drive, she avoided my gaze, staring silently out the window at the passing cars. I finally broke the silence.

"It was a wonderful night. "

She glanced at me with indifference, then turned her eyes back to the street. "Are you okay? "

"What do you mean, 'a wonderful night'? What night? "
"All right... If you don't want to talk about it, we won't. But what we did was incredible. I still can't believe it happened. "
"And what exactly happened? I'm trying to remember but I can't. " "Don't be shy. You should call me more often, like you did yesterday. " She looked at me in disbelief. "I didn't call you. "
"Then who left these marks on my neck? " I pointed to the bite and scratch marks she'd left. "I did that? I don't believe it. "
"What part don't you believe? Shall I remind you in detail what you did to me? "
"All I remember is waking up late, finding your gift, doing some work online, then going to the bathroom. And after that... "

Souad fell silent, thinking. "And then what? "

"That's what I've been trying to figure out since I woke up this morning. "
"You really don't remember leaving these marks on me? " I asked again, touching my neck. "I did that? "
"Come on, don't deny it. Should I remind you of my favorite part? When you said, *Relax... Leave it to me.* "

She blinked, stunned. "No. I didn't say that. "

"You said it. "
"Shut up. I don't want to hear any more. I must have been unconscious. "
"It was a wonderful birthday. "
"Although I don't remember anything you say, I feel strangely happy today and in need of meditation. "
Souad got out of the car, and I watched her walk away briskly, her dress swaying left and right, her bag swinging at her side. There was something different about her. And when she turned her face, smiled, and waved, I realized I loved her even more.

That was yesterday.

Tonight, I feel insulted and Souad knows it. She also knows I'm trying to provoke her because of that.

I was surprised and shocked by her behavior with that man. Was it because I'd just discovered what a few tender words from a stranger could do to her? Or because I was seeing a new side of her, I hadn't expected?

I had believed she was immune to emotional manipulation. This wasn't what I expected from her. But I think what truly disturbed me more than anything was my jealousy. I wasn't used to feeling jealous, and I didn't want to show it or appear weak in front of her.

I realized that Souad, like any woman, could be swayed by a flirtatious word from a professional lover and that man fit that description perfectly. Everything about him pointed to it: his looks, his voice, that charming smile. It all appeared so effortless and captivating it set off every alarm in me.

"Look at his car, " Souad screamed suddenly. "It's swaying. Be careful. "
"What's going on with him? "

His car was indeed swerving left and right. I sped up to get closer and make sure he was okay. He was holding the bottle of perfume, spraying it inside the car.

"What's up with the perfume? " Souad asked, surprised.
"I don't think the problem is the perfume. The problem is what he wants— and what he wants is you. It would've been better if you'd just sat beside him and saved the perfume. "
"You are becoming unbearable. "
"We shouldn't have accepted his invitation. "

I wanted to tell her that I felt like I was leading my wife to her lover. But that would've made me sound foolish. I was irritated.

She reached out and stroked my hair.

"It's the first time I've seen you so jealous. "

We had passed Ibn Battuta Mall, halfway to the hotel. His car was swerving wildly back and forth. We kept watching, but all we could see was his silhouette through the windshield. He was waving nervously, as if talking to someone.

"Do you think someone's with him? " Souad asked.
"It seems so, though I don't see anyone next to him. " "It looks like they're arguing. "
"Yet, but I don't see the other person. "

I sent him a warning signal. I flashed my high beams and honked a few times, but it didn't help. On the contrary, his car kept swerving erratically.

"Oh my God, Souad screamed, I'm afraid he's lost control. "

I slowed down and tried to keep my distance to avoid a crash. His car veered suddenly to the right and left the main road. Luckily, no other cars were nearby. There were roadwork and potholes on the shoulder, and he seemed to be trying to avoid them. He succeeded to some extent, but the car kept plowing inward, into the sand. It was clear he no longer had control his car spun, tilted to the side, and finally flipped over.

Souad screamed in alarm as a cloud of dust billowed up, filling the air. His car vanished behind it, fading into the darkness.

I pulled over to the side. A few speeding cars passed without stopping.

I jumped out, and so did Souad. We dashed into the dust cloud. His car had landed upright, and the engine had stopped. When we arrived, the door was open, and that strange man was standing beside the car silent and calm. He wasn't tense or panicked, just distracted, his mind somewhere else.

I grabbed his hand and shouted, "Are you okay? "

He looked at me in surprise and asked, "What happened? "

I tried to pull him away from the car, but he resisted and pointed toward it. "I'm fine. What matters is her. Is she okay? "

I looked at the car and asked, "Who is she? Was someone with you? "

He didn't answer. He was swaying, so I helped him sit down on the ground and hurried back to the car. I checked inside. No one. I returned to him. He was lying on his back, blood trickling from his nose. He pointed at the car again and asked, "Is she okay? "

I told him, "There's no one in the car. Were you with someone? "

He looked at me, as if trying to remember, but said nothing. "Can you stand? "

"I think so, " he replied, struggling to his feet.

I supported him and led him to my car, where Souad was waiting. He closed his eyes, as if about to faint. Souad rushed over and took his other arm. He turned toward her, trying to open his eyes.

"You crazy girl... You almost killed us. "
"Me? " Souad said, startled. "What did I do? "
"Don't worry, I said, he's delirious. We need to get him to a hospital fast. "

She said, worried, "The hospital is far. Let's call an ambulance. "

He was drifting in and out of consciousness, between reality and delirium, scanning the area as if searching for someone. We had no choice but to call the police. I reported the incident and asked for an ambulance.

I stayed beside him, resting his head in my lap. A tear rolled from his eye as he stared at Souad. Then he smiled and whispered weakly:

"You're made of cotton candy and girls' madness. " "What is he talking about? " Souad asked, confused.

"I don't know. He's delirious. "

"I'm not delirious. Please stay close to me... "

The sound of police sirens and ambulances began to approach, growing louder. He turned to me and muttered something I couldn't make out. Then he grabbed my hand and whispered in my ear:

"The bag! It's in the car. Please bring it. "

I hurried back. Sure enough, a tough leather bag was on the floor. I picked it up and handed it to him. He took it, then handed it back to me.

"Please, put it in your car. Keep it safe for me. I think I'm about to faint. " I handed the bag to Souad, who took it hesitantly.

"Please, " he said, "I'm afraid it'll get lost." "Is there money in it? Jewelry? "

"No, no. Nothing like that. "

He fell silent for a moment, closed his eyes, then continued in a weak, low voice, "Still, everything is there. "

Then he lost consciousness.

Souad complied and put it in the car. Just then, police cars and an ambulance arrived.

It didn't take long. The paramedics took care of the man, gave him oxygen, carried him to the ambulance, and took him to the hospital.

When the police officer asked me if I knew him, I immediately denied it. Indeed, we didn't. I only mentioned the circumstances of the accident. Without mentioning that we had met at the mall, I didn't want to get involved in the investigation.

In the car, Souad silently hugged the bag.

As for me, my mind was awash with questions and question marks. Was there actually someone else with him?

Who was he talking to and gesticulating with? Was he arguing with someone?

Who did he mean by asking if she was okay? Then why did he blame Souad? What made him say, "You almost killed us? " What does Souad have to do with what happened?

Fourteen

I couldn't sleep all night thinking about what had happened. Souad was also tossing and turning irritably. I knew what was bothering her and what was going through her mind. When she thought I had fallen asleep, she quietly got out of bed and walked out of the room to the living room. I guessed what she wanted to do, as I knew her curiosity. I got out of bed and followed her quietly into the living room. I found her sitting in front of the bag, staring at it silently. She sensed my arrival and said, touching it with her hand: "What could it be inside? "

I said firmly, "Don't even think about opening it. It's a trust. The man has trusted us. "

"I know, I know, " she said with a sigh. "But I was just wondering what's in it? He was keen to save it. Do you think there's money in it, bundles of dollars like those we see in movies? "

She placed her fingers on the lock. "Do you think it's locked? "

"Don't think about it too much, and please don't touch it. Forget it, put it out of your mind. We won't mess with it. We'll deliver it to its owner just as we received it. Let's go back to bed. "

I was careful not to let her catch me off guard and mess with the bag. However, I failed. I fell into a deep sleep and was awakened only by the sound of Souad's screams.

I got up quickly. She wasn't in bed. "Where are you, Souad? "

She didn't answer. I hurried to the living room, but she wasn't there, nor was the bag. The sound came from the bathroom, but it was locked from the inside.

"Open the door, Souad. "

No one answered. I knocked with both hands. "Open the door. "

I heard the lock click open. Souad opened the door and quickly left, very scared. I looked inside the bathroom. There was nothing out of the ordinary except for the bag on the floor.

It was locked. I took it and followed Souad to the bedroom, where she was sitting, crying. I sat beside her and tried to calm her down.

"What's wrong? What happened? "

She didn't answer and continued crying. "Did you open the bag? "

"No, I didn't open it. "
"Then why are you trembling and crying? "It's the mirror. "
"What's wrong with it? "

But Souad didn't answer and continued crying.

I left her and went to check the bathroom and the mirror. There was nothing out of the ordinary. I returned to Souad and repeated my question.

"What's wrong with the mirror? "Did you look in it? "

"Yes, it's a mirror and there's nothing in it. Tell me what happened? "What did you see when you looked in it? "

"What would I see? I said, laughing. I saw my reflection. Come with me and see for yourself. " I pulled her by the hand into the bathroom. But she closed her eyes.

"Look in the mirror. Don't be afraid. "

She opened her eyes reluctantly. "Look carefully. Do you see anything else? " "No. "

"Then what? "

"Nothing. " "Nothing. "

"Tell me what scared you. " But Souad didn't answer.

"Didn't we agree not to open the bag? " "I want to sleep. " I just want to sleep. "

Souad slept clinging to me all night, hugging my arm and not letting go.

Early in the morning, I got up quietly, took the bag, put it in the closet, and locked it with the key. I put the key in my pocket and left the house while she was still asleep.

But before going to the office, I had to check on that man in the hospital When I entered his room, he was in his bed—asleep or unconscious, I don't know. In his hands were tubes, IV fluid, and a heart rate monitor.

The nurse entered and smiled when she saw me. "Fortunately, he didn't suffer any injuries or fractures. "

She checked the IV lines and added, "He's fine, but he needs to rest. He's still in shock. " "Has he been unconscious since yesterday? "

"No, he woke up, but he was nervous and raving all night. The doctor just gave him a sedative to help him sleep and rest. Is he a relative of yours? "

"No, he's a friend, " I said hesitantly.

Then she asked curiously, "Do you know a woman named Ahlam? "
"Ahlam? No, why? "

"He was raving and talking to a woman named Ahlam. " "I have no idea. "

I looked at him closely. There was something about his calm face and gray hair that left a lasting impression, filling me with a sense of reassurance and trust. "

I left the hospital and went to my office in Dubai Media City, where I run a small website and web design agency. But all day, my thoughts were focused on that man, wondering about Ahlam. "Is she the one behind that perfume? Was she his wife? His lover? Was she the same woman he was asking about when he got out of the car? Was she with him? Had they been arguing in the car, causing the accident? And where had she disappeared to?

Souad called me to say she was feeling tired and wouldn't be going to her work today. She would rest at home instead.

When I returned that evening, I found her waiting for me, eager to visit the man in the hospital. She was quiet the entire drive, her face tinged with sadness.

"Did you sleep well? " I asked. "Yes. "
"Are you still shaken by what happened last night? " "No, I've already forgotten it. "
"Then why so silent? Why do you look so sad? "
"I'm not sad, " she said softly. "I've just been thinking about that man. "

We entered his room. He was asleep, with no tubes in his arms, no equipment attached to him. Souad stood at his bedside, watching him in silence. Then she leaned closer, gently stroked his face and forehead, and sat on the edge of the bed. She took his hand in hers and stayed there quietly. I couldn't understand her behavior toward a man we had only met the day before.

The man began to stir, moaning and muttering words I couldn't make out, his fingers tightening around Souad's hand. At last, he opened his eyes, startled to find us so near. Fixing his gaze on her, he whispered, "Don't leave me. "

Souad's face filled with confusion. She tried to pull her hand away, but he gripped it harder. His breathing grew heavy—gasping, uneven. Alarmed, I called for help. Nurses rushed in and administered a sedative. Gradually, his body relaxed. His eyelids drooped as though he were fighting to stay awake. Finally, he looked at Souad, managed a faint smile, and drifted into a deep sleep.

We left the hospital after the doctor assured us he was fine, only suffering from fatigue and exhaustion. On the way back, silence hung between us. My mind, however, was restless, tangled with questions. I glanced at Souad, who seemed lost in thought.

"Have you known him before? " I asked. "Of course not. "
"Then why this attention? Why such concern? " "That was spontaneous. "
"His reaction suggested otherwise—as if he already knew you. "
"I don't know him. I've never seen him in my life. But if you knew his story, you'd sympathize with him too. "
"His story? "

Right then, I realized she had opened the bag. A guilty smile played on her lips, the kind of smile that confessed a secret.

"Honestly, " she said, "I read his diaries. " "Which diaries? "
"The ones in the bag. " She hesitated, then added, "I couldn't resist. "

So you opened the bag? Didn't we agree not to? "

"Sorry, I couldn't help it. I had to know more about him. " "And what was in it? “

“Nothing important… just the diaries. What a strange story. “

At home, the closet door was open. Somehow, Souad had managed to unlock it I still don't know how. She went straight to the bag, pulled it out, and opened it with a rush of excitement.

Inside were stacks of papers and various legal contracts tied to his work. From them, we learned that his name was Salah and that he was an engineer. There was also a small, elegant leather-bound booklet memoirs, written in a careful hand with strikingly beautiful penmanship.

 “Read it, “ Souad urged. “Read it. What a strange memoir. “

Chapter

Fifteen

For whom am I writing these memoirs? For myself—or for others? I no longer know.

Sometimes I ask: Why should I write them for others? What's the use? What would the world gain from my story? What difference would it make?

Could the world ever give me back a woman without a name or address? A woman with no features, no face except the one etched in my memory? Could the world return to me a woman without an identity, whose only trace was a username—*Ahlam*?

How could a real woman be woven out of the virtual threads of the internet? How could she step out of a dream and into reality? Such a woman vanishes at the first light of dawn, and when you open your eyes, the illusion slips away. Then you wonder: is it truly the light you long for, or the dream you've just lost?

Perhaps I write only for myself to keep time from erasing the memory of what happened. To prevent the day from coming when I ask myself if it was ever real, or if the woman who stole my life and disappeared was nothing more than an illusion spun from my own mind.

I don't write to keep from forgetting—she is unforgettable. She is engraved deep within me. Her glances, her smile, her words still tremble in my blood and stir me from my sleep. Time has not softened the wound of her absence. On the contrary, it has deepened it. The scar she left grows sharper each morning I wake to find her gone.

I write because I can't breathe because writing is the only breath left to me. Since she vanished, I have been haunted by nightmares of narrow, suffocating spaces where no air or light can reach me.

I write so I won't lose my mind. I write so I won't lose my grip on what happened. I write so that day never comes when I'm forced to believe she was only a dream. That is why I cling to every detail, every small nuance. I don't write for sympathy or pity they cannot heal me. The helpless gaze of loved ones watching you drown does nothing to ease the suffocation.

My ship has sailed for years, scanning oceans for a single island. I have the latest navigation systems, the finest technology, computers, satellites yet still I cannot find her. Though her coordinates are simple: her longitude is a glance, her latitude is a smile.

I've come to dislike passwords. They are barriers we hide behind, fortresses we build around ourselves, masks that conceal others' smiles and keep them at a distance. Why does vulnerability terrify us? And why are others afraid of us?

What lies behind their garden walls? Nothing we don't already have dreams and ambitions, instincts and desires.

So why do we wear masks online? Why do we reveal ourselves to strangers yet hide our feelings from those closest to us? How can a woman, with a single click, press "Cancel " and erase someone she once cared for deleting their name from her friends list as if they had never existed?

Before that, I didn't believe in love.

To me, love was an illusion a feminine invention with no place in a man's world. Sex was real. Sex belonged to men.

Love was an illusion, a form of poetry, and longing. Sex was touch, union, and ecstasy.

Love meant deprivation for women. Sex meant fulfillment for men.

Women seduce men with sex to gain love. Men seduce women with love to gain sex.

I played the game perfectly. I wanted a causal relationship—no strings, no commitments. I had crafted clever plans and backup exits to withdraw quietly, leaving no trace, no damage. I wanted a civilized battle one that ended not with hatred, but with a handshake and mutual parting.

No prisoners.

That was the plan.

I told her from the beginning, *"You are free. "*

And so, she left free, unbound. She told me, *"Go, you are free. "*

But to my surprise, I remained her prisoner.

I wanted her to leave my life without clinging. My freedom was precious even selfishly so.

I wanted her to leave quietly, leaving no scars, no residue.

It was a brilliant plan.

And the problem was: it worked.

Ahlam vanished just as I had intended to vanish myself. She honored the contract perfectly. She disappeared.

And I remained her prisoner.

I'm still waiting for her to set me free. I'm still waiting—alone at the station.

Trains come and go. Passengers board and depart. But Ahlam never appears.

Time passes until I become addicted to waiting. Addicted to my seat.

Addicted to searching every smile, every face hoping for her smile, her gaze.

If only she would return, even just to say goodbye. I ask for nothing more than a few seconds.

I want to see her so I can forget her.

I want her to return so I can prove to myself that she's only a woman an ordinary woman and then let her go.

I want to convince myself she belongs to this world, so I can stop searching for her in another.

I don't want justification. I don't need an apology. She never lied.

She never deceived me.

She never made promises she didn't keep. She never disappointed me.

All I want is one moment. I want to see her.

Smell her perfume.

Touch her hair.

And ask her, *"What are you made of? "*

And she replies, *"I'm made of cotton candy and the playfulness of girls. "*

Now here is my story:

Chapter

Sixteen

Souad watched me all evening as I read the diary. I kept catching glimpses of her moving quietly around me, hovering, occasionally glancing to see how far I'd gotten. She was eager for my reaction and she had every right to be. The story, with all its strange turns, stirred something in me. Ahlam's character fascinated me. Slowly, I began to understand why he was so bound to her.

"What do you think? " Souad asked impatiently the moment I closed the notebook. "She's amazing. "

"Who? "

"Ahlam, of course. Strange... but captivating. "

Souad frowned, clearly irritated. That wasn't the answer she had expected. "You find her amazing? "

"She looks like you, " I added quickly, before her anger could deepen. Her cheeks flushed, and she smiled, suddenly delighted.

"She looks like me? "

"I can understand what he went through. "

"He didn't deserve what happened to him, " she said softly. "He seems kind… gracious. " "It's a pity that he lost her. Imagine someone like that, really existing. "

"What do you mean? "

"I mean… she's a woman worth seeking. "

Souad didn't answer. She was waiting for me to go on, and I knew what she was waiting for. I couldn't let the silence stretch too long—she would have exploded. So I added quickly:

"A woman like you. "

Her face grew redder, and she smiled again.

But then she frowned. "She made him waste his youth. He could've found happiness with someone else someone more beautiful, more loyal. "

"And yet, he wanted her. Something about her captivated him. " "Like what? " she pressed, a little angrily.

"I don't know. Maybe her boldness. Her courage. Her experience. "

"If it's experience you want, then go to prostitutes. Many of them are more beautiful, bolder, more experienced if that's what attracts you. "

"Are you jealous of her? " "Jealous? Me? "

"Then why are you angry? "

"Why should I be jealous of a woman who threw herself so easily into his arms? Not even prostitutes do that. "

"And what's that got to do with me? I'm not the one she threw herself at. "

"But you wished you were in his place, didn't you? "

She hurled those words at me, then stormed out of the bed, slamming the bathroom door behind her.

That night, she ignored me completely. She wouldn't accept my excuses that I wasn't involved, that it was just a story but she gave no reply either. She stayed that way until morning.

Over coffee the next day, I tried to break the silence. "What made you angry yesterday? "

"Oh, I wasn't angry. "
"You're mistaken if you compare yourself to her. You're special there's no comparison. "

She kept her back to me, sipping from her cup while staring out the window. But I caught the shy smile she was trying to hide. Finally, as she was leaving, she said quickly:

"I'll call you when I finish work. "

What unsettled me wasn't that she had made a scene because I admired some unknown woman in a stranger's story. It was the fact that nothing escaped Souad. No matter how hard I tried to hide it, she sensed what was in my mind. She read it in the tone of my voice, the way I moved my fingers even the way I scratched my nose.

She must have sensed the danger behind my fascination with Ahlam. And perhaps she was right. Had I, even for a moment, wished to be in Salah's place?

The shadow of Ahlam haunted me all day. That strange story kept distracting me. Ramesh, my young Indian assistant, noticed it too as he set a cup of coffee on my desk. "You look sleepy and tired. "

"Not tired or sleepy, just lost in thought. " "Want me to finish the project for you? " "No, no I'll handle it. "

I tried to bury myself in the work, but the words blurred and my thoughts wandered. "You're not yourself today. "

"True—something's on my mind. " "A woman, isn't it? "

"Yes. A story about a woman. " "I'm curious. Tell me. "

"All I know is… she's unlike anyone I've ever known. "

He raised an eyebrow. "She's gotten under your skin. Be careful. " "What do you mean? "

"You're newly married, and already your thoughts drift to someone else? " "Don't get me wrong. I love Souad. I've loved her since we were children. I can't imagine life without her. She's the one I want to grow old with, the one I want to build a family with. " "And yet… this other woman still draws you in? Is she really that beautiful? "

"I don't know. I've never even seen her. " He stared. "That makes no sense."

I struggled for words. Nothing fit. Finally, I murmured:

"She's something else. It isn't about beauty. " "Then who is she? "

"Her name is Ahlam. Another man loves her he's searching for her. " "Then you love her too, " Ramesh said with a laugh.

"It's not like that. How could I love someone I've never met? But there's this strange feeling as if I know her. As if I were the one searching. "

"You'll have to tell me her story. "

"I can't. It's someone else's private confessions. "

He smiled knowingly. "You're not in the mood to work. " "You're right. I can't focus. "

I left the office abruptly not to rest, but because I needed to be close to the case that haunted me. I went straight to the hospital, hoping Salah had woken up.

The moment I stepped off the elevator, I smelled Souad's perfume that strange, alluring scent.

I wasn't mistaken. She was already in his room. A wave of unease swept through me. For the first time since our marriage, she felt distant, like a planet drifting away from its orbit. She moved around Salah as if he belonged to her, as if she belonged to him.

She was startled when she saw me. Uneasy.

Salah lay on the bed, awake at last. His face lit up when he noticed me. Souad propped a pillow behind his back, helping him sit.

"Thank God you're safe, " I said.
"Hello, hello—how are you, Mr...? "
"Ahmed, " I supplied quickly. "I'm fine. " "I'm Engineer Salah. "
"How are you feeling today? "
"Well, enough. I'm sorry to trouble you both. You've been incredible. I'm lucky I met you. " "The accident was no small matter, " I said. "It's a miracle you survived. "
"Thanks to you two. Without you...I don't know what would've happened. "

He paused, his expression clouding with memory. Then suddenly:

"The bag... is it safe? "
Souad and I exchanged a quick, embarrassed glance. I answered first:
"Don't worry, Mr. Salah. It's safe. With us. "

Salah noticed our discomfort. He asked:

"Did you look inside? "

"No, of course not, " Souad replied, glancing at me. "It holds very personal things. No one's seen them. " I changed the subject. "What about the car? "

He laughed. "Nothing that can't be fixed. Insurance will handle it. " A long silence followed, but a question kept circling in my mind.

"Was someone with you in the car, Mr. Salah? "

He hadn't expected that. He looked at me, then at Souad. His expression tensed, fingers fidgeting. He stared at the ceiling, then shut his eyes.

"There's no need to answer, " Souad said gently. "You look tired. "

Salah opened his eyes, visibly disturbed. "What made you think someone was with me? "

Souad responded, "While we were following your car, I thought I saw another shadow maybe someone beside you. It looked like you were talking to someone. "

"Seriously? " he laughed. "I must've been singing along to the radio. I was alone. " "There was no music playing when I pulled you out. "
"Then I guess I wasn't listening to music. "

I couldn't hold back. "But you were talking to someone. A woman. You asked me to save her. " His face darkened. He withdrew again into silence.

"Was it Ahlam? " I asked. "Ahlam? "

He looked puzzled. "You're the one who should tell me was Ahlam there? I wish you'd say yes. I wish you'd tell me she was beside me. "

"But we found no one else. No trace of anyone. " "I know. There was no one but me. "
"Then, who did you ask me to save? "

He gave me a strained look, then smiled. "You don't give up, do you? " "It's the way you said it. So urgent. Like someone *was* really there. "

"Leave him alone, Ahmed, " Souad said, sighing.

But Salah continued, "I must've been hallucinating. I was alone. "

"You weren't hallucinating, " I insisted. "You were conscious. You even asked me to save the bag. "

He searched for a way out of the conversation, but when no answer came, he stayed silent. "It's fine if you don't want to explain. I only want to help. "

"Having you both nearby is all the help I need. "
"Would you like us to call a friend? A family member? " "No. No need. "
"Maybe your wife? "

He looked at Souad and replied, "I'm not married. " "Isn't there anyone close to you? "

"No one. "

He paused, then smiled. "I'll be discharged tomorrow. The invitation still stands I'd love to have you both for dinner at the hotel. "

I tried to decline, but he insisted.

"Maybe you can bring the bag with you. "
"We can bring it now, if you like. " "No, no need. Tomorrow. "

Just before we left, he added, "I hope you've read the diaries. "

Souad's face paled. He went on, "I don't mind. I feel close to you both, and I trust you. " On the way home, Souad was quiet, humming to herself. I broke her reverie.

"Why did you go to the hospital? "

She turned to me, surprised by the question, but answered calmly. "I wanted to help. "

"You could've told me. "
"I didn't think I had to. It's normal it's a humanitarian thing. He's a lonely man. "
"You used to fear strangers, avoid them. And now, suddenly, you rush to this man. I don't understand. "

"You're right. I don't even know why. Sometimes I feel like I'm not in control like things just happen, and I can't explain them. "

"Like the day before yesterday? When you called me in a panic? " Souad laughed softly, then turned her face away, embarrassed. "You know you can trust me. I can help you. "

"Of course. You're the only one I trust. "

"Then why won't you tell me what happened in the bathroom? " She went pale, silent.

"What about the mirror? Did you see something? " "No. "

"Then what scared you? Why won't you tell me? " "I told you—I didn't see anything. "

"Then why were you afraid? "

She hesitated. Then, quietly, "Please stop asking. I told you—I didn't see anything. I didn't see anyone. "

Her words cut through me. I let it go, but her last sentence chilled me.

I didn't see anyone.

What did she mean by that?

Chapter

Seventeen

n My Corner (after Charles Aznavour) He watches you from the corner of his eye. You shift, uneasy, caught in the depth of his gaze— and you surrender to his game.

And I, in my corner, say nothing, Though I see everything. He stalks you, pressing closer, and you welcome it with a smile, as if you were sorry I was here.

And I, in my corner, though silent, read your game perfectly, hiding the weight of the breath that strangles me.

He looks at you with furtive fire, while you laugh freely, carelessly, glad of his hidden desire.

He flirts with you through me and you rejoice. Your laughter rings.

And I, in my corner, though I say nothing, feel my heart tremble on the verge of tears.

I drink my sadness, watching the end draw near, for love is never still It always changes tomorrow.

Salah was waiting for us at the hotel entrance, his posture and elegance resembling that of an artist or politician arriving at a festival. The moment he spotted us, he hurried forward, smiling warmly.

 "I'm glad to see you both, " he said.
"We are, too, " I replied, handing him the bag. He took it, then turned to Souad.
"And how are you today, Madam Souad? " "Fine, thank you, " she answered briefly.

He studied her intently.

"No, no something is bothering you. I can sense it. I hope I'm not the cause."
"I could never be bothered by you, " she said politely. "You're very kind. I appreciate your concern, but I'm fine. "

His attentiveness grated on me, setting off alarm bells once again. At that moment, I wished I hadn't come. Their exchange of pleasantries was unsettling, and I dreaded how the rest of the evening might unfold.

But everything shifted the instant we reached our table. The surprise awaiting us altered my mood entirely, steering the evening onto a lighter, more cheerful course.

There, waiting, was a beautiful woman in her thirties, with striking blonde hair and distinctly Western features. She rose as we approached, smiling shyly as she extended her hand.

"I present to you, Nicole, " Salah said.

The introduction caught me off guard. Turning to her, he continued in

English, smiling as he gestured toward Souad:

"She's a dear friend. "

Souad greeted Nicole warmly, even exchanging kisses. But when Nicole approached me and kissed my cheeks, Souad's smile stiffened, if only for a moment.

"Do you speak French? " Nicole asked me in English.
"No, " I replied quickly. Souad, however, answered in French, hinting that she knew a little.

We sat around the dining table. Nicole was lively and spoke with infectious enthusiasm, while Salah listened with quiet attention. She leaned toward him often, holding him with a familiarity.

That was difficult to ignore. Her words flowed mostly in English, though now and then she addressed Souad in French.

Souad was delighted, basking in the attention and the air of distinction it lent her.

Conversation turned naturally to our impressions of Dubai. Nicole spoke at length of her admiration for the city its beauty, its markets, and the vast allure of the desert. She told us she had lived there for several years, working for an insurance company.

Souad asked her, "Where in France are you from? " "I'm from Grasse, in the south. Do you know it? " "No, " Souad replied, a little wistfully.

Nicole's eyes lit up. "It's the city of perfumes. They manufacture scents for France and for the world. "

"It must be a beautiful city, " Souad murmured.

"You should visit one day. The air is filled with the scent of flowers and perfumes wherever you go. The landscape is breathtaking—hills, plains, and endless farms, all a patchwork of roses and blossoms. You can even tour the perfume, soap, and essential oil factories. My father owns a small one there. "

She spoke with nostalgia; her voice tinged with dreamy romanticism. "So, what brought you to Dubai? " Souad asked.

Nicole burst out laughing.

"Everyone asks me that question. " She paused, then added in French, still laughing: *"C'est l'amour. "*
"It's love, " Souad translated.

Annoyed, I whispered, "I got that. I'm not stupid. " "To love, " Nicole said, raising her glass toward Salah.

Dinner ended, and I couldn't shake the thought: *All the women are in love with Salah.*

Souad got along well with Nicole, but I could tell she wasn't entirely comfortable being pushed out of the spotlight.

Salah suggested we have coffee elsewhere. Nicole leaned in, whispered something to him, then stood.

"I'll pass on coffee, if you don't mind. I have to leave. "

Souad, unable to fully hide her relief, said, "So soon? Stay with us a little longer. "

"Thank you, I wish I could, but I must go. " Then, turning to Salah with regret, she added, "I hope my leaving doesn't upset you. "

Salah kissed her hand, answering with his usual courtesy. "Of course it does. I would have loved for you to stay all evening. "

"Oh, Salah, I'm so sorry. "

"It's all right. What matters is that you're comfortable. "

Well, he's not supernatural, I thought with a quiet smile. *Some women aren't completely taken in by him. He's just a man, like me.*

Nicole kissed Souad and me goodbye, then slipped her arm around Salah's waist, her head resting on his shoulder. At the door, she pressed a passionate kiss on his lips before leaving.

When Salah returned, he laughed. "Now we can relax and continue our evening in Arabic. " "She must love you very much, " Souad said.

"Who? " He looked genuinely surprised. "Nicole! "

"Nicole? Do you think so? " Salah smiled faintly, his eyes drifting toward the door. "You must be old friends, " I said.

Salah laughed. "Who's Nicole? No, not at all. I only met her today at the insurance company. She's nice, isn't she? "

I exchanged a glance with Souad and smiled. "She's nice. I thought you two were engaged. "

He shook his head, looking toward the door once more. "I'm not that type. I don't think I could ever get engaged to anyone. "

"Why not? " Souad asked. "Many women would love to be with a man like you. "

I shot her a disapproving look it wasn't the most appropriate thing to say but I added, "Indeed. "

"All the women in the world aren't worth a single glance from Ahlam, " Salah said softly. "Just as all the perfumes of Grasse aren't worth a single drop of hers. "

I frowned. "The same perfume Souad wears? " "Yes. "

Suddenly, he shot up, slamming his palm on the table. His voice rose sharply. "The bottle! The perfume bottle! "

Souad and I stared at him, startled.

"It was in the car, " he went on, agitated. "What happened to it? Did it break or is it still there? " "We have no idea, " I said.

"It must still be in the car. I'll call Nicole she knows where the car is now. " He picked up his phone and dialed her number.

Souad leaned toward me and whispered, "That's strange. There's no need for all this fuss. It's just a bottle of perfume. "

Salah spoke with unusual concern. "Nicole will call the repair shop. Her insurance company sent the car there for repairs. "

"Don't worry about it, " I said. "We'll get you another one. What's the name of this perfume, Souad? "

"I know its name, " Salah said before she could answer. "It's 999—triple nine. I've known it for a long time because it's Ahlam's perfume. "

"Then it's fine, " I replied. "We'll get you another bottle. "

Salah smiled faintly. "No need. Just tell me where you bought it. " "You can find it in any perfume shop in the malls, " Souad said.

"Are you sure? I've searched for it for years. No one knows it or has ever even heard of it. " "That's strange, " Souad murmured.

"It's okay, " I said. "Souad can buy you another bottle from the store where she bought it. " Souad turned to me, surprised. "But you're the one who bought it for me. "

"Me? " I asked, startled.

"Yes. It was your gift, along with the necklace, on my birthday. " "What? I didn't do that. "

"How could you not? Weren't you the one who gave me the necklace and the perfume? " "I gave you the necklace, yes but not the perfume. I thought you bought it. "

"No, I didn't. "

"That's… very strange. So where did it come from? "

We stared at each other in confusion. I asked, "Tell me where you found it. " "The bottle was next to the necklace on the bathroom counter, by the mirror. "

"I did put the necklace there I wanted to surprise you. But I didn't bring the perfume bottle. " "Stop joking. Then who put it there? Where did it come from? "

"I was surprised at the time because the bottle was unwrapped. "

Salah, who had been listening intently, said in shock, "That's really strange. Does that mean someone entered the apartment and placed the bottle there? "

"That's impossible. No one else has the keys, " I replied. "So, who brought it? " Souad asked fearfully.

"I think maybe one of your friends gave it to you to try, and you kept it without realizing, then forgot about it. "

She hesitated. "Maybe, I don't remember, but it's possible. "

Just then, Salah's phone rang. "It's Nicole. "

He spoke briefly, then returned smiling.

"They found the bottle in the car, and it's intact. She'll bring it to me tomorrow. " He looked as happy as if he'd won a grand prize.

"Now we can show it to the perfume sellers. They'll surely identify its source. " "It's clear this perfume means a lot to you, " Souad said.

"More than you can imagine, " Salah replied. "The existence of this perfume is the first real proof that Ahlam existed. This perfume is her identity. No one else ever wore it. Until you came, madam. Fate brought you to me. I wonder if it was a coincidence… I don't know. But the moment I entered the mall that day, my nose caught that scent. I couldn't believe it. My heart raced. I expected to find her, but instead, I found you. And you smelled like Ahlam. Look how our lives intersected how perfume brought us together. "

"Have you tried looking for her? " I asked.

Salah laughed softly and pointed toward the beach. "Do you like to walk on the sand? "

Souad eagerly agreed. We left the restaurant and headed toward the shore. "Is this the beach that…? " Souad began.

Salah smiled. "Yes, it is. "

"Then let's walk on the sand, " Souad said, laughing.

She slipped off her shoes and ran ahead, teasing the waves sometimes chasing them, sometimes retreating, kicking the water so that droplets glittered in the air.

Salah watched her and murmured to me, "That was Ahlam. "

"I don't think so. Souad is different. Her nature is different, " I replied. "You think so? "
"Yes, of course. "

Does he want to replace Ahlam with Souad? I wondered. Or does Souad want to take Ahlam's place?

Still watching Souad as she played, Salah said quietly,

"I searched for her a long time. Everyone abandoned me, thinking I'd gone mad. I don't blame them my story is strange. They think I invented it. "

Souad returned and walked with us.

"I believe you, " she said, "but I don't understand her. I don't understand why she disappeared. "

"I resented her at first, " Salah admitted, "but I couldn't help forgiving her, even making excuses for her. "

Before I realized it, I blurted, "Do you want me to help you find her? "

Souad stopped short, her expression both startled and faintly pleased. "Are you serious? "

Salah turned to me, intrigued.

"How can you help when I know nothing about her? Can you actually find any trace? "

"I don't know. But we can try. I believe every problem has a solution. Searching always leads somewhere. I'll consult my assistant he's far more skilled with computers and the internet than I am. Together, we might devise a plan. If you agree, come to my office and we'll discuss it in detail. "

Something inside me warned that I should wait, that I should keep Souad and myself out of this stranger's life. Was I really bringing the bear into my own vineyard?

"Do you know I've left no stone unturned? " Salah said. "Every time I failed, the frustration grew. But now, with you, I feel hopeful again. "

"You're making me feel I was too hasty in offering, " I replied uneasily. "What if I only frustrate you more? "

"Don't say that, " Souad whispered. "Please, try. "

All the way back, Salah kept pressing me about what I planned to do. I had no clear answer. If I were honest with myself, perhaps I only wanted to impress Souad especially after Salah's strange story, and his cinematic presence had begun to captivate her.

At least the outcome pleased her. She embraced me, reassured by my initiative.

"Will you give me the diaries for just one day? " I asked Salah. "There are a few details I want to review. "

"Of course, " he said quickly. "I feel that this time with your help I'll finally reach a conclusion and find her. "

A wave of fear hit me at his words. I cut him off sharply.

"Please don't put too much hope in me. It's only an attempt. I don't want to disappoint you. "

"Don't worry, " he said calmly. "I can't be more disappointed than I already have been, nor more shocked. Don't carry that burden. I'm no longer fragile. Think of me as a phoenix: every time I burn, I rise again to search once more. I will never despair, because I know she's out there.

Somewhere. Perhaps searching for me, perhaps running from me—I don't know. But I want her. I want Ahlam. "

On the way home, Souad sat close beside me. She seemed excited by the idea of searching for Ahlam, though I doubted her motives.

"Is this really what you want? " I asked. "To find her? " "Of course. Why even ask? "

"And do you truly believe she exists? "

She looked at me in surprise. "What do you mean? " "Perhaps you only want to prove she doesn't exist. " "And why would I want that? "

I smiled faintly. "I don't know. Maybe so he can finally erase her from his mind—bury her—and give himself to another woman. "

She looked at me in shock and disapproval. "I can't believe you think of me that way. Do you think I'm after him? "

 "I don't think anything of you. I didn't mean you by 'another woman.' "

Souad's face reddened, confusion flickering in her eyes. "So, who did you mean by 'another woman'? "

"Any woman. Maybe Nicole. "

My words didn't calm her. She remained restless, agitated. Something inside me whispered a warning: I had to be cautious with Salah. He was dangerous without meaning to be. Yes, I trusted Souad, but women were drawn to him his charm, his air of mystery. I couldn't afford to close my eyes.

Later, Souad turned off the lights and slipped into bed beside me. My attempts to awaken the jinni within her the jinni that had been unleashed two nights before failed. She stayed still, distant, resigned. Finally, she turned her back and drifted into sleep.

"Can you hear me, Ahmed? Wake up. "

I opened my eyes to find Souad leaning over me, whispering my name. "Ahmed, wake up. "

The room was dark.

"Are you all right? " I asked, concerned. "Yes and no. I don't feel comfortable. " "What's wrong? What happened? "

"I'm sorry, " she whispered, her voice trembling. "What are you saying? What time is it? "

"Forget the time. Did you hear me? " "Could you turn on the light? "

"I don't want the light on. " "What were you saying? "

She rested her head on my chest and whispered, "I said I'm sorry... sorry because I didn't live up to your expectations tonight. "

"You woke me at this hour just to say that? Couldn't it wait until morning? " "Why are you upset? "

"I'm not upset. You just pulled me out of a deep sleep, that's all. " "You know I love you. "

"Yes, I know. And I love you too. " "Then don't be angry with me. "

"Why would I be angry when you wake me just to tell me you love me?

That makes me happy very happy. "

"I want to discuss something with you. "

"Now? In the middle of the night? Fine, if you insist… but turn on the light. "
"I don't want you to look at me. I'm embarrassed. "

"What's making you feel like this? "

"I want you to answer something: Do you feel that I don't live up to your expectations? " "What expectations? "

"You know… your fantasies, your desires, the things we do together. Do you feel I'm not enough? "

"Of course not. What makes you think that? "

"Tonight I tried, but I wasn't… I wasn't good enough. I could feel it. "

"I love you no matter what. Don't burden yourself with this. Go to sleep. "

"I still can't remember what happened that strange night, " she went on. "But I've thought about it endlessly. I can't imagine how I could've done all the things you told me. It's not in my nature. Even if I tried, I couldn't repeat them. It's impossible. "

"I understand. Don't let it trouble you. " "I stayed awake until I found the reason. " "Really? And what is it? "

"The reason is… that night, it wasn't me, " Souad whispered. "I mean, it was me, but not me. My body was there, but someone else was inside it. It was another woman. "

I laughed softly.

"You mean another woman borrowed your body for the night? "

Her eyes brightened. "Exactly. That's it. You understand me perfectly. "

"Alright… and where were you while this other woman was borrowing your body? " "What do you mean? "

"I mean, when she moved in, where did you go wandering without it? "
"Are you mocking me, Ahmed? "

"And why would I mock you? Your words are perfectly rational. " I smiled.

"Go to sleep, my love. Don't worry. Everything is fine between us. "

"You're still angry. I can't talk about this when you're like that. Just go back to sleep. Good night. "

"Good night, Souad. I love you-you, or whoever else might be living inside this beautiful body. "

"Take your hand away and stop mocking me. "

"Good night. "

"I love you too. "

In the silence, I could hear her breathing against my ear, her whisper brushing the dark: "Ahmed... Ahmed. "

"Yes? "

"Do you think I'm cold? "

I didn't answer immediately—I only wanted to sink back into sleep but she pressed on: "I want you to be honest with me. What happened that night was something extraordinary,

something I can't repeat. Still, I'm trying trying my best to be perfect. I want you to feel that I am every woman on earth to you. "

"You are, my dear... and even more. Now rest. Sleep. "

She didn't reply. My words neither convinced nor reassured her. But at last, she drifted into silence, and then into sleep.

Chapter

Eighteen

One is always startled by the hidden desires and lusts that simmer within. It's as though another, stranger world lies inside us a being we know nothing about. It could be an angel... or a monster whose true face no one can predict until it rises. Sometimes it remains locked away forever, silent and unseen. Other times, it bursts forth without warning. And when it does, there's no telling what might follow.

Before Salah arrived at the office as scheduled, I told Ramesh his story in full. Ramesh listened attentively sometimes smiling, sometimes grave. When I finished, I asked,

 "What do you think? "

His only comment was: "It's an entertaining story. " "Entertaining? That's all? "

 "What do you want me to say? It's a common tale. A young, inexperienced man clueless about life and sex meets a mature woman who ushers him into the world through the wide gate. With her, he loses his virginity, both physically and emotionally. "

"Oh my God, you've given it the driest interpretation possible. " Ramesh laughed. "That's how I see it. Plain and simple. "

"And where is the romance in your reading? You've only seen the stem, the leaves, the colors the photosynthesis of the rose. You've missed its beauty, its mystery, its living breath. You, Ramesh, are a disgrace to romance. "

He grinned. "So what do you want from me? "

"I want to help this man. I was hoping you'd help me find the woman. "

"You must be joking. That's impossible. This has been going on for more than ten years. There's no email address anymore, and even if there were, it would be long dead. The chat programs of that time have vanished, replaced by others. You know as well as I do no one can track down someone who doesn't want to be found, " Ramesh said flatly. "Even intelligence agencies can't chase a ghost who's erased herself from the net."

"In short, I want a solution, " I insisted. "Don't complicate things. "

"Honestly, if this woman doesn't reveal herself if she doesn't step out of hiding she can't be reached. "

I already knew that. But I trusted Ramesh's talent for finding answers. I wasn't about to give up.

"Fine, " I said. "Give me your best ideas. Don't tell me you're helpless against something this simple. I'll take anything just give me a starting point. "

He saw that I was baiting him, and I knew he loved a challenge. He laughed.

"I don't have anything just now. But leave it with me I'll think of something. "

That afternoon, Salah arrived, cheerful and brimming with energy. Settling into my chair, he gazed out at Sheikh Zayed Road.

"You have a beautiful view here. Tell me what have you two accomplished?"

I turned to Ramesh, who answered:

"We can't rely on her old internet address; it's a dead end. I'm sure you tried already, without success. What we *can* do is post a 'Woman Wanted' notice on social media and wait for her to respond wait for her to step out of the shadows. "

Salah didn't seem enthusiastic. A look of disappointment crossed his face. "I've done this before many times. It's never gotten me anywhere. "

"I'm telling you, " Ramesh said,
 "if she doesn't reveal herself, there's no way to reach her. All we can do is try again. "

I remained silent, listening. Salah noticed. "What are you thinking, Mr. Ahmed? "

"I'm afraid you won't like what I'm about to say. "
"Speak. Don't worry about my feelings. Any idea will help. I need to get a handle on this. " I said plainly, "Couldn't she be dead? "

Salah's face darkened, and he didn't answer. He just stared at me as I continued,

"Couldn't she have left the hotel and been hit by a car, for example? Or that something else bad happened to her? Did you ask about her at the hospitals at the time? "
"Yes, " he said at last. "I searched every hospital for her. I don't think she was hit by a car. She disappeared of her own free will. "
 "I think if we want to begin this search properly, we should start with a question. If we knew the answer, it might lead us to her. "

"Okay, ask. "

"What makes a woman run away from a man she loves? Women, in particular, usually cling to the man they love they don't let go easily. "

Salah's face reddened, and he frowned.

"Do you mean she's the flirtatious type? That I was just a passing man in her life? "

But after a moment, he reluctantly admitted,

 "Maybe that's true. "

"But if we assume she did have feelings for you and I favor this idea, because it's clear from the context of the memoirs then I'd say she couldn't abandon you. "

Salah interrupted, agreeing, "Unless something bad happened to her. "

Ramesh nodded.

"Isn't it possible she was suffering from a terminal illness, so she chose to stay away from you and die quietly? "

Salah turned toward the window, hiding his face. He looked down at the street and the surrounding buildings. Without turning back, he said softly,

"This is the worst and harshest explanation. And although it is, unfortunately, the most likely assumption, I wish you wouldn't consider it. I've considered it for a long time, and it hurt me deeply. But I want you to dismiss it. I don't want us to ever dwell on it, because it will kill our hope. I have a feeling she's alive and well, and I will find her. "

"In any case, " I said,

"this is just one more possibility. We're reviewing everything that comes to mind. "

Ramesh added,

"It could be much simpler. Perhaps she has a family and doesn't want to abandon them, so she keeps her adventures secret. "

Salah leaned back in the chair and said quietly, almost to himself,

"If I knew now that she was dead, I would grieve for a while and then eventually forget her. But she has even deprived me of the blessing of forgetfulness. Her sudden disappearance has kept her constantly on my mind. And just as I was about to come to terms with her absence, her scent came back into my life and rekindled my feelings. "

Just then, Salah's phone rang.

"It's Nicole, "

he said, answering quickly.

He spoke to her for a while, then turned to me with a bright expression. "She has the bottle. "

He hung up.

"Do you have a car so you can get it? "

"No, unfortunately, I still don't. "

"Do you want me to drive you to her? "

"No, I'm not in the mood to meet Nicole. I won't be able to get away from her. " I smiled. "Why do you want to get away from her? She's nice and pretty, too. "

Salah laughed.

"I know, and I really like her. But for the last two days, I haven't been able to think about any woman but Ahlam. "

"Where is she now? "

"At her workplace in Deira, near City Center. "

"I have an idea. Wait a minute, "

I spoke.

I called Souad. She worked at City Center. "I need you to do me a favor. "
I already knew her reaction.

"I'm busy. I'm exhausted. I can't. "

"It won't take long. "

"Oh, Ahmed… there's too much work today. "

"The place is close to your office. "

"I told you, I can't leave stacks of papers sitting on my desk. "

 "Fine, as you wish. "

"Maybe another day. "

"It's okay, I'll go to Nicole's myself. " "Nicole? "

"Yes, I'll pick up the perfume bottle from her for Mr. Salah. Don't worry about it. "

There were a few seconds of silence. Then her voice came, firm and unexpected:

"Okay. "

"Okay, what? "

 "I'll get it. "

"No need, you're tired. I'll go myself. "

"No, I said I'll go. "

"But what about all the papers? "

"Oh, for God's sake, enough! I'll call her now and go before lunch. Give me an hour, then I'll meet you at the Mall of the Emirates. "

I smiled at Salah. "Relax—you won't be seeing Nicole today. "

"Thank you both. You saved me from a big mess. " Then he brightened. "I want you to start today by publishing the ad. I won't hide from you, ever since I smelled that perfume, I've been optimistic. I feel she's close. "

"Do you want us to mention your name? " Ramesh asked. "For example: *Salah is looking for a woman named Ahlam*? "

Salah thought for a moment, then said, as he was leaving,

"Do what you think is best. I have great faith in you. "

At the door, he paused. "Do you think there's any chance? "

 "Only if Ahlam reads the ad and responds, "

Ramesh replied. Salah smiled before leaving. "I feel thrilled and optimistic again. "

The perfume bottle the reason we'd met Salah also became the reason Souad grew closer to Nicole.

Souad called to say she'd be late coming home because Nicole had invited her to dinner. It was a perfect chance for Souad to get Nicole talking about her relationship with Salah.

But events kept getting stranger.

I had my lunch alone, then went home. I felt very sleepy, but I didn't want to give in. I lay down, trying to stay awake until Souad returned. When I finally opened my eyes, the room was dark, and the air was heavy with her perfume.

I went to the bathroom and found the perfume bottle by the mirror. That meant Souad was back. I hadn't noticed her sitting in the chair opposite the bed, silent and still, staring into space.

"Souad? "

She didn't answer. As if she hadn't heard me, she remained silent. I switched on the light. She seemed to wake from her reverie, hiding her face in her hands, looking at me with half-closed eyes.

"When did you get back? " I asked. "Just a while ago. "

"Why were you sitting in the dark? What happened? " She glanced at me,
then turned her face to the floor. "How was your meeting with Nicole? "

"She gave me the bottle of perfume. "

"I know. I saw it in the bathroom. What's wrong? You look upset. "

 "I'm tired. "

"Did something happen? Did she upset you? "

 "Please, leave me. Go to work and let me be. "

"How can I leave you like this? "

"I'm fine. I'll lie down for a while. Go. "

 "Okay, if that's what you want. "

I moved closer to hug her, and a strange smell clung to her. "What's that?
Is it alcohol? "

"It's Nicole. She offered me wine with dinner. Now please, go. "

She was in a nervous, unnatural state. I didn't press her to talk she
wouldn't have spoken in that mood, anyway. I let her rest. Then I called
Salah and told him we had the bottle. He invited us to meet him at the
hotel and spend the evening there. Souad resisted at first, but I insisted,
and she finally agreed. Something must have happened between her and
Nicole to sour her mood so badly. Sooner or later, she would tell me
everything.

"I have a strange feeling about tonight. I'm not comfortable with it, " she
said hesitantly.

"On the contrary, you should come. It will help you shake off the sadness
you've carried all day. "

But she was right her instincts were sharper than mine. The evening turned out to be extraordinary, though not in the way I had expected.

As usual, Salah was waiting for us at the door. He smiled broadly.

"We're going to an oriental restaurant tonight. They say a belly dancer is giving a wonderful show. I'd love to see it together. What do you think? "

Souad's faint smile disappointed him.

"What's wrong, Madam Souad? You don't seem excited. "
"I don't care for belly dancing, especially in public. I find it vulgar. " "You don't seem in the mood today. "
"I'm not well. I was planning to apologize for not coming. "
 "She's been down since this afternoon, "
 I explained.
"That's exactly what belly dancing is for, "
Salah said brightly.
"The perfect cure for a bad mood. So I won't accept any excuses. "

Inside, the music was deafening. A female singer was belting out an Umm Kulthum song. Souad and I weren't used to this kind of nightlife. We sat at a table, Souad beside me, tense and withdrawn. The clapping and cheering around us did nothing to rouse her; she remained silent, unmoved.

The music was so loud that even Salah and I could hardly hear each other. Still, he leaned toward her.

"You look pale. Are you sick? " "No. "

Her answers were curt.

I whispered, "Why don't you tell me what's wrong? "
 "Nothing's wrong. "
"We can leave right now if you want. "

Suddenly, Nicole appeared in front of us. Souad's face drained of color; her features froze. Nicole, too, stood stiff, startled at the sight of her. She offered a cold greeting.

Salah urged her to sit, but she declined. Instead, she pulled a key from her bag, placed it in his hand it was his room key and left quickly without a word or a glance back.

Salah slipped the key into his pocket with a smile. Souad's face darkened, pale and tight. He opened the menu. "I'm very hungry. What will you have? "

"I'm not hungry. "
"You should eat something. "
"If she says she doesn't want to, then she doesn't want to, " I cut in. "They serve excellent fish. "
"I'd rather not. Just orange juice. "

She reached into her bag, took out the perfume bottle, and set it in front of him. "This is for you, " she said.

Salah stared at it for a long time without touching it. Finally he said, "Please, keep it. " "No, it's yours now. "

 "Honestly, I'd be afraid of losing it again. I'd feel safer knowing you have it. You'd take better care of it than I could. "

He lifted the bottle, brushed it across his cheek, and closed his eyes.

"What's the point of keeping it without a woman to wear it? Do me a favor. " "What? "
"Wear some now. "

Souad blushed, pride and embarrassment mingling on her face. She took the bottle, then excused herself to the bathroom to freshen her makeup.

A strange unease came over me. I knew the source, though Salah hadn't crossed the bounds of politeness.

He pulled his chair closer, watching Souad walk away, and grinned. "She's a wild tigress. "

"What? "
"Would you believe she raped me today? "

My face burned. I stared at him, stunned, mouth half open, throat dry. "Who? "

I managed to croak.

"Nicole. "

I exhaled sharply as he showed me his room key.

"This afternoon, there was a knock at my door. When I opened it, there she was. Nicole. "
 His voice brimmed with satisfaction.
"So? "
"She shoved me inside, closed the door, and raped me. Just like that. No words, no greeting, nothing. "

I hesitated, suspicious. "Nicole? "

"Yes, Nicole. What do you think? "

"Strange. She doesn't seem like that kind of woman. "
"I thought the same. She caught me completely off guard. "
 "You're lucky… Nicole? "

Salah laughed and sipped some water.

"I admit that you have a special charm and charisma that captivates women. "

"Are you jealous of me, Mr. Ahmed? "

"What's the point of jealousy? I'm married now, and I won't pursue women. I've had my share of adventures. "

"No one is ever satisfied with women. What if Nicole came knocking on your door? Would you reject her? "

I smiled and didn't answer. "You see, you're hesitant. "

"I'm not hesitant, but I imagine the situation when I open the door and see Nicole in front of me. "

"Would you close the door in her face? Yes or no?

I laughed and said,

 "It's shameful for a guest to come to you and for you to turn them away. Where is the hospitality? "

 "You're evading the answer. "

"In any case, she won't come to me. I lack your charisma. I recall putting a lot of effort into attracting women. But you women flock to you. "

"That's not true at all. I don't seek them out, nor do I try to attract them. "
"Then how do you explain Nicole's behavior? "

"I don't know. "

Then he laughed and asked,

"Do you think I bewitched her? "

"That's for sure. "

We were silent for a moment, then he said,

 "She's a wonderful woman, despite everything. But I hope she doesn't come back. " "Why not? She might be the right woman. "

He smiled.

"There's only one right woman. No one else has a place in my heart. I've avoided women for so long that sometimes I miss them as much as I miss life itself. But even if I tried, I couldn't. Believe me, it isn't my choice. It's as if she cast a spell on me and vanished. "

I shook my head.

 "A new love might make you forget Ahlam. "
"I hope so. But love comes to you you don't go seeking it. I just wait. "
"Then open your heart. Live your life. "
"That's what I've been trying to do all this time… until I came across you. "

Suddenly, he closed his eyes and drew a long, calming breath. "Oh my God she's here. She's come. "

 "Who? "
"Ahlam. "

I turned, and there she was, approaching from afar Souad. She swayed with a graceful,

feminine gait, her hair flowing, her smile radiant. Beautiful, magnetic. When she sat down, her scent filled the room, strange and unmistakable.

"Thank you, " Salah murmured.

She smiled without a word, her eyes meeting mine with a glow that unsettled me. "How are you now? " I asked.

She didn't reply. Instead, beneath the table, her hand found mine, giving it a gentle squeeze. Her smile deepened, carrying something of the jinni that seemed to have returned.

Turning to Salah, she rubbed her hands together playfully. "I'm almost dying of hunger. "

"Finally, " he laughed, "a woman who admits she's hungry. "

While we ate, she was cheerful, far more than I had expected. I leaned toward her and whispered,

"Did you take something? A drug? "
"Of course not, " she said, her eyes wide with surprise and a strange, radiant smile stretching across her face. "What makes you say that? "

Her sudden joy was overwhelming, and under the table her hands and legs searched for me, all while her face wore a mask of innocence.

Then a belly dancer took the stage, hips swaying to the pulse of Middle Eastern drums. Souad's eyes lit with wonder.

"This is the first time I've seen a belly dancer live, " she said.

She clapped, swayed in her seat, hands rising with the rhythm, completely enthralled. Suddenly she exclaimed:

"Let's dance! "
"What? "
"You and me come on! "
"Are you mad? You're too shy to dance in public. "

But she wasn't listening. The music had claimed her. She rushed to the center, moving as though no one else existed, as if she had been dancing all her life.

The belly dancer stepped aside, applauding with admiration. The audience joined in.

When she danced, the music seemed to celebrate, the universe swayed its hips, The samba grew envious, the waltz turned into a lover, and the tango quietly retired.

I looked at Salah, who sat transfixed.

"She's brilliant, " he whispered. "She's stolen the show. "

A woman from the crowd approached, untied her scarf, and fastened it around Souad's waist. Souad danced on, higher and higher, as if among the stars, carried by the applause. I could hardly believe this was the same Souad.

Salah leaned toward me.

"Her mood has improved rather quickly. " "Yes—suddenly, strangely "

But for me, the evening was unraveling. I forced a smile, burning with embarrassment.

The music stopped. Souad, breathless, returned the scarf to its owner and came back to us amid thunderous applause. She sat, panting, cheeks flushed, sweat glistening on her neck and chest.

The woman returned with the scarf, embraced her, and kissed her cheek. "Your dancing delighted us. You're an angel. Please, keep this scarf. "

She draped it over Souad's shoulders and left. Souad glanced at us, then looked away.

 "I did it for you, " she said softly though whether to me or to Salah, I could not tell.

Salah laughed.

"You've won everyone's admiration. I think the only one who hates you now is the dancer you stole her audience. "
"Do you think I looked like Ahlam? "

I always remind myself to forget you Morning and evening, night and day, Summer and winter But I always forget to forget you.

Salah fell silent, surprised by the question. He studied her face for a long moment. She continued, "I mean... when she danced that night at the hotel. "

Salah glanced at me, confused, then shook his head. "No. You don't look like her at all. " Then, after a pause, he added quietly, "That night she was sad. Very sad. When I held her on the dance floor, I felt pain flowing out of her body into mine. "

"Was she in pain? "

"I don't know. I never tried to find out. My pride my vanity kept me from caring for her the way I should have. I was selfish. "

"Don't blame yourself. Maybe she didn't want anyone's help. "

"Or maybe she was desperate. That's why I blame myself because instead of drawing her close, I pushed her away. And I lost her. "

"Don't worry. We'll find her. " "You really think so? "

"I feel it. Sometimes I sense she's here with us. Her shadow has haunted me ever since I read the memoirs. "

A silence fell between us until Souad said softly, "I'm sorry. I shouldn't have brought up Ahlam now. "

"Never mind, " Salah replied. "The perfume made her present anyway. Thank you for wearing it. "

It's no use. I can't get you out of my mind. You're a stubborn melody, Humming, humming A persistent song caught in a whirlpool.

As I expected, the *jinni* returned that night, taking hold of her again. I couldn't stop it, nor could I understand her strange behavior. As always, I surrendered to her sudden madness until daybreak.

When your love rains, Flowers bloom in my eyes, The scent of jasmine fills the universe, Grapes ripen, wine flows, Butterflies rest on my chest, And a rainbow radiates from your eyes.

I woke late. Souad was beside me, the shawl draped over her shoulders, watching me. She smiled when my eyes opened.

 "Good morning. "

I looked at the clock it was late. "Why did you let me sleep so long? "

"I was tired, " she said, kissing me lightly. "Thank you for the shawl. " I
frowned. "What do you mean? "

"The shawl is beautiful. "

"You don't remember how you got it? "

"I have these vague images dreamlike, scattered. I was… dancing. " I
laughed.

"No, really. They're not just images. Did it happen? Did I actually dance? "

"Is it possible you don't remember? You were completely conscious. "

"It feels like someone else's dream. And what about the other things? Were
they real, too? " "What things? "

"You know… in bed. " "Oh yes, those were real. "

"My God… I did all that? All those crazy things? That was almost…
debauchery. Why didn't you stop me? "

"Do you think I'm mad? "

"Oh, stop it, Ahmed. Something's happening to me. "

"A little madness never hurt anyone. "

"I'm serious. I'm frightened. I feel like I've lost control like I'm a
sleepwalker. I don't know when it happens, or why. "

 "Don't make it into a big deal. Sometimes it's good to let go, to give in to
your whims. " "No. These aren't whims. I'm afraid it's something deeper…
"

"What do you mean? "

"Something else happened. I haven't told you. Something weird. " "What
happened? "

"When I went to Nicole to get the perfume bottle. "

She shifted in her seat and leaned closer, her face just inches from mine.
Her eyes flicked around as if someone might be listening.

I whispered, "Is anyone watching us? "

"This is serious. Please don't mock me. That day, I called Nicole and told her about the perfume. She asked me to come to the office immediately because she was about to leave. Minutes later, I was there. She offered me coffee, and we talked. She was kind, open, and warm-hearted I liked her immediately. Then she brought up Salah. She seemed obsessed with him. She asked how well I knew him. I told her we'd been friends for a long time. "

"So you lied to her. "

"Just a small detail. She said she fell in love with him at first sight. " Then she leaned in and whispered,

"Do you know what she confided in me? "

"What? "

"She said, *When he talks, I feel like throwing myself into his arms.* " "She really said that? "

"You know how women confide in each other. I asked her, *What do you like about him?* She said, *Everything. He's my type.* Then she smiled and whispered, *When he talks to me, I get this tingling sensation all over my body.* "

"She must really trust you. "

"She's easygoing, and I was glad she opened up. But what I'm about to tell you now is serious and embarrassing. So please don't interrupt. "

"When it was time to leave work, she invited me to lunch at her place. She insisted said she wouldn't give me the bottle unless I came. She lives in Dubai Marina, in an apartment on the twentieth floor overlooking the sea. One bedroom, a spacious living room with a glass wall facing the marina. Soft music played through the speakers as we sat and chatted. She started preparing spaghetti with tomato sauce. Then she brought out the perfume bottle. "

'This is strange,' she said. *'I've never heard of this perfume before* "999. "' She uncapped it, sniffed, shivering. *'Oh my God it's wonderful. Unlike anything I've smelled before.'* She dabbed some on her neck and behind her ears, then reluctantly handed me the bottle. *'I should get one like it,'* she added.

"We ate, and I was enjoying myself. But then something shifted her mood changed. She had been cheerful and full of life, but suddenly she grew quiet, sad, and withdrawn. She started talking about her childhood, how lonely she had been—and still was. Then she apologized. *'Sorry if I'm bringing the mood down.'* I told her, *'You're just tired. I should go.'* But she said, *'No, no. Stay a little longer. I need a friend to talk to.'*

"I told her I was glad she considered me a friend, that I understood I'd had a lonely childhood too, though maybe less painful. She said, *'It must be the music it's making me melancholic.'* Then she sat closer, leaned her head back, closed her eyes, and rested her head on my shoulder. And then… she began to cry. "

'Are you okay, Nicole?' I asked.

'I feel like I'm floating,' she whispered. Then she took my hand. *'I feel like crying.'*

"She was silent for a moment, then stood and said, *'I need to dance.'*

"She began swaying to the music. *'Come on, dance with me.'* She grabbed my hand and spun me around the room. I was drawn in we moved together, arms in the air, bodies swaying.

She spun me and pulled me close again. When the music stopped, she hugged me tightly. "

'Inside me is a vast, deep chasm that stretches from space to eternity,' she whispered. *'I need a complete presence to fill it.'*

"Silence fell. Her tears soaked my neck. I felt her breath, her warmth, the perfume's scent. Her arms squeezed tighter. Her lips brushed my neck. Her fingers slipped beneath my dress. I forgot where I was. I gave in it felt like part of the dance. But when I realized what was happening, I was lying on the couch she was on top of me. "

"I panicked. I shoved her away hard. She didn't resist. She just stepped back, shaken, breathing heavily. Fear was written all over her face. I stood up, adjusted my clothes, grabbed my bag, and left without a word. "

Souad fell silent. Her eyes searched my face for a reaction. Then she asked, "What do you think? "

"That's... really something. I wouldn't expect that from her. She's a strange woman. " "I didn't know she was a lesbian. "

"I don't think she is. "

"Of course she is—unless you don't consider me a woman. " "Of course you're not a woman. "

"What? "

"You're my little bird. " "Be serious. "

"It's really confusing. "

I smiled at her. She looked at me, puzzled. "What? Why are you looking at me like that? " I couldn't help but laugh.

She frowned, clearly annoyed. "What's so funny? What's making you laugh? " "Are you sure she was the one who... "

"What? Are you suggesting I was the one who harassed her? " "Maybe some man borrowed your body and "

She didn't let me finish. She threw a pillow at me and lunged. I held her off, laughing. "I'm just kidding. "

But she kept pushing at me, furious.

"You're making a joke out of something serious and dangerous! "

I hugged her and said, half-seriously,

"It *is* serious. Look at my neck. Do you see your teeth marks? "

She pushed me away, then looked closely at my neck.

"You're so annoying. I was wrong to tell you this story. "

After a moment, she calmed down and leaned closer to examine the marks. "Oh my God, did I do that to your neck? "

"You see, you're more dangerous than Nicole. Anyway, what's even stranger than your story is what happened after you left Nicole. "

"What happened? "

"That same day—right after you left—she went to finish what she started. She went to Salah's hotel. "

"In Jebel Ali? "

"Yes. It was in the afternoon, I think just after you left her. She knocked on his hotel room, stormed in and... "

"What? "

"She raped him. " "What? "

"Exactly what I'm telling you. That's what Salah told me. What she did was nothing short of rape. But,..Of course, he didn't resist. How could he push away a woman in that situation? " She scowled at me.

"I would pushed her away. "

I burst out laughing. "But you're a woman. " "And would *you* have surrendered to her? "

"That's a tough question. "

"Tell me honestly what would you have done? "

"I don't like hypothetical questions. And that one's embarrassing. " "So you *would* have cheated on me? "

"That's also a hypothetical conclusion. I told you I don't know how I'd react. Do you want me to lie and say I'd have thrown her out? "

"You don't love me anymore. I can feel it. You're thinking about other women. If you truly loved me, you'd have said no right away. "

"I'm trying to be honest. You're the one turning this into a fight. Can we just get back to the story about Nicole and Salah? "

"No promise me first you won't give in to her if she comes to you. " "Why do you assume she'd come to me? Are you jealous? "

"She's clearly unstable. Her behavior is unpredictable. "

"You're calling *her* crazy? And who danced on the table at the restaurant? "

She narrowed her eyes.

"So you think I'm crazy too? "

"What Nicole did to you is almost the same as what you did to me on your birthday. Surprising, strange, completely illogical. "

"Don't remind me of that night. I swear I wasn't myself. I still don't know what came over me. What happened to me was almost identical to what happened to Nicole. Isn't that strange? "

"I don't like hearing you compare yourself to her. You're not like her. "Her cheeks flushed, though she smiled.

"Do you really think so? What's the difference? " "You're crazier and more stubborn. "

"I'm not talking to you anymore. "

"But you're more beautiful, more feminine… and your smile enchants me. "

"Don't flatter me. I want to know—truly—where I stand in your eyes compared to other women. "

"You want the truth? " "Of course. "

"Even if it's not what you want to hear? "

She hesitated, her voice trembling.

"No… I mean, yes. The truth won't disturb me. "

"Alright. The truth is… you're at the very top. That's what you wanted to hear, right? Now can we sleep? "

"See? You admitted it. That means there are others. " I looked at her helplessly.

"Oh, Souad… you truly confuse me. "

Suddenly, her phone rang. She glanced at the screen, in disbelief. "It's Nicole. "

The phone kept vibrating in her hand. "I wonder what she wants from me? "

Feigning seriousness, I said, "Maybe she wants me. Let me talk to her. "
"No, I'll talk to her. "

Souad's tone was dry, reserved, almost cold. Finally, she said firmly, "Okay, whatever you want. But my husband will be with me. "Then she hung up.

"What does she want? "

"She wants to meet… and talk. I don't want to go alone. You'll come with me. " "When? "

"In an hour. In the cafeteria across the street. " "Maybe she'll bargain with you over me. "

Souad frowned but didn't answer. Instead, she whispered, "I'm really scared. "

We didn't have to wait long. Nicole arrived soon after we did, greeting us with visible unease. I sat down. She leaned forward and began at once:

"Forgive me for bothering you so late, but I can't sleep until I speak. You should know first and foremost I am not a lesbian. I still don't understand how I did what I did. "

Souad said nothing, only listened, her eyes avoiding Nicole's.

"I can never explain what happened. The thought terrifies me that I might be crazy or losing control of myself. "
We stayed silent.
"The worst part, " Nicole continued, her voice breaking, "is that I knew exactly what I was doing. I knew it was wrong, yet I couldn't stop myself. It was as if someone else had taken control. "

Souad glanced at me from the corner of her eye. Nicole spoke through tears, wiping her face constantly.

"Your behavior shocked me, " Souad finally said. "It scared me. I didn't know what had happened to you. "
"I'm so sorry. I swear, I'm not a lesbian. And I understand what you feel… because something similar once happened to me. I won't blame you if you hate me. "

"How? " Souad wondered curiously "It was years ago. I was a teenager, staying with a friend while her family was away. We drank, and we danced until I was completely drunk. Sometime in the night, I felt her beside me in bed touching me, doing unnatural things. But I wasn't fully conscious. The next day, it was all a blur. I decided to bury it, to pretend it never happened. I never spoke of it, not even to her. I just walked away. "

"And how did you feel? "

"I was very upset and angry. But as time passed, the incident didn't mean much to me. Then I completely forgot about it. What makes me angry now is that I tried to repeat what had happened to me. I don't know why. "

"Maybe I look like that friend of yours. "

Nicole looked at Souad for a long time, then said,

"I don't think so. But even if you did look like her, I'm not driven to women. I was drunk, that's all. "

"Now what do you want from me? "

"I want you to forgive me and try to forget this incident. We could have been good friends if it hadn't happened. "

"Then let's forget about it as if nothing happened. Let's be friends. "

"Do you really mean it? "

As we walked home, Souad said triumphantly,

"Now what do you think? Are you convinced now that something unusual and unnatural is happening to Nicole and me? "

"Don't exaggerate. These are things that happen to everyone. Just whims that either of us might experience. "

"But for this to happen to both of us together? "

"Just a coincidence. "

She didn't comment, but she wasn't convinced.

I arrived late at the office. Ramesh was waiting for me, looking exhausted. He greeted me with a tired smile.

"What's up? "
I asked.

"I haven't slept yet. I posted your ad on more than two hundred sites Facebook, Twitter… "

I smiled. "I knew I could count on you. "

He handed me a piece of paper. "Here your username and password. Responses will come to this account. You can log in anytime to check them. Now we just wait. I've chosen the most popular and widely read sites social media, newspapers, magazines, and media outlets. "

 "Do you think we'll get a result? "

"We have to be patient. Repost the ad regularly, for a long time. It's a slow process, but persistence pays off. "

"I'll leave it to you. Keep posting until we get a result—or until Mr. Salah gives up. "

Chapter

Nineteen

There is a historical mistake. Human qualities do not align with the teachings of the gods. When I see a woman's smile, the divine sky shatters, and a new sun rises—one from another history. A history that never passed through the Ten Commandments, the Last Supper, or Mount Arafat.

What would we have been like if history had taken that other path? Would we be more miserable than we are now? Is a person, freed from restraint, more bloodthirsty than he already is?

What if history changed its course?

We stood frozen before the computer screen. I could not believe what I was seeing. Salah was silent, rereading the message again and again. Ramesh, however, smiled triumphantly. At last after days of waiting and frustration, and years of despair Salah rose and read aloud the long-awaited sentence:

"I am Ahlam. What do you want from me, Salah?"

"What a cold sentence… and what a ridiculous question," Salah muttered.

He turned toward the window, lost in thought. *What do I want from you, Ahlam? Is that really a question? What do you expect me to want?*

Ramesh broke the silence. "Remember, Mr. Salah, we don't yet know if this message is really from Ahlam. It could be a hoax."
"I know."
"Think carefully about how you want to respond."
I added, "Yes. Take your time. Ramesh and I will leave you alone"

Salah sat before the computer, fingers hovering over the keyboard. He hesitated, then typed something. Minutes later, he stood up with a faint smile.
"What happened? Did you get anything?" "Not yet. But today we'll know the truth." "What did you write?"
"I asked her something only Ahlam would know. We'll see."

His optimism did not last. That evening, he called me in a disappointed voice—it wasn't Ahlam.

After that, dozens of replies arrived. All false—some mocking, some critical—men and women alike. Finally, Salah told me to drop the matter.

"The whole thing is ridiculous," he said bitterly. "I don't think we'll ever find her. Maybe she never even saw the ad. And even if she did—why would she reveal herself?"

"Maybe fear," I suggested.
"Ahlam is strong. A woman like her isn't afraid."
"Then maybe something else is holding her back—something darker."
"What do you mean?"
"This is a woman we know nothing about. Anything is possible." "Like what?"
"Don't laugh if I say this." "Go on."
"She could be a fraud… a bank robber… even a spy.?"

Salah stared at me incredulously. But I continued.
"Think about it. She wanted to meet you so quickly. She chose the airport.

She booked the
hotel under your name. Then she vanished without a trace. Isn't that the
behavior of spies and agents?"
"Are you serious?"
"It's only a possibility. I'm considering every angle. You said you searched
her bag it was empty."
"That's natural. She didn't want me to identify her."
"And she had money. Large sums. Why would she carry so much?" "Is there
a woman who doesn't love money?"
"And the knife?" "What about it?"
"A knife kills silently. It doesn't attract attention."
"Oh my God. You're scaring me and making me laugh at the same time.
Ahlam? A spy? Mossad? A murderer?"
"It's just a thought. Maybe she was involved in something and needed to
disappear. She used you for cover for two days."
"Absolutely not. Ahlam can't be that. Forget it. Erase it from your mind." He

stood up abruptly, annoyed, and left without saying goodbye.

The next morning, he called.

"Do whatever you believe can help us find her. Keep going until we solve
the mystery."

Two days after we met with Nicole, Souad was still restless. She tossed in
bed at night, troubled by something she wouldn't say.

I was fast asleep when she shook me awake after midnight. "It's the
perfume."
"What about it?"
"There's something magical about it." "Sleep, Souad."
"I'm telling you—there's something magical about it." "Yes. Magical enough
to keep us both awake."

All night long, she whispered the word *magical*. I let her voice carry me
back to sleep.

In the morning, Souad was still sitting with the perfume bottle in her hand,
eyes closed, fast asleep. She opened them with difficulty and said she'd be
late for work she hadn't slept all night.

I called her during the day to check on her. Strangely, her phone was off. I tried the home number, but no one answered.
Maybe she was still asleep or sick.

I called again, several times, spacing the calls out. Still, nothing.
Finally, I phoned the magazine where she worked. The manager said she hadn't shown up. A colleague from her office didn't know anything either.

Uneasy, I left work and went home, hoping to find her sleeping. But she wasn't there. The bed was unmade, her clothes lay scattered where she'd taken them off the night before, and her bag lay on the table in the middle of the room. Only the perfume bottle was missing.

It wasn't like her to vanish without telling me where she was going. The only exception had been when she went to visit Salah in the hospital. Could she have gone there?

I didn't feel right about it, but I called him.
His voice was calm, friendly, as always. I didn't mention Souad—I just asked about his health. He spoke about work. A normal, boring conversation. No sign of Souad in his tone. If he'd known anything, he would have said so.

Where could she be?
Nicole, maybe. Could she have taken the perfume bottle to her, to test her

theory? But Nicole hadn't seen her either.

A sudden chill gripped me. Something was wrong. Very wrong. Her phone being off left the mind open to every dark possibility.

I was on the verge of calling the police when my phone rang. "Hello?"

It was Souad's light, childish voice. "Souad? Are you okay?"
"Yes, I'm fine."
"Where are you? I've been so worried." "I'm fine, don't worry. Listen... I saw her." "Who did you see?"
"Ahlam."
"What?"

"Yes, Ahlam. I have to see you now. Where are you?" "At home."

"I'm at the mall near home. Let's meet at the metro station. Call Salah to

come too." Her voice was bright, brimming with excitement.

I hurried out and made my way toward the mall. On the way, I called Salah, repeating Souad's words. He couldn't believe it.
"How? Where? When?"
"I have no idea. That's what she said. Let's meet at the metro station at Mall of the Emirates, and we'll find out."
"Are you sure she said Ahlam?" "That's what she said."
"It's incredible…"
"We'll know soon enough."

Souad was waiting at the station like a schoolgirl, her long dress flowing, her hair tousled as if she had just woken up.
"Are you alright?" I asked.

She looked at me with that innocent, radiant smile. "I'm fine."

"I was worried sick. I called your office, your friends—no one knew where you were. Where did you go?"

She laughed softly, almost giddy. "To the beach."

"The beach?" "Yes."

"What were you doing there?"

"The sea is so beautiful in the morning. You can see the ships on the horizon, and the air is cool and refreshing. I love walking barefoot on the sand, letting the waves play around my feet. Have you ever tried it? We should do it more often."

She smelled faintly of perfume. "Are you feeling well?"

"I'm not sick. I'm fine. Why are you so worried?"

"Because you're acting strangely. You'll drive me mad with this talk. Why would you go to the beach so early?"

"The sea was calling me. I love walking on the sand, playing in the waves. I would have undressed and gone into the water, if it hadn't been for a young man walking behind me."

My temper flared.
"What? Someone was following you?"

"I don't know if he was following me. But I felt embarrassed to undress in front of him. The beach was otherwise empty."

"Embarrassed? To undress? Why? Doesn't everyone take off their clothes in the street? Isn't that normal?"

She frowned. "You're joking, aren't you? Are you angry?"

"Why should I be angry? My wife wants to undress in public but feels shy because a stranger might be watching."

Souad's eyes followed me as I paced nervously.
"Weren't you afraid he might harm you? What's happening to you, Souad?"

She came closer, rested her head on my shoulder, and clutched my arm. "I'm fine. Don't exaggerate."

Her embrace carried the scent of the sea, mingled with the perfume I knew

too well. "Here's Salah!" she exclaimed suddenly.

She let go of me and ran toward him. "I saw her. I saw Ahlam!"

Salah stopped, startled by her intensity. She spoke breathlessly, with shining eyes:
"She's fair-skinned, with long brown hair, honey-colored eyes, and a smile that lights up her face."

Salah frowned. "You're repeating what you read in the diaries, aren't you?"

"I'm telling you—I saw her. She was holding the perfume bottle. '999.'"

"Where?"

"At the metro station. She was right there, all along! How could we have missed her? Her picture is hanging on the wall—smiling, holding the bottle."

"You mean… you saw a perfume advertisement?"

"Yes, yes! But it's her—I'm sure of it. Ahlam is the model in that ad!" Salah

shook his head, uncertain.
"I've never seen such an ad. And I practically live on the metro, riding from station to
station."

"And yet it's there," Souad replied with certainty. "I have to see it for myself. Will you take us to it?"

We boarded the first train heading to the city center. Salah stood silently near the carriage door while Souad sat, humming her song.
He asked her, "How do you know the woman in the ad is Ahlam? You've never seen her face before."
"It's her. I'm sure. She was looking at me and smiling."

Salah smiled without commenting. After a while, he asked, "Do you remember which station it was?"
"No, but we won't miss it. We'll pass by it for sure. It's one of the stations between Mall of the Emirates and City Center."

Salah's anxiety was obvious his nerves were on edge. At each station, he scanned the walls, carefully inspecting every picture and ad, searching in vain for Ahlam. When we reached City Center without finding anything, he was clearly disappointed. Souad, meanwhile, sat detached, eyes closed, still humming.

"Could you have been mistaken?" Salah asked, losing patience.
"No," she said confidently. "This is the line I took. I'm not mistaken. Maybe it was on the return line. Let's go."

But the return trip brought no better luck. We didn't see any station with the ad she described. Disappointment showed plainly on Salah's face, and he glanced at me with suspicion. I felt embarrassed and unsure of what to say. He turned again to Souad, trying to assess her seriousness, but she smiled and said,

"Do you know what I just realized? There's a similarity between you two I hadn't noticed before."
"Similarity?" I asked. "What similarity?"
"Your love of women," she said. "You both love passionately."

Salah wasn't in the mood to hear any of it, but she went on,
"There's a big difference in how you love, though. Salah is loyal to one woman one who ran away from him."

Then she fell silent.
I said, slightly reproachful, "Are you implying I'm not loyal to you?"
"I mean Salah doesn't think of anyone else anymore. He's made up his mind." "And I haven't made up my mind with you?"

She said nothing, leaving the question hanging in the air. We remained silent the rest of the way. When we reached the Mall of the Emirates, Souad said,
"Come on, let's eat. I know a good restaurant here."

We walked in silence, Salah and I both frustrated, following behind Souad. Suddenly, Salah stopped in front of a large perfume shop.
"Could this be the ad?"

In the display window was a massive advertisement featuring a girl holding a perfume bottle. The bottle resembled the one Ahlam had. Salah rushed toward it. The image was huge. He stood there, studying the girl in the picture. She was pale, with jet-black hair, and the bottle had a number on it—but not "999."

I said,
"There are lots of perfume ads with different models holding bottles. What you saw could have been any of them."

Salah looked back at Souad, who was still inspecting the display with a puzzled expression. He said, disappointed,

"None of these are Ahlam, and that's not the same perfume. You must've

imagined it." Souad didn't answer. She stared at the photo with skepticism.

At the restaurant, Souad said,
"No, I wasn't confused. You're right, though—it's not the same ad. That woman is
completely different. It's not her. The number is different, and the ad I saw was at the station, not inside the mall."

Salah said firmly,
"You've confused everything. Probably from overthinking."

"No," Souad insisted. "I remember every detail. She was looking at me, smiling. Next to the bottle was a line in French: 'Happy Birthday.' She held the bottle in her palm like this" she demonstrated with her hand "—and pointed to the number: 999."

"'Happy Birthday'?" Salah said. "Then maybe you were just thinking about your birthday." "You don't believe me."

For the first time, Souad looked embarrassed. She ate slowly, without appetite. A heavy silence settled over the table until, suddenly, as if struck by a revelation, she said:

"It's my birthday. She was wishing me a happy birthday. Isn't that sweet of

her?" Salah said nothing. He didn't even look up, just kept eating.

Souad rose abruptly, agitated, her eyes shining with excitement.
"Oh my God, how did I not realize? She was talking to me. It's clear now—can't you see? It's my birthday. Everything started on my birthday. My date of birth is September 9, 1989—three nines!"

She turned to Salah, who had finally lifted his gaze, listening more attentively.
"And the metro opened on September 9, 2009—also three nines. It's all connected. Don't you see?"

Salah paused mid-chew, his tone thoughtful.

"And she wasn't talking to you? What does any of this have to do with

you?" "I don't know… But didn't you say the date you met Ahlam was…?"

"September 9, 1999."

"Exactly! September 9, 1999. All nines. Don't you see? The nines are the
answer. We're all connected by these numbers—you, me, Ahlam, and the
perfume."

Salah studied her, a faint smile playing on his lips.
"This is truly strange. A strange coincidence… or is it really a coincidence?
Three nines."

"It's not a coincidence," Souad said firmly. "I'm certain Ahlam was luring

you through me." "Luring me to what?"

"To meet."

"Then that means she was here?" Salah asked, suddenly excited. "I'm sure

of it. This perfume was a message. A date."

"A date?"

"Yes. I have a strong feeling she was watching us. She was waiting for you,

Mr. Salah." She placed the perfume bottle on the table and said with

conviction:
"The perfume was the bait. She gave it to me on my birthday so I would
wear it, so you would notice, and then she would appear."

Salah examined the bottle, then looked up at Souad.
"But she didn't show up. The moment passed, and she didn't appear."
"Because you missed the appointment. The car flipped over."

His voice rose in frustration.

"But why all these complications and riddles? Why wouldn't she come to me directly? Why through you?"

I spoke calmly.
"Let's not jump to conclusions. Many questions remain unanswered. And remember—we're still talking about an advertisement no one else has seen. We haven't come across it ourselves."

Souad insisted, her eyes blazing. "It exists. I saw it. It's real."

"Then where is it?"

"We need to scour the stations." Salah turned to me.
"What worries you? Why are you still unconvinced?"

"There are too many questions. Like, how did the perfume even reach us? Or how did you just happen to be at the mall on opening day?"

"Those are minor details. What matters is we've caught a thread."

"Don't get carried away. I don't want to discourage you, but honestly, I don't think we've caught anything yet. If we think about where this could lead us I'll tell you I don't think it takes us anywhere. None of this has brought us any closer to Ahlam."

Salah's voice softened.
"Don't be pessimistic, Ahmed. Be optimistic. Let me dream—let me be happy, even if just for a while."

Chapter

Twenty

The message blinked on the screen:
"Mr. Salah, are you looking for a specific woman Ahlam or just any

woman?" My reply was swift. "A specific one. Are you Ahlam?"

"I'm not Ahlam, Mr. Salah. Unfortunately. But the ad caught my interest. I
want to help you find her."

For a moment, my chest tightened I thought we'd finally caught her. But
the hope dissolved into disappointment.

"Who are you?" I typed. "And why do you want to help?" "My name is

Maria. I may be useful in your search." "How?"

"I have my own ways."

"It won't help if you don't know her personally, or at least her address.
We've already tried everything."

A pause. Then her following message came:
"I only have one question." "What is it?"

"Why didn't you post her picture?"

My fingers froze over the keyboard. For a moment, I hesitated, weighing whether to answer. Finally, I decided to speak plainly.

"Listen, I'm not Salah. He's not here to tell you his story. I'm his friend, helping him with the search. The man loved this woman, but she disappeared. He's been looking for her for a long time. He doesn't have a picture of her. So if you have any information, you can tell me."

Her reply came quickly, calm and decisive:
"I need specific answers that only Mr. Salah can provide. I want to deal with

him directly." "Well, he's not available at the moment."

"Goodbye."

And just like that, the screen went silent.

I was still worried about Souad. The past two days had weighed on her in ways I couldn't name. Something unusual stirred inside her—something she wasn't sharing. For the first time, I felt she was hiding her feelings from me, not being completely honest.
"Take me to the sea," she said that evening. "I feel a desire to see the sea."

"What is it with the sea?"

"It's beautiful. It has no limits. It stretches to infinity. I want to swim, to dive into the water, to taste the salt. Could you take me to a deserted beach? I want a sea that's mine alone."

It was night when we drove out to a distant, abandoned shore. I steered along a dark, sandy, uneven road, its edges faintly lit by the faraway glow of old houses. The road finally opened onto a black void, endless and impenetrable, where only the roar of waves told us the sea was there—retreating, advancing, unseen.

"Where are we?" she asked.

I stopped the car and pointed toward the pitch-black horizon. "Here is your friend, the sea. It all belongs to you alone."

Souad leapt out, stood still for a moment, then walked forward until her feet touched the water.

"Come with me."

We strolled along the sand, then began to run. She slipped out of her dress and flung it aside. "Let's get in."

"Aren't you afraid of swimming in the dark?"

She laughed softly, dipped her foot into the waves. "The sea is the sea—day or night. Come on."

"I don't dare. The sea has moods. I don't like to disturb it for fear it might get angry. It's like you."

"Like me? How?" "Mysterious. Just like you."

She turned, her eyes wide. "Me? Mysterious? That's not true."

"You're mystery itself. How do you explain going alone to the beach the day before yesterday? Or seeing an ad that doesn't exist?"
Souad looked at me, incredulous.
"Do you still not believe I saw it? I told you I was on the train when it stopped, the door opened, and Ahlam's picture was on the wall. Do you think, like Salah, that the station exists only in my imagination? How do you explain the details I gave? Do you think I invented
them?"

"I'm not saying you made it up. But maybe… it was your imagination." "I

don't know. I can't explain it."

"Weren't you afraid that morning, alone on the beach?"

"No. Not at all. It felt like a dream. The autumn clouds on the horizon were stunning. I felt I owned the universe."

"You don't share it with me," I said quietly. "You live it alone, and shut me

out." "Don't be jealous. You're always with me."

"You're living a strange dream. I'm afraid you'll drown in it and never wake up. I want to understand what's going on inside you."

"Don't worry. I'm okay—you see?" "I'm not so sure."

"Come on, let's swim. Tonight, the sea and I are in good spirits." "I'll watch.

Just stay where I can see you."

Souad ran into the water. I heard her laughter rise, then fade, as she drifted farther out until she was swallowed by darkness. Her voice echoed across the waves:
"Come on! The water's refreshing!"

I hadn't planned on swimming, but at last I stripped down and waded toward her. She floated on her back, staring up at the stars, her arms stretched wide across the surface. I reached her and held her in my arms, but her gaze was still lost in the sky.
"Do you know what happened here, on this night ten years ago?" she

asked. "What happened?"

"In these waters, Ahlam swam just as I do now. She tasted the salt, as I do. She gazed at the sky, as I gaze now. I feel her inside me, as if she's become a part of me. Her tears run on my cheeks, her thoughts drift through my mind. I feel I understand her completely."
She closed her eyes.
"

Chapter

Twenty-One

You look distracted today," Souad said softly, chewing while her eyes lingered on my face. "Why do you say that?

"You're staring at your plate without eating." "I'm not thinking about anything in particular."

She reached out and brushed her fingers across my cheek. "Something's on your mind."

"You're all that's on my mind," I said with a smile, kissing her fingers. "Me and someone else. Do you still love me?"

I laughed. "No."
"Women sense these things," she said. "Sense what?"

"Danger."

"And do you feel that now?"

"Maybe you've met another woman. Men do that all the time."
"I meet women every day, but that doesn't mean I'm involved with them."

"But you compare me to them, don't you?"

"In what way?"

"Do you regret marrying me? Do you find them more beautiful, more

exciting than me?" "Tell me exactly what's bothering you, Souad."

"Fine, I'll say it: you were flirting with another woman." I froze. "Me?"

"Yes. We saw her at the station. She came closer to you, and you flirted
with her as though I wasn't there."

"When? Where?"

"In my dream yesterday." "In your dream?"

"Yes. And it was disturbing it made me furious with you."

"Souad, that's unreasonable."

"So there isn't another woman?" "Of course not. Don't be silly."

"Then why do you seem so distracted today?".

Before falling asleep, she lifted her head and whispered,
"I can't bear the thought of you holding another woman. The very idea is

killing me." "You know there's no one in my heart but you."

"That won't stop your arms from holding someone else. If I saw it, I'd die.
Do you hear me?"

"You're being unreasonable tonight. Where do you get these ideas?
Anyway, don't worry I won't let you see me with anyone else. Are you

happy now?"

"You're mocking me, not taking my feelings seriously. You don't love me the way I love you. Say you love me."
"I love you, Souad." "A lot?"

"Very much."

"I know," she whispered. "And I love you too."

"Oh God, Souad. If you know, why put me through this interrogation when I'm tired and half-asleep? You know I love you. I won't let you die of loving me I want you to live so you can keep loving me."

"I just like to make sure sometimes. Good night."

"Good night."

A few minutes later, she stirred again, whispering against my ear, "I dream of you loving me the way Salah loves Ahlam."

"I love you even more," I said. "But right now, I only dream of sleeping.

Good night." "Will you dream of me?"

The next day, Maria was the first to message me on Messenger.
"I couldn't sleep all night. I kept thinking about Salah and Ahlam. Their story haunted me. He's a rare man chivalrous, noble, almost knightly in this sordid age. Today, love is fleeting, shallow, and disposable. Men no longer devote a lifetime to pursuing a woman.
Where are men like him anymore?"

"Who are you?" I asked.

"Don't ask me anything personal. I won't answer."

"Let's be honest with each other. I don't think you can help. Forgive me, but I think you're just a lonely woman with no real life outside this screen. You live online because you have neither family nor friends. You're isolated, introverted. You're pretending you want to help just to fill your time."

Maria ended the conversation.

I regretted pushing her away. Any help no matter how small was better than nothing. But was she truly capable of helping? I wasn't sure.

For the next two days, Souad was restless. She abandoned work to wander through markets and perfume agencies, carrying the mysterious bottle everywhere she went. She showed it to perfumers, executives, and experts none recognized it; none had even heard of it. She returned each evening more frustrated than the last.

But one night, she came back different excited. She placed the bottle on the table, sat in front of it, and stared at it as if it were alive.

"You're too obsessed with this perfume," I told her. "It's just perfume."

"Something happened today," she said, her eyes shining.

"What?"

"Do you know the Arabian Perfume Company?" "Yes. What about it?"

"I went there and showed them the bottle." "And?"

"They didn't recognize it either. But one of them the director, I think

offered to buy it." "Really?"

"Yes. For a large sum of money." "How much?"

"Enough to shock me. He grew angry when I refused to sell it." "So it is

something rare, after all."

"It's more than rare. It isn't just perfume. There's something... different about it."

I laughed bitterly. "You should see yourself right now, gazing at that bottle like it's a lover. You've been strange ever since you brought it home. I wish you'd sold it."

"I'm perfectly normal," she said firmly. "And just wait let me finish. When I left the company, one of the Indian employees who had been watching from a distance followed me outside. At first, I thought nothing of it, but when I realized he was behind me step for step, I grew nervous. I quickened my pace toward the metro, but he stayed close so close I could hear his breathing. I turned, ready to scream, when he suddenly smiled, handed me a card, and said, 'Go to this address.' Then he walked away."

She opened her bag and handed me the card. It was for a perfume shop. Both sides, printed in English and Hindi, read:
Indian Perfumes — Preparing and selling all kinds of oriental and western perfumes.

The address: Naif Souq.

"Do you know Naif Souq?" she asked. "Of course."

"Will you come with me tomorrow?"

Naif Souq is like a piece of India in Dubai. Arabic and English fade into the background; the dominant tongue is Malayalam, sometimes Urdu. When you step into Naif Souq, you step into India. Shops and stalls line every street, selling everything from fabrics and perfumes to electronics and household goods.

Spice shops surrounded us, the aroma of curry drifting from small restaurants and overwhelming our senses. No one spoke Arabic or English. Suspicion, indifference, and guarded stares met us at every turn.

I showed a shopkeeper the perfume bottle. He shook his head, neither knowing nor caring, and disappeared inside. Had Souad not been with me, no one would have bothered to glance my way. It was only her beauty that made people reluctantly respond.

Finally, Souad pulled the card from her bag and showed it to a porter dragging a two- wheeled cart piled with boxes. He stopped, set the cart down, examined the card, then smiled and motioned for us to follow.

He led us through several alleys, past fabric stalls, and into a lane scented with incense. At last, he stopped before a shop and pointed to the name: **Indian Perfumes.** With a polite nod, he turned to leave. Souad pressed money into his hand. At first, he refused shyly, then accepted, and rolled his cart away.

We stepped inside. Shelves lined the walls, crowded with perfume bottles and small jars. Barrels of dried flowers, sandalwood bark, and incense filled the floor.

At the front stood a young Indian man, who greeted us with a warm smile. Around him hung rows of hand-filled bottles. A soft cloud of incense smoke floated in the air.

He welcomed us, then asked something in a language we didn't understand. Souad showed him the card. He nodded, confirming we were in the right place. Then he took out a perfume bottle, sprayed some onto a tissue, and offered it to Souad.

She gently waved it away. The young man looked puzzled. Then Souad reached into her bag, pulled out the mysterious bottle, and placed it in his hand.

The young man examined it, shook his head indicating he didn't recognize it and sniffed it. We watched closely, searching for a reaction. Aside from evident admiration for the scent, there was no sign of recognition.

He asked in a mix of Arabic, English, and his native accent what exactly we wanted. I wondered if he had anything similar. He shook his head, then started showing us samples of different perfumes, trying to sell them.

We left the shop. Souad looked deeply disappointed. "What did you

expect?" I asked.
"I don't know... But the man who gave me the card was so confident."
"Confident in what?"
"I don't know. I just hoped we'd find something maybe information about its ingredients, its source, its distributor anything."

We hadn't gone far when a voice called out behind us. We turned to see the young salesman waving for us to return.

He stood at the shop's entrance, smiling, and motioned us inside. An old man now sat where the younger one had been. It was clear he had been waiting for us.

As we entered, he looked at us over the rim of his glasses, studying Souad's face. Then, with a disappointed tone, he said,
"You're not who I was expecting. I'm sorry."

The young man stepped in.
"This is my father," he said. "He was lying inside, but the scent of your perfume woke him up. He asked me to call you back."

The old man nodded.
"I can recognize that perfume from among thousands. It pulled me from a deep sleep. I thought I was dreaming."
"So you *do* know it?" Souad asked eagerly.
"I never thought I'd smell it again in my life. Who sent you to me?" "A young man from the Swiss Arabian Perfume Company."
He smiled. "That's my other son Pravit." "So what do you know about the perfume?" "Unfortunately, nothing."

Souad's expression fell.
"But you recognized it," she said hopefully.

She handed him the bottle. The old man opened it, brought it to his nose, closed his eyes, and inhaled deeply.

"Yes," he said. "It's the same."
"Do you know where it comes from? What's in it?"
"It's pure oil. Not a blend. A single, undiluted extract from one flower. But I don't know which flower, or where it grows."
"How can you tell?"
"It's my profession. I grew up surrounded by perfumes. I learned to recognize every ingredient. It cost me my sense of smell."
"Then how are you smelling this now?" I asked in astonishment.
"That's the strange part. It's a puzzling scent like nothing I've ever known. I'm sorry I can't tell you more."

Souad's disappointment was evident. I felt the same hope slipping away just when it felt we were getting closer to the truth.

She looked at me as if to say: *There's no point. He doesn't know anything.*

But just as we turned to leave, the old man said,
"The woman who brought it to me the first time was also disappointed."
"The woman?" Souad gasped. "Ahlam?"

the man said gently, "I didn't know her name." "But you met her?"
"A long time ago."
"What did she want?"
"The same as you. But she had the flower itself, not the perfume. She wanted to know about it but I'm not a botanist. I don't know plants. I was heartbroken that I couldn't help her. At her request and insistence I gathered everyone I knew in the field. But no one could identify it. It was a strange, unique flower."

I asked, "If she brought the flower, why was she asking you about it? Where did she get it from?"
"We asked her the same thing. She said she found it by chance. She didn't say where or how."
"Didn't she leave an address?"
"No. All I know is that she was beautiful, kind, friendly. She laughed a lot... worried a lot... and dreamed a lot. A remarkable woman. I'll never forget her smile or her eyes. We talked about many things."
"You never learned where she was from?"
"I think she was just passing through. She didn't live in the Emirates." "How do you know that?"
"She was in a rush. She didn't want to wait even a day while I continued researching. She apologized and said she had to travel maybe for good."
"Did she say where?" "Yes, to India."
"India?" Souad echoed.
"She said she was going to visit the Konark Temple and study the *Kama Sutra*."
"The *what*?"
The old man chuckled. "Look it up. You'll like it."

Souad turned to me, stunned. "India?"

We left the shop, convinced there was nothing more to learn. The old man walked us out. He looked sorrowful.

"If you know anything about her, please tell me. And if you ever see her again, tell her about me. Maybe she'll visit. I would love to see her again and talk to her."

His words moved me. I turned to Souad
"Did you hear that old Indian man? The way he spoke about her I think he's in love with her."

On the metro, Souad sat quietly, watching the passengers Indian, European, Asian. Her gaze drifted to the passing cars and billboards along Sheikh Zayed Road. The shops and towers lining the street were beginning to glow with evening lights.

Then she turned to me and smiled. "Why are you smiling?" I asked.
"Nothing. I'm just touched by what happened today. It gives me hope. I'm sure we've gotten closer to her. The perfume led us to her it's her message to us. She wants to be found."
"Honestly, I think I've started looking for you more than for her or the perfume."
"Don't say that. I'm always with you. But you have to admit this woman is special. She's like a perfume... leaving a trace wherever she goes."
"You really think we've found a clue?"
"I don't know. But at least now we know someone else saw her. We're more certain than ever that she's real. I'm so happy."
"You sound more interested in her now than Salah ever was." "I think we should tell Salah the news."

But Salah was away, and all we had was his phone number. That evening I called, but there was no answer. I tried his office, and the answering machine picked up. I left a message:
"Call me. It's urgent. I have good news."

I was sure it would be the best news he'd had in years. But the next day passed, and still he didn't call. I began to worry. He'd been gone a week, and we'd heard nothing. I left several more messages. In the last one, I said:
"It's about Ahlam."

Meanwhile, Souad grew distant. She worked long hours, spoke little, and seemed always deep in thought. Her appetite vanished. She left early in the morning and returned late in the evening, only to sit silently at her computer. Unless I reminded her, she didn't eat. I started cooking and doing the dishes not that she noticed. It wasn't like her.

One evening, I said, "Even beautiful birds have to eat."
"I'm not hungry."
"But I'm the poor bird and I am hungry."
She smiled faintly. "And why isn't my bird eating?"
"Because his beautiful bird didn't cook for him." "I'm sorry. Please eat something."
"We're going out for dinner. You look exhausted."
"No, I'm not in the mood. I have work to do. Let's stay in."

I made cheese sandwiches, but she barely managed two bites before returning to her computer.

The next morning, I found her asleep on the couch beside it. I made coffee and woke her gently. She sat up with difficulty, still half-asleep, sipping in silence.
"Looks like you slept late," I said. She didn't answer. She just sipped. "Want me to drive you to work?"
"No, I'll take the metro like always," she replied calmly, before disappearing into the bathroom.

Her phone rang, but she didn't hear it. After several rings, it stopped. On the screen were multiple missed calls all from her workplace. Then it rang again. I answered.

"Hello?" a woman's voice asked. "Hello."
"Is Mrs. Souad there?"
"Yes, but she's in the shower." "Is she alright?"
"Yes."
"I'm her colleague. I was worried. She hasn't been to work for two days. Is she sick?"

Her words startled me. Souad hadn't said anything. I stammered, "She had a sudden illness, but she's okay now."
"Why hasn't she answered my calls?"

"Maybe she was asleep when you called." "Will she be coming in today?"
"I think so."
"Alright.
We're waiting for her. Thank you."

I hung up, stunned. She hadn't been at work for two days. So where had she been? What had she been doing?
When she came out of the bathroom, drying her hair, she smiled. "You're still here? Aren't you running late?"
I hesitated. Should I confront her? Her pale face, her exhaustion, and her silence held me back.
"I'm just worried about you. You look pale. You seem tired." "I'm fine."
"How's work?" I asked, feigning casualness. "It's okay."
"Alright... I'll go then."

But I had already made up my mind. I would follow her.

It wasn't easy the road to the metro was open. I drove ahead, parked near the entrance, and went inside. I bought a ticket and waited in the corner of the platform, hiding behind a newspaper I'd brought for cover.

Several trains came and went. Then she arrived.

She wore a long, loose, colorful dress, flat shoes, and glasses. Graceful, confident, she stood tall, eyes fixed ahead, not glancing left or right.

I watched her, and a wave of emotion swept through me. I wanted to walk over, kiss her, tell her I loved her. It felt like seeing her for the first time.

And yet I felt ashamed. Ashamed for spying. Ashamed for doubting her.

But my heart was pounding. With fear. And with anticipation of whatever truth awaited me.

The train arrived. Souad entered the women's and children's carriage. I stepped into the one next to it and positioned myself by the door, making sure I wouldn't miss her stop.

The train departed from the Mall station toward Dubai Deira. It stopped at the first station, and the carriage door opened. I prepared to get off, but

Souad didn't leave her seat. The train took off again. It stopped at the next station, but she still wasn't among the departing passengers.

I assumed she was going to her job at City Center. But she didn't get off there either. So where was she going?

The train was headed to the airport and the Mushrif area. I remained in my carriage, watching the passengers get on and off, until we reached the last station.

Only one passenger remained in my carriage when the train finally stopped. The radio announced the end of the line and instructed all passengers to disembark.

I waited to exit, wanting to make sure Souad had gotten off before me. But no one did.

I stepped out onto the platform and cautiously walked toward her carriage. I entered and looked around. It was empty.

Disappointment settled over me followed by anger at myself. How could she have slipped away from my sight without me noticing?

It couldn't be that she had left the carriage without me seeing her. And yet, she had vanished.

Still, her trace remained in the carriage a faint scent of her distinctive perfume. A perfume that only Souad, and before her Ahlam, wore. A perfume that only she could identify.

I looked for her everywhere I could. I even went back to City Center, where she worked. I didn't find her there.

I told them she was sick and that I had come to inform them of her absence.

I called her mobile phone, but she didn't answer.

She had no friends outside of work, except for Nicole. I called Nicole, but

she knew nothing. No one knew anything about her. And how could they, if

I her husband knew nothing?

I had no choice but to wait for her return, as usual.

I went back to the office and tried to distract myself with work, but Ramesh noticed something was off.

"What's wrong, Boss?"

"I'm not well. I think I'm a little sick."

"Is it still the story of Ahlam that's bothering you?"

"It's bothering me and my wife even more. I don't know what we've gotten ourselves into."

Ramesh smiled and looked at me from behind his screen. "Just like Indian

movies." "By the way, I want to ask you something. What do you know

about the Kama Sutra?"

Ramesh laughed and looked at me, surprised. "You mean the *Kama Sutra*? Who mentioned it to you?"

"An Indian person. But he didn't explain what it meant." "It's something

related to Indian culture."

"What do you mean? Is it something like yoga?"

"You could say it's a kind of *sexual yoga*. A cultural philosophy for adults. It's a way of life that includes sexuality."

"Is it a philosophy book?"

"It's more of a lifestyle a collection of thoughts and poems about virtue, sex, love, and life."

"Virtue and sex together? Isn't that strange?"

Ramesh left his desk and sat in the chair across from me, clearly intrigued by the topic.

"It's even stranger to think they *don't* go together. Yes, it's the art of sex and love methods of sexual positions, the art of intimacy. It's expressed through paintings, ancient statues, and wall carvings in some palaces and temples."

"You mean pornographic paintings and statues?"

"Some might see it that way, especially if they haven't read the book. The images and sculptures came after the book to complement and illustrate its teachings."

"There are teachings?"

"More like *rules*. The *Kama Sutra* roughly means 'rules of sex.' But sex, as I told you, is only part of the book. Its main goal is to offer advice on the art of living. It's rooted in ancient Indian philosophies.

"To the untrained eye, it might look like just a book on sex or even pornography. But in ancient India, it was considered both culture and science. A girl who was allowed to study this art and learn its philosophy was considered lucky."

Ramesh paused, then asked, "But tell me what made you bring up this

subject?"

"Ahlam."

I spent the rest of the day trying to contact Souad, but neither her phone nor the home phone answered.

Maria appeared online. I ignored her; I wasn't in the mood to chat, especially with her. But it wasn't long before she messaged me:

"Hello, why are you ignoring me?"

"I think you're wasting your time. I don't see how you can help."

"What if I give you her picture?"

I was shocked. "Her picture?"

"Wouldn't that be a major step in finding her? Without a picture, you won't

get anywhere."

"Her picture? So… you know her?"

"No, but my job is to draw faces. Give me her description, and I'll draw her.
I can also use some technology The kind used by Criminal Investigations to
reconstruct faces and I'll give you an exact portrait. But I need details. That's
why I need Salah's help. He must describe her to me
himself."

"I must admit, that's a great idea. Do you work for the Criminal

Investigation Police?" "That's none of your business."

"Okay, but how will we meet?" "I deal with Mr. Salah only."

"Fine. I'll send you his email address."

"I want his phone number, too."

I gave her his phone number, knowing he hadn't answered since he

returned to Syria. They'd all disappeared: Ahlam, then Salah, and finally

Souad.

I felt a shiver run through me as that thought crossed my mind. I couldn't
stay in the office any longer I decided to go home. I had no choice but to
wait. At least I was somewhat reassured: she'd been absent from work the
past two days, but she always returned home by evening. I told myself I'd
wait. If she didn't come back, I'd call the police.

When I entered the house, her shoes were by the door, and I heard water running in the bathroom. Relief washed over me. I knocked gently, letting her know I was there, then headed to the kitchen to prepare dinner. But she took her time. I called out, asked her to hurry, but there was no answer. It was as if she were deliberately avoiding me. I knocked again, softly, but all I could hear was the relentless trickling of water.

I pushed the door open and was met with a wall of steam. Heat pressed against me, blinding me. "Why all this steam? Where are you? Are you okay?" My voice echoed in the haze. I felt my way forward, hands brushing against damp tiles until I reached the sink. The faucets were gushing full force. I shut them off, then stepped back, uneasy. Something sharp crunched under my foot. Glass. My heart seized. "Souad!" I shouted, my voice cracking. There was no reply. I flung the door wide open, desperate to clear the steam. The bathtub brimmed with scalding water, but it was empty. The mirror was shattered, its shards scattered across the floor like ice.

Panic overtook me. I tore through the apartment living room, kitchen, bedroom. Empty. Her clothes lay tossed on the bed. Her phone rang faintly when I called, coming from inside her bag on the couch. My chest tightened; my thoughts collided in chaos. Souad had become the axis of everything strange—the perfume, the metro, the sea, Salah, Nicole. What bound it all together?

I staggered to the door, unsure where to go, unsure even why I felt an urgent need to find Salah. Maybe he'd know what to do. Then an odd memory struck me, a fragment of Salah's story with Ahlam. My stomach twisted. I spun around and ran back to the bathroom.

There, behind the door, Souad sat naked on the floor. Her head rested on her knees, her arms locked tightly between her legs.

"You're here?" I breathed, stepping closer. "Why didn't you answer me? Why are you here like this?"

She didn't look up.

"Souad," I pleaded, placing a hand on her wet hair. "What happened? Look at me."

Slowly, she lifted her face. Her eyes, heavy with exhaustion, met mine. Drops of water slid from her skin, falling to the tiles—dark drops, red now against the floor.

"Are you hurt?" My voice trembled as I bent down, trying to lift her.

But she resisted, clutching her hands tightly between her thighs as if guarding something. "What are you hiding?" I tried to pry them loose.

Her legs locked tighter. "Souad—show me."

At last, after a long struggle, she yielded. She opened her palms. Between them was a jagged shard of the broken mirror, her hands slick with blood.

I reached for it, but she pressed harder, squeezing until fresh blood spurted from her palms. "I'm a bad woman," she whispered.

"Souad, please," I begged. "Let go of the glass. Let it go."

But Souad didn't respond. She was clenching it tightly in both hands, as if she wanted to stab someone or herself. "You'll hurt yourself. Give the piece of glass."

I carefully removed the piece of glass from her hand and placed it on the floor. Then I brought a towel, wiped the blood off the floor, and put it away in a corner.

I held her bloody hand and helped her stand in front of the sink. I washed her hands and then wrapped them in a towel while she watched me silently, as if she weren't concerned, or as if she weren't the one hurt, but someone else.

"Hug me," she said in a frightened voice.

I took her in my arms and held her close to my chest. "Run your hand over my body. Do you feel me?"

"Of course I feel you, and I feel your heartbeat in my chest." "So I'm back."

"Back? What do you mean?"

But she collapsed in my arms, so I picked her up and put her to bed. When she felt a little better, I dressed her, and we went to the hospital.

"How did that happen?" the doctor asked her. "I hit the mirror and it broke."

We left the hospital. She was calmer and more collected. On the way back, she leaned her head against the window and just stared silently at the cars and streetlights. When we got home, I asked her, "Is that what really happened? Did you hit the mirror?"

She answered calmly, "Yes."

"And the piece of glass in your hand? Why were you holding it?" She said hesitantly, "I was scared."

"What scared you?" "The mirror."

"What's in the mirror? This is the second time this has happened. What's so scary about it? What did you see?"

"I didn't see anything. I didn't see anyone." "What do you mean you didn't see anyone?"

She frowned and said fearfully, "I looked and didn't see myself. Everything was there except me. I wasn't there! Scary, isn't it?"

"You must have been exhausted."
"I feel tired and want to sleep."

I took her to the bedroom. I made her stand in front of the vanity mirror.

"Do you see yourself now?"

She looked at herself in the mirror and smiled faintly. "Yes, I see a bad woman." "Don't say that. You're the kindest woman I know."

"I'm having strange sensations and wild thoughts that tempt and excite me at the same time and that terrifies me."

I guess you're thinking a lot about Ahlam. She's probably gotten into your

head. I tucked her into bed, pulled the covers over her, kissed her, and let

her sleep. "I want you next to me."

I lay down beside her. She rested her head on my chest and closed her
eyes. She slept like a child—a child wrapped in secrets, until she became
one.
I didn't get the chance to ask why she'd been absent from work. The

moment wasn't right. In the morning, I woke up to the sound of her voice.

"I'm leaving."

I opened my eyes and saw her smiling, already dressed and getting ready to

go. "When did you wake up?"
"I have to go. Go back to sleep."
"How are you feeling today?" "I'm fine. I really have to go." "Where are you
going?"
"I'm late. See you later."

She left in a hurry, without saying where she was headed—to my confusion
and disappointment.
I heard the front door close. She didn't even give me a chance to ask about
her absence from work.

I didn't wait. I got up quickly, dressed, and decided to follow her. I wouldn't
lose her this time like I had the day before.

I hurried out of the house and jumped into the car. On the way to the mall,
I saw her walking in the distance. I knew I could beat her there. I reached
my usual hiding spot just before she arrived.

The metro came. I waited for her to board, then made sure to get on the
next carriage, just like I'd done before.
But this time, I was more determined not to lose her.
I got off at every stop to check if she had slipped away. The train passed

station after station she stayed on board. Until we reached the last stop.

I waited until everyone got off. But she wasn't among them. I stepped into

her carriage. She wasn't there.

Fury welled up inside me. She had vanished again—despite all the precautions I'd taken. How could she have gotten off without me noticing? I'd watched every stop, every platform. She hadn't left the train—I was sure of it.

Where was she?

I went back to my office.

I called her as soon as I got there. No answer.

Just like the day before, she didn't show up for work.

Something was wrong. This wasn't normal behavior. Was she aware I was following her? Had she found a way to evade me?

But why? Why avoid me? Why didn't she want me near her? The questions spun in my head like a whirlpool. My face flushed with heat. My mind raced.

I left the office, avoiding Ramesh's worried questions—he'd noticed my anxiety. I went home, feeling useless and unable to focus on anything.

The house was empty. Loneliness set in.

I began wandering around. I opened the closet and stared at her clothes, her shoes, her bags. I studied them as if I were discovering her for the first time. I sat at the dressing table she had arranged, examining her lipstick, eyeliner, perfume, and other cosmetics.
A lump rose in my throat anger and longing tangled together. What had changed?

Then I heard the key turn in the door.
Souad walked in, calm, with a faint smile. My early return from work didn't

surprise her; she acted as if it were perfectly normal.

"It was a busy day,"
she said.
"They told me at work you'd been absent for two days. Why didn't you tell me?" "I didn't want to bother you. You would've worried too much."

She slipped off her sandals and lay down on the sofa. "But I had to. I had to get off at that station."
"And does the train stop at that station?"
"Yes, it stops. Every time it does, the door opens and closes—but I don't dare leave the train."
"Why not?"
"Because it's always empty. No one ever gets off. The people on the train are always
preoccupied, as if they don't notice it at all. Only I hear the soft music. Only I'm drawn to the lights. Only I'm captivated by the advertisement by its joy and liveliness. The woman in
the ad smiles at me alone, beckoning me to get off."

"It's just an illusion. I've been to every station, and I've never seen that one."
"I thought I was imagining it too. But this morning, I decided to take the risk and I got off." "You got off at that station?" I asked in disbelief.
"Yes."

I looked at her skeptically. "And what did you find there?" "You won't believe it."
"What?"

She smiled, reached into her bag, and pulled out a flower. "A flower?"
The flower," she emphasized. "Have you ever seen anything like it?"

It was a strange-looking orchid with blue and yellow petals.
"It smells like that perfume," I said, stunned. "Where did you find it?"
"When I got off. At the station. I was afraid especially when the train pulled away and left me standing there alone. There was no one else. Just me, the announcements, the music, and the lights. I saw a long, brightly lit corridor with a sign at the end that read *Exit.*

"I started walking, slowly and cautiously. Halfway through, there were restrooms. From the men's room, I heard panting. Curious, I cracked the door open and peeked inside. A young man and a woman were there. She was pressing him against the wall, kissing him. The man sensed something and whispered, *'I hear someone.'* The woman spun around, flung the door open but didn't see me standing behind it. Embarrassed, I ran toward the exit without looking back."

Souad spoke with excitement, her eyes shining, eager to pull me into her discovery. Then her expression softened, her voice tinged with awe.
"And when I stepped through that door… everything was there."
"Everything?"
"Stunning nature green meadows, waterfalls, orchids. Vast fields of rchids."

I laughed. "Souad? Where did you *buy* this flower?"

Her face darkened with disappointment and anger.
"I can't believe you don't believe me. Not after everything I told you."
"And I can't believe you expect me to. If you don't want to tell me where you've been, that's fine. But don't feed me some fantasy about a magical station. You're describing a place that exists only in dreams."

Souad's face fell. Tears welled in her eyes.
"It seems you don't want to hear the rest of the story."
"No. I'm tired of stories. It's become boring. I just wanted you to be honest with me. I worry about you. You haven't been yourself lately. You don't share your thoughts with me anymore. You don't confide in me like you used to."
"I'm going to bed. I'm tired."
"That's exactly what bothers me. You're always tired. Always silent."

She gave me a reproachful look, then turned away, went into the bedroom, slipped into bed fully dressed, and shut her eyes.

In the morning, Salah finally called. "Hello, Ahmed. How are you?"
"I'm fine," I said, still disoriented. "I've been trying to reach you—left messages on your Damascus number."
"I heard them. I'm fine. But something strange happened—too strange to explain over the phone. I'll tell you when we meet. You mentioned in your message that there's something important. What is it?"
"We've found someone who knew Ahlam. Who met her, even." "Really?

Who?"
"An Indian perfumer."

I told him briefly about the perfumer, Ahlam, and the flower.
"Oh my God—that's incredible. Honestly, this is the best news I've had in a long time. Thank you."
"It's all thanks to Souad. She led us to him."
"Please give her my regards. I'll call you both later—once I settle in. I've got important news, too."

Chapter

Twenty-Two

Salah called in the evening to check on Souad. We agreed to meet at the Mall of the Emirates for dinner. He sounded cheerful, energetic, and optimistic and he mentioned he was bringing a guest.

"Who's this guest?" Souad asked curiously.

"It's Maria. She's going to help us draw a picture of Ahlam." "Is she a friend

of Salah's?"

"Does that matter to you?" "No. Is she beautiful?"

"I don't know. But don't worry she won't be more beautiful than you."

Souad dressed in her finest clothes, layered on nearly every kind of makeup, and adorned herself with jewelry. It was instinctive a woman never likes competition. Still, I couldn't tell if she wanted to impress me, or Salah.

I watched her in the mirror as she applied a final touch of lipstick. "Don't you think you're going a little overboard?"

"Why? Don't you like how I look tonight?"

"You're not used to going out like this. You'll attract attention—and I know you'll feel embarrassed if people stare."

Her face flushed red as she studied herself in the mirror. "Do you really think so? What should I do?"

"Be natural. Even without makeup, you're the most beautiful woman in the world to me the most beautiful of all."

Souad smiled shyly.
"Alright. I'll tone it down. I don't want to attract too much attention."
We left together, her arm tucked in mine, satisfied with herself and confident she could easily outshine her supposed rival.

At the restaurant, we arrived before Salah. Souad kept glancing around nervously, never missing a chance to see how her beauty might affect the other guests.

We didn't wait long. Salah soon appeared, Souad's eyes fixed on the woman beside him, scanning her from head to toe.

"Oh my God, who is that?" Souad whispered.

Maria was of average height, slightly plump, with short black hair. Her looks were ordinary. She wore jeans and a plain T-shirt. Clearly, she wasn't in Souad's league.

"This is Maria," Salah said with a smile.

"Welcome. Finally it's you," I said, shaking her hand warmly. She smiled

faintly, her face reddening, but said nothing.

"You two must already know each other," Salah teased.

I quickly corrected him, extending my hand again.
"No, we haven't met in person. Only through our conversations about you, and Ahlam. This is my wife, Souad."

Maria greeted Souad with a small, polite smile. Souad's beauty had clearly taken her aback, but she seemed relieved to realize she wasn't here to compete.

"Your wife is beautiful, Mr. Ahmed," Maria said. Souad smiled coldly.

"Thank you."

"How are you both?" Salah said. "I missed you."

"And we worried about you," I said. "What happened? You said something strange had happened. What was it?"

"I'll tell you later, after dinner. Maria wore me out today didn't you, Maria? And I wore her out, too. But her work is incredible different from anything else."

Souad asked, "What is your field of work, Miss Maria?" "Miss Maria," Salah

corrected her.

Maria ignored the correction and answered calmly. "I'm an artist. I draw and paint faces."

"Why bother drawing them? Why not just take photographs?" Souad asked.

"I draw people's faces based on descriptions when there's no photograph

available." "And are the results usually any good?"

"Yes. With the help of some technology, the likenesses are fairly accurate. It's an effective tool in police work. But in our case, the challenge was time and how memory fades."

Salah said,
"I was frightened when she started asking for details. I was shocked to realize that Ahlam the woman I had never forgotten, not in dreams nor in reality had become almost featureless in my mind. I never imagined her image could fade so much. I would close my eyes and try to recall her, but nothing came. I panicked. I was afraid she would vanish from my imagination after already disappearing from my life.

I went back to my diaries and old notes, searching for anything any detail that could bring her image back. Thank you, Maria. You brought color and life back into her face. Now, I'm waiting for you to show me her portrait."

"Not before I meet the other person you said had seen her," Maria replied. "He must go through the same examination you did. Two memories, two perspectives together, they can create a truer, more accurate image."

"You seem to love your work," Souad said.

"Yes," Maria answered calmly. "And I'm good at it."

During dinner, Maria was visibly nervous. She kept her eyes on her plate, speaking little. In person, she was nothing like the sharp, confident woman I had known online here she appeared shy, awkward, even struggling to chew her food, sipping water to help her swallow.

Souad broke the silence. "May I ask why you're not married yet?" Maria

took a sip of water, then, without raising her head, replied,
"It hasn't happened yet." She smiled faintly. "Or maybe it did, but…" "How

so? What happened?"

"There was someone. But that was a long time ago—an old story." "Did he

get married?"

"Yes. He even had children." "Do you still love him?"

"Stop, Souad," I said gently. "You're embarrassing her."

"It's all right," Maria said. She lifted her eyes for a moment, then lowered them again. "It all turned into a beautiful memory. Sometimes I hate him. Sometimes I blame myself for loving him so much. But back then, I couldn't help it. Afterwards, my heart no longer beat with the same strength as if it were tired… as if its flame had gone out. Love requires energy, and I fear I no longer have enough. Everyone has their share of love. I had mine, and I'm satisfied with it."

She fell silent. One hand clutched her fork, the other traced circles on the rim of her glass. Her eyes stared blankly at her plate. The table grew heavy with silence until Salah, chuckling, broke it:

"Draw me a picture of Ahlam, and I promise I'll find you a groom."

Maria laughed softly. "Then I'd better get to work immediately, day and night. But for now, excuse me I can't stay any longer." She turned to Salah, smiling. "We have an appointment tomorrow morning with the herbalist, remember? Don't be late. Good night."

She left the restaurant. We watched her disappear into the crowd. That was the last time I ever saw her or heard from her.

The next day, she went with Salah to see the Indian herbalist, then left, promising to email him the results of her work. Her brief appearance had been significant. The portrait of Ahlam she later sent would alter the course of events and give Salah's journey a mighty push forward.

"Now, tell us," I said. "What was that important incident that happened to

you in Syria?" Salah smiled faintly.
"I was imprisoned."

"What?"

He laughed. "Yes, I was imprisoned." "But why?"

"It's a strange story."

"Was it related to your work?"
"I don't think so." "So, what happened?"

"Two men arrived at the office claiming to be security officers. They asked
me to go with them immediately to the branch. I tried to ask why, but they
wouldn't explain. They also refused to let me call anyone. They said it
wouldn't take more than an hour, and then they'd bring me back."

"Did they assault you?"

"No, not at all. They were polite, but firm. They took me to a security
branch, led me into a large room with a desk and a leather chair, and left
me there alone for hours. Finally, a man in his late forties came in. He
stared at me in silence, then sat behind the desk and asked, in a dry voice,
'Are you Engineer Salah?'"

'Yes.'

'You work in Dubai?'

'Yes, I worked there. Then I founded a company called'"

"He cut me off sharply: 'Enough. I know everything about you... I know you
well.'

He looked through some papers, then studied me again with a silent,
unnerving gaze that sent fear down my spine. Without a word, he rose and
left the room.

Later, they moved me to another small room—just a bed, a chair, and a
bathroom. I asked if I was going to be released, but they didn't answer. No
one knew anything. I felt terrible.
Eventually, they brought me food. It was surprisingly good, better than
what I'd heard about prison meals. After eating, I lay down on the bed and
waited. No one came. I fell asleep.
When I woke up, I found that someone had placed a wool blanket over me
during the night.

In the morning, they took me back to the investigator's room. He was there
again, behind his desk, looking serious as if he didn't know how to smile.

He stared at me for a while, then called a guard and told him to release me.

I tried to shake his hand, to ask why I had been brought in. But he ignored me and muttered, 'My advice to you is this: forget the past. Don't dig into it. It won't lead you anywhere.'

Salah fell silent, staring at us. "Is that it?" I asked, surprised.

"Yes, that's all. They released me."
"That's strange. I wonder what he meant by 'the past'? What past was he talking about?"

"It's obvious," Souad said. "He meant Ahlam. He's warning you to let her go. To move on with your life."

"But what does security have to do with my personal life? What do they know about Ahlam?"

"Maybe she's a suspect in some case," Souad said hesitantly, "like we once feared. Or maybe she works with them?"

"If that were true, they wouldn't have let me go. They wouldn't have treated me so kindly. I'm really confused. I don't understand their purpose. They didn't interrogate me. They didn't ask me anything. Isn't that strange?"

"It's very strange."

Salah smiled. "But there's one positive thing you're all forgetting." "What's

that?"

"I left unharmed."

"Now I have a surprise for you," said Souad. She pulled the flower out of its bag and placed it in his hands.

Salah took the flower, turning it gently between his fingers before lifting it to his nose. A look of astonishment crossed his face.

"It smells exactly the same perfume. Where did you get it?" "From the

station I told you about. Do you believe me now?"

Salah glanced at me as though asking for my verdict. I shrugged. His eyes
lingered on the flower before he finally said, after a pause:

"I don't know what to believe. But one question keeps haunting me."

"What is it?"

"What's the connection between the three of us—me, you, and Ahlam?
Why did the perfume come to you?"

"I think she simply chose me. She came to me." "Maybe. But why you?"

We parted with that question still hanging in the air.

That evening, Souad was restless. Something weighed heavily on her,
though she tried to mask it. Her fingers twitched, her eyes followed me
from kitchen to living room to bedroom, always on the edge of speaking.

"What's wrong, Souad? What is it?" "Nothing."

"Say it, and stop following me around like a cat."

She hesitated. "I… spoke to Nicole a little while ago." "And?"

"I'm going with her to France." "What?"

"Just for two days. Over the weekend."

"Two days? To France? Why don't we go together during the holidays, visit

Farid?" "I can't wait. I already left my passport at the French embassy."

"What? Why?"

"Nicole's taking me to Grasse. We'll visit the perfume factories and show them the perfume. Their expertise might help us. We'll find Ahlam."

"You're obsessed with Ahlam." "Let me go. Please."

"When do you plan to travel?"

"By the end of the week, if the visa comes through. I'll only be gone two

days." "It seems you've already made up your mind."

"Please. I'm so excited about this trip, and I have a good feeling. I'll die if I

don't go." "...Alright, go."

"I'll bring you back a bottle of French perfume, straight from the factory."
Two days later, Souad left for Grasse, and I was alone. For the first time, the house felt hollow. I had grown used to her presence to waking and finding her eyes on me, quiet but watchful. I should have felt free again, relieved to have my solitude back. But I didn't.

I kept thinking of her.

She called on her first day, saying she and Nicole were heading to Nicole's father's factory. The next day, she sounded thrilled, telling me everything was going well, that she had glimpsed the truth—but she didn't explain further.

When two more days passed and she hadn't returned, I grew uneasy. Another two days, and her Emirati phone went silent— "out of coverage or unavailable."

At first, I wasn't too worried. She was with Nicole, after all, and in France. Undoubtedly, she was enjoying herself.

But after a week, my anxiety deepened. I tried calling Nicole. Her French number was off. Finally, I tried her UAE number—and to my surprise, she answered.

"Hello?"

"Hi, Nicole. How are you?" "Fine. How are you and Souad?" Her words

froze me.

"What? Aren't you two together?" "No."

"What do you mean? Didn't you travel with her?"

"Yes. But she only stayed with me two days. Then she left for Syria." "Syria?

Why? Didn't she find what she was looking for in Grasse?"

"Yes, she got what she needed on the first day. After that, she was eager to travel to Syria. She told me she knew where Ahlam was. I assumed she had already told you."

"She knew where Ahlam was? Where exactly?" "I don't know. She said

she'd tell us later."

"But she didn't call. I don't know anything about her, and I'm worried. What happened in Grasse?"

It takes hundreds of flowers to yield a single drop of perfume just as it takes a single smile to inspire hundreds of lines.

Nicole said:

"We arrived in Grasse in the morning. Souad was so excited that she wouldn't even let us rest; we went straight to my uncle's factory. It was a small workshop where he worked mostly alone, sometimes with one or two assistants. He made body sprays, aftershaves, oils, scented soaps, and deodorants, which he sold to tourists.

He was stunned by the perfume Souad showed him it was unlike anything he had ever smelled. He didn't recognize the flower, though he suspected it might be a rare orchid unfamiliar to him. Eager to learn more, he contacted some friends who owned other factories. The whole morning was spent huddled together, analyzing the perfume, but they reached no conclusion. They stood before the flower and the fragrance in awe.

Souad grew restless and disappointed. She even thought about leaving Grasse altogether and visiting Farid in Besançon. Then I received a call from Monsieur Gallimard, owner of the largest perfume oil factory in Grasse—a respected man, known for his seclusion.

The first thing he asked me was:
'Tell me about the woman and her perfume. Is she Syrian?' 'Yes.'

'I must see her. Can you bring her now? I'll be waiting.' 'Of course.'

Souad wasn't optimistic after the failure with my uncle's friends, but she didn't want to miss an opportunity that might bring her closer to Ahlam.

When we arrived, Monsieur Gallimard was waiting at the factory entrance. He looked at Souad for a long moment.
'You're young.'

'What do you mean?' she asked.

'The other one was the same age but that was more than twenty years

ago.' 'Which other one?'

He didn't answer directly. Instead, he led us inside.
'We'll go straight to the lab. They told me you brought a flower.' 'Yes.'

Souad opened a book she carried and carefully removed a dried flower pressed between the pages. He took it gently, studying the stem and leaves.
'My God. It's the same one.' He inhaled its scent deeply. 'Yes—it's the same. Come, follow me.'

He led us into a hall that looked like a flower museum. Pictures of countless species—roses, orchids, and other plants covered the walls. He walked directly to one frame and pointed. 'Here it is. I named it Orchid Syria. A Syrian scientist found it accidentally last year. He called it the Bull Orchid, because the lower lip of the flower has two protrusions that resemble bull's horns.'

Souad compared her flower to the photo.
'It's identical. The same colors white, blue, and yellow.'

'You don't realize the importance of what you're holding in your hand.'

'What do you mean?'

'That flower is only the second one ever found in the world.' 'The second?'

Yes. The Syrian scientist found only one. Here is its photo. He searched everywhere but couldn't find another. It was discovered in the forests of a village called Sarstan, east of Tartus in Syria. Despite his efforts, he found nothing more. He even asked for my help. I went myself, searching Sarstan, its surroundings, and every nearby village. But I returned empty-handed, defeated.

Souad hesitated, then said softly:
'Actually, I have more than this.' She handed him the perfume bottle.

Gallimard received it as though it were a holy relic. He held it with both hands, staring at the liquid within before raising it slowly to his nose. He inhaled. His eyes widened.

'I can hardly believe it. This means there are vast fields of these flowers somewhere. Tell me where did you get this bottle?'

'It was a gift.'

'It must be from Madame Ahlam, isn't that right?' Souad's breath caught.
'Ahlam? You know Ahlam?'

'Yes—and how could I forget her? After I returned from Syria, having given up on ever finding the flower, a young woman your age came here. Beautiful, passionate, carrying a suitcase full of orchids. She offered me a generous sum to teach her how to extract the perfume from the flower. She stayed here until she learned.'

'But what's so special about it? Isn't it just another flower?'

No, it's truly unique. Its fragrance is a pure, singular essence, not a blend like other perfumes. It's more than just a scent though men enjoy the smell, it seeps into the woman's soul and flows through their blood cells, disrupting the very balance of their mind Just like Ahlam does; Occasionally, I dream of this orchid, and it turns into Ahlam. A woman like her… is unforgettable.

'Then you must know where she is now.'

'Unfortunately, no. After Ahlam perfected the perfume extraction, she left immediately. But before leaving, she gave me her address and said there were endless fields of this flower. She promised to take me there. Later, I discovered her name and address were false. There was no woman named Ahlam at that location, and no orchids anywhere nearby. I've never found her. For twenty years now, Ahlam and her flower have remained just a dream.'

'Couldn't you grow the flower in your lab using the seeds you had?'

'It's a rebellious, delicate, and difficult flower. I tried everything. All my cultivation attempts failed, and I lost all the seeds. I went back to Syria many times. I even met the scientist who discovered it and told him about Ahlam. We searched for her, and for the bull orchid.
Nothing. No trace of her. No trace of the flower. You have the second one

remaining' 'I'm happy to share this perfume with you, since it means so

much.'

'If I were you, I would keep it for myself and hide it from the world. Please… just tell me where you got it.'

'The bottle was a gift.' 'From whom?'

I don't know.

Monsieur Gallimard looked at her in surprise. "And the flower?"

Souad answered without hesitation: "From the metro station in Dubai."

Monsieur Gallimard laughed for a long time, then said, "You must be making fun of me."

Gallimard couldn't believe Souad's story about the source of the perfume and the flower. Nevertheless, he contented himself with taking the dried flower and a few drops of perfume. When we left the factory, Souad decided to travel immediately to Syria. I failed to dissuade her from this decision, and I made a great effort to convince her to stay the night.

The next morning, I took her to the train station. She called me from the airport that same day to tell me her plane would be taking off shortly for Damascus. I never heard from her again.

Chapter

Twenty-Three

I didn't wait long. After hearing Nicole's story, I traveled to Syria. It was clear that Souad no longer thought of anything but the flower and Ahlam, ignoring me and the rest of the world.

But where could Ahlam be?

Umm Tawfiq told me she had gone to Tartous on a business trip. "She arrived unexpectedly a few days ago, stayed only a few hours, and left quickly. She hasn't returned and hasn't called," she said, more upset than worried.

"Did she leave an address?"
"Yes, the Grand Tartous Hotel. I call her constantly, but she's always out. I don't know what's keeping her from contacting me."

"Let's call her now."

The hotel receptionist answered:

"She's not in her room. She hasn't returned yet. We'll let her know about your call as soon as she gets back."

Later, I called Salah and told him I was in Damascus. When we met, he was so agitated that he didn't even ask why I had come. He was radiant, clutching a rolled sheet of paper.

"Do you know what this is? You won't believe it. Finally—I got it. I have her picture. Ahlam's picture!"

"Really?"

"Maria is incredible. She's a gifted artist. She sent me the portrait online. It's her—the same Ahlam. Maria brought her back to life, after time had nearly erased her from my memory. I will never be able to thank that woman enough. Look."

"It's a beautiful portrait," I said. "And the woman herself is just as

beautiful." "Yes—that's Ahlam."

I studied the picture carefully.
"Don't you see a resemblance between her and Souad? The smile is the

same." "The hair, the eyes too. Where is Souad now?"

"In Tartous."

"What is she doing there?"
"Searching for Ahlam. She went to France last week for that very purpose, and there she found a clue that led her to Tartous," said Nicole, who had accompanied her.

"If she had waited for the portrait to appear, she would have spared herself all this trouble. I don't know how to repay you."

"She has become completely obsessed with Ahlam—and with the perfume. I'm planning to travel to Tartous tomorrow."

"We'll go together. I'm eager to see what she's discovered."

Chapter

Twenty-Four

The next day, we left early in Salah's car and drove straight to the Tartous Hotel. "Mrs. Souad isn't here," the receptionist said. "She never stayed at the hotel."

"What do you mean?" Salah asked sharply. "She gave us this address. I even called you, and you confirmed it. Isn't this the Tartous Hotel?"

"Yes, sir. She reserved a room—but she never checked in. She arrived, left in a hurry, and a taxi was waiting for her. That was a week ago."

"Where did she go?"

"I don't know. She never came back. But she left a bag—we put it in the safe."

The bag held only clothes. No note, no clue to where she'd gone. The whole thing unsettled me.

We circled the neighborhood, asking shopkeepers and restaurant owners if they'd seen her. No one had. At last we went to the police. They, too, had nothing. The chief tried to reassure us: "No news is good news it means nothing bad has been reported."

We checked into the same hotel, hoping for a miracle.

After midnight, I heard a soft knock at my door. My heart jumped Souad, I thought it was Souad. But it wasn't her. A tall, muscular man with a hard face stood outside.

"Are you Salah?" "No."

"Where is he?"

"In the next room."

He went and knocked. "Mr. Salah?" "Yes."

"Come with me."

"Who are you? What do you want?"

"Someone wants to see you. Come, and you'll find out." Then he turned to me. "You're Ahmed? You can come too. I'll wait for you downstairs."

Minutes later, we found him in the lobby. Outside, a black Mercedes with tinted windows idled by the curb. He opened the back door.

"Please. Get in."

We sat in the back. He took the wheel; another man sat beside him, smoking silently. Without turning around, the smoker said:

"How are you, Mr. Salah?"

"Who are you? What do you want from us?" Salah demanded. "Didn't we warn you to forget Ahlam's story?"

"So you're the ones who summoned me to the branch last week?" "Why

dig up the past?"

"What does it matter to you?"

"It matters to her. And to everyone close to her."

"I don't want to harm anyone. I only want to know who she is, where she is."

"But the harm is already done. Her picture is online. Her name is on

people's lips." "Is this about politics, Security, or intelligence?"

The two men exchanged a laugh.

"What do you really want from her?" "I just want to know who she is."

"And then?"

"I don't know."

"Fine. We'll give you what you want—if you promise to close this file once and for all. No publishing. No questions. Do you agree?"

Salah nodded. There was no other choice.

The car slipped out of Tartous, along the seafront, then turned onto a side road hugging the beach. After several kilometers, it stopped near a rocky stretch of coast.

The man got out. "Come. We'll walk on the beach."

We hesitated. He added, almost gently, "Don't be afraid."

We followed him up a hill, the rocks sharp beneath our shoes, until we reached a high ledge above the crashing waves. Spray burst into the night air. My stomach clenched; nothing could stop them from killing us and hurling us into the sea.

Then, from the distance, we saw her.

A woman stood on the rocks, gazing at the furious waves. She wore a long, flowing dress, her figure still and solemn against the storming sea.

We continued walking toward her. Her hair blew wildly in the wind, her face still hidden. I felt a spark of recognition and exclaimed, "Souad? Is that you?"

She turned toward us and pushed her hair from her face, revealing her features. She looked to be in her twenties. She smiled and said, "No, I'm not Souad."

Salah stood frozen, staring at her in astonishment. Then he whispered, "Ahlam? That's not possible."

The woman laughed. "I'm not Ahlam either."
"You're Ahlam. My eyes don't lie. But how could that be?" "You're Salah.

Uncle Salah."

"Uncle Salah?"

"You used to sing me 'Tick-tick-tick' Umm Suleiman when I was five. Do you

remember?" "Oh my God... you're Ahlam's daughter."

"Yes. I'm Hala, Ahlam's daughter."

She pointed at the man, and he quietly climbed down the rocks before walking away. The girl approached Salah and studied his face.

"Aren't you tired of looking for Ahlam?" "She's everything in my life."

"Do you love her that much?" "Where is she?"

She turned toward the sea. "There." "What do you mean?"

"You arrived too late, Mr. Salah."

Salah looked anxiously at the sea as the girl continued:

"I regret to inform you, but Ahlam is dead." "Dead?"

"Two years ago, she came to this rock, went into the water, and never came out. We found her clothes and her bag here. But she never reappeared; the sea swallowed her."

"Drowned?"

"Yes, unfortunately. Even though she was a skilled swimmer." "Do you

mean she committed suicide?"

"I don't know. No one knows. Her death remains a mystery."
"How could you not know? You're her daughter. You must have known her best—known her intentions."

"And you, who loved her—did you truly know her? Did anyone know what was going on in her mind? What lived inside her?"

He turned toward the sea, eyes fixed on the horizon.

"Searching for her consumed my life. It became a purpose in itself. How can I go on living without the hope of finding her? What should I do now? I've become addicted to the search. But who am I searching for now?"

He turned to Hala.

"Do you have any idea what Ahlam did to me? She changed the course of my life. I wish she had never answered that ad. Would you tell me about her—you knew her best."

My mother was a mystery. I can't claim I knew her well, but I can tell you what I do know. Her real name was Fawzia. That was the mother I knew—

the one I understood and loved. Ahlam was the other side of her, the unknown side. She brought pain to both herself and me. I'll tell you about her because I understand your suffering. Ask whatever you want to know. Where should I start?

"From the beginning."

Chapter

Twenty-five

Fawzia was an only child. Her mother died when she was ten, leaving her in the care of her father.

Hala took an old photo album from her handbag, opened it, and pointed to a picture.

"Here she is in her school uniform. They say she was an outstanding student bright, always at the top of her class."

Salah pointed to another picture

"Isn't that a photo of her in a bridal gown?" "Yes, it is."

"But she looks very young. Did she marry young?" "That was her first

marriage."

"Her first?"

"Yes. And it was tragic." "What do you mean?"

"My grandfather Fawzia's father was a timber merchant. He owned a large warehouse and a sawmill. He was financially secure. But one night, he received a call that the warehouses had caught fire. Everything was destroyed wood, equipment, all of it. No one knew what caused it, but it ruined him. He lost everything. Even selling the house wasn't enough to cover his debts. He was on the brink of prison. But Hajj Radwan, his friend—and one of the largest timber merchants—stepped in. He offered to pay off the debts and provide whatever money was needed to get back on his feet."

"That was generous." "It came with a price." "What price?" "Marriage to

Fawzia."

"Her father refused, didn't he?"

"At first, yes. The Hajj was fifty; Fawzia was only fifteen. She dreamed of being a doctor or a scientist."
"What was her response?"

"She was shocked when her father brought it up. He didn't force her, but there was no other way out. They had no options. So she agreed. But that wasn't the worst part. No one knew she had been madly in love with a young man from the neighborhood. They wrote letters and dreamed of marriage once he finished university. Fawzia kept it secret. She didn't say a word. She went into her room, lay down, and spent the entire day in silence no food, no drink, not a sound. The next morning, she emerged carrying a bundle of letters. She burned them in the stove, went to her father, kissed his hand, and told him she agreed to marry Hajj Radwan."

"That's heartbreaking."

Her father knew how deeply she loved him and what she was willing to sacrifice. But there was no other choice. The marriage took place.

From that day forward, people said she changed. She became distant, even from those closest to her. Over time, she withdrew, and the spark in her eyes faded.

"How was her relationship with her husband?"

Hajj Radwan wasn't an evil man he was respected and admired for his virtues. But he was utterly captivated by her beauty. Who wouldn't be? Every man who saw her was drawn to her. He treated her with kindness, showered her with gifts, and kept her apart from his first wife and children. In return, Fawzia showed him obedience and respect so much so that he grew suspicious. He began to think she was hiding something. He had the servants watch her, and he himself would burst into her room unexpectedly, only to find her praying or reading the Qur'an.

"Eventually, she wore the veil. She secluded herself, stopped visiting relatives, and lost all desire to leave the house. A few months after the wedding, her father died perhaps of guilt and sorrow, for watching the light drain from her."

"Couldn't she have asked for a divorce after his death? She didn't have to stay with Hajj Radwan."

"She could have, and Hajj Radwan most likely expected that. But she reassured him, *'I married you of my own free will. No one forced me. I am now yours, so you need not be jealous. When I chose to marry you, I gave you my life. I will remain loyal to you as long as I am your wife.'"*

"What a remarkable woman," Salah said in amazement. "I don't think Hajj Radwan ever dreamed of a wife like her."

"Her devotion only deepened his doubts. He couldn't comprehend the strange sincerity of such a young woman. He questioned her constantly, pressing her to reveal what she was
hiding. But her answer was always the same: *'I entered this marriage contract with you, and I will honor it faithfully.'*

"But that didn't convince him."

"What more did he want from her?"

"He wanted her to love him. It was true she had given him her body and her loyalty, but he sensed her heart remained closed."

"She must have suffered."

"She did—silently. She isolated herself, devoting her days to prayer,

reading, and drawing." "Drawing?"

"Yes. Drawing and reading helped her survive the long, empty hours. Hajj Radwan could find no fault in her; she met his moods with only kindness and forgiveness. Once, he asked her, *'Why are you so patient with me? Why don't you ever get angry when I mistreat you?'*

"Her answer astonished him: *'If I make you angry, I lose my chance at heaven. I want you always to be pleased with me.'*

Salah laughed. "What a strange idea."

"Yes, strange indeed. But instead of softening him, it made him more suspicious and jealous. He imagined she despised him, that she was only using him as a stepping stone to heaven— where she would be joined with another man. He told her angrily, *'That will never happen. You are mine in this world and the next. I will never abandon you, and you will never belong to anyone but me.'*

"This is the most unusual marriage I've ever heard of," Salah muttered.

"She fell into despair and frustration," Hala continued. "She neglected food and drink, living in a state almost like Sufi asceticism. But then something happened that changed everything.

"Two years into the marriage, Hajj Radwan fell gravely ill and was confined to bed. His condition was so severe that his first wife and children gave up hope. They neglected him, already planning for life after his death. They accused Fawzia of trying to seize his wealth. When they felt the end was near, they forced her to sign away all her inheritance rights.

"Fawzia, however, was indifferent. She gave up everything in exchange for being allowed to continue his treatment. She didn't abandon him—on the contrary, she served him tirelessly, bringing doctors, administering his medicine herself, caring for him day and night.

"Everyone was certain he would die. His wife and children even left to prepare for the
funeral. But thanks to Fawzia's stubborn devotion, Hajj Radwan recovered completely. And that was the turning point.

"From that day on, everything changed. She became the first lady of the house—pampered, unquestioned. He even allowed her to resume her studies. But a year later, he died suddenly of a heart attack."

"An eighteen-year-old widow," Salah murmured. "A beautiful widow, an

orphan, and alone."

"So you're not Hajj Radwan's daughter?" Hala smiled. "No."

She went on: "Fawzia had no one left. She left her husband's house and returned to her father's, giving up everything to his first wife."

"She gave it all up just like that?"

"Didn't I tell you she was extraordinary? She never cared for wealth. She said his wife and children deserved it more, and all she wanted was to be left in peace. They gave her what they considered her legal share a small sum and some neglected properties. She didn't care. What she truly wanted, she revealed only after she returned to her father's house."

"And what was that?"

"She wanted to reclaim her first love." "That was her right. But how?"

"She went to him." Salah laughed. "Bold."

"Nothing could stop my mother. She told him she was free now, that she still loved him. She expected warmth, eagerness. But she found a different man—cold, strict, harsh. He had graduated, risen to an important post, and received her with utter indifference. Her explanations meant nothing to him. She left his office in despair, moved to Beirut, and enrolled in the Faculty of Fine Arts at the American University."

"So, who is your father?"

"The same man she once loved."
"That means she kept pursuing him until she married him. She never gave up."

"It's not as you think. She didn't pursue him—it was a coincidence. He had become an intelligence officer with the Syrian Deterrent Forces in Lebanon. He met her by chance at the university. His heart seemed to stir again. He proposed, she accepted, and I was born."

"Luck finally smiled on her."

"I doubt she truly got what she wanted, or that luck ever smiled on her. My mother never knew peace or stability. Her thoughts were always restless and uneasy."

"How did she die?"

"One day, she left Damascus for Tartous. She often spent days there alone. But that time she never returned. After days of searching, they found her clothes and belongings on the beach rocks, on a stormy winter's day."

"My God… I can't imagine it. You don't believe she drowned by herself, do

you?" "No one knows. The sea was rough."

"But you said she was a skilled swimmer."

The sea, as you know, is never safe; you can't trust it. Did it betray her? Or perhaps did she willingly throw herself into its depths? I think that will remain a mystery.

Salah didn't respond. He remained silent, flipping through the pages of the album, his eyes wandering over her photographs.

'
"That was Fawzia," I said. "That was Ahlam. May God have mercy on her

soul."

Hala added,
"That was Fawzia's story. As for Ahlam—that's another story entirely. I
don't know much about it. I was little when I first heard that name. My
father and mother used to throw it around during their arguments."

"Do you know what's funny about this whole story?" Salah asked, deep in

thought.

"What?"
"The funny thing is... I never felt involved in it at any stage. When you were
telling me her story, I kept asking myself: Where do I fit in all of this? And it
gradually became clear to me—I didn't."

"What did you expect from her," I asked, "or from any woman, after only
one meeting, over twenty years ago?"

"Don't say *only* one meeting. It wasn't ordinary. It was a turning point in
my life. And I still believe it was for her, too. Something must have been
stopping her from contacting me. But now it's clear... I was never on her
mind. She was living her life normally without me, while I suffered every
day and searched for her. I lived with the hope of seeing her again,
imagining she'd be waiting for me to say reproachfully: *Why did you take
so long to find me?* Now, I see I've been living a lie. I built an entire life on
an illusion. I wish I'd never known the truth. I wish she'd remained a
beautiful dream in my mind—a dream I could shape as I pleased, to live my
happiness in."

Hala closed the album and put it back in her bag.
"I think it's time, Mr. Salah, for you to live your life realistically."

"It's too late for that. I'll never be able to remove her from my heart. I'm
addicted to her love. I don't know how to live without the hope of meeting
her again."

"We've all suffered from dreams. As much as I was proud to speak of
Fawzia, I was ashamed to speak of Ahlam. Do you think my father was
happy to marry her? I don't remember a meeting between them that

didn't end in a fight. I wish she had stayed Fawzia."

She slung her bag over her shoulder and gave us a farewell smile. "You can go back where you came from. The car is waiting for you."

Salah stepped toward her, looking deeply into her face. "Do you miss her?"

"She was my mother. When she was near, I wished she were like other mothers. I envied my friends with their calm, steady mothers. I couldn't find her when I needed advice. I always wondered—was she my mother, or was I hers? Now… I miss her foolishness, her mischief, her fun. I miss her madness."

She walked away. After a few steps, she turned to Salah. "I wish she'd met you first."
"Me too," he replied.

She disappeared into the distance. Salah stood there, staring into the darkness of the sea. Then he walked to the edge of the rock and watched the waves below.

The water in the sea, sweeping you away—waves upon waves. The seagulls in the air, following you—flocks upon flocks.
Your whims in my veins—beating, pulse upon pulse. The lust in your eyes burns me—poem after poem.

Chapter

Twenty-Six

We returned to the hotel. Salah was silent, troubled, with something heavy on his mind. As we headed to our rooms, I asked,

"What's wrong? What are you thinking about?"

"Do you believe she's dead?"

"Why wouldn't I? If her daughter says so? Why would she lie?" "I don't

want to believe it. I'm sure she didn't tell us everything."

"What more do you want?"

"Imagine—she left us without her address, without her father's name or

job." "And what does that matter to you?"

"They don't want us to search anymore. All they wanted was to make us stop—to get rid of us."

"I don't think so. The girl was clear: Ahlam is dead. You have to forget her and get your life back."

"I can't. She's still here—" he tapped his temple. "I feel she's still alive. I feel her around me. No, I don't believe she's dead."

"You must stop thinking about her. Please."

"My heart says otherwise. The perfume and the flower say otherwise." He

truly believed it, and I couldn't convince him. At last I said,
"As for me, all I want now is to find Souad."

The next morning, as soon as we woke, we went to the police station—only to return disappointed. Salah considered going back to Damascus since we had no leads, but I decided to stay.

Despite my anxiety and depression, I still held on to hope for a miracle. And I felt that miracle stir when I saw the receptionist hurrying toward me, smiling, holding out a small piece of paper. On it was a phone number.

"What is this?"

"It's the number of the driver who picked up Madame Souad. Maybe he knows something about her."
"Oh my God, how did you get it? Does he work for you?" "No, but he left

his number so we could call him." "Why?"

It seemed Madame Souad hadn't paid her fare when he dropped her off. He had come several times asking about her, and finally left his phone number in the hope that we would call him when she returned.

This was encouraging news. It renewed our hope.

I called the number immediately and spoke to the driver. I told him I was Souad's husband and that I was waiting at the hotel to pay him. The man didn't delay—he arrived about an hour later. He was around fifty years old.

He told us he had picked her up in Damascus and that she had first asked to go to a hotel, then requested that he take her to a village called Sarastan.

"Sarastan?"

"It's a small village near Tartous. She got out there and asked me to wait for her, but she disappeared and never returned."

"Why didn't you report her missing to the police?"

"I didn't think it was serious enough. I thought it was just fare evasion. It never occurred to me she might be in danger; there was nothing to suggest that."

I offered him money

"Would you take us back to where you dropped her off?" "Now?"

"Yes, now."

The driver glanced at the money and smiled. "Let's go."

The distance to Sarastan was short, but the road was harsh—mountainous, rugged, and narrow. We drove along winding passes that overlooked deep valleys, with forests and grassy meadows spreading on both sides, orchards scattered among them, and old houses clinging to the slopes. The village lay hidden in the folds of the mountains, veiled in fog. Clouds drifted lazily through its alleys and over the few scattered houses.

At the entrance of the village, the driver stopped; the car could go no further. The road ahead was nothing but dirt and stone.

"Here," he said. "She got out and asked me to wait. She walked toward the village until she disappeared. It was cold and stormy. I stayed for hours, but when she didn't return, I asked

around. The villagers denied seeing her. I was furious, especially when night fell and the cold became unbearable. At last, I drove back to the hotel, hoping to find her there. But she never came back."

Salah and I got out while the driver waited. We wandered through the fog, between houses with smoke rising from their chimneys. The scent of bread, wild thyme, and damp forest wood drifted on the breeze. Smoke and mist mingled with the salty breath of the sea, sending a sharp freshness through the air.

On a narrow lane, we met a group of elderly villagers walking together, laughing softly. They greeted us warmly, as though expecting us, and invited us to join them. They were dressed festively, heading to a celebration.

I took out Souad's photo and showed it to them. They passed it around indifferently, then handed it back. One of them finally asked:
"Was she looking for the flower?"

The question stunned me. "Yes," I said quickly.
"Then perhaps you'll find her there." "Where?"
"In the forest."

Soon we reached a wide square shaded by tall trees, the village's meeting place. A fire burned in the center, and tables were laid with food— tabbouleh, fresh bread, plates of appetizers. Children in new clothes darted between the tables, laughing. Men were stringing lights overhead while others arranged loudspeakers at the corners. The whole village seemed busy preparing for a wedding.

They invited us to a table.

An old woman sat beside me. I leaned closer. "What's the occasion?"
"A wedding tonight," she said, eyeing me curiously.

I showed her Souad's picture.
"She's my wife. She came here days ago. I've lost contact with her." "Was she looking for the flower?"
"Yes."
"Everyone is. I only hope she didn't enter the forest alone." "Why?"
"She could lose her way."

The forest clung to the mountain slope, overlooking a valley on one side and the sea on the other. Mist curled between the trees, their branches interlacing so thickly that in places sunlight barely touched the mossy ground.

"Do you think she went there?" Salah asked. "If she decided to, nothing would stop her."

A young girl nearby glanced at the photo. "I think I saw her," she said.
"When?" I asked, my pulse quickening.
"A few days ago. I believe she was heading toward the villa." "Which villa?"
She pointed uphill. "Follow the path. You won't miss it. There's only one."

I turned to Salah.
"What do you think?"
"I think we may finally be very close."

We promised the villagers we would return for the evening's celebration, then set off up the rocky mountain path. The cold air stung our faces. Ahead, a silhouette emerged from the mist—first a vague shadow, then slowly, the outline of an old villa.

"That must be it," Salah said. "But who would live here, so far from everything, in a forgotten place like this?"

The house revealed itself as we approached: enclosed by a stone wall topped with iron spikes, its heavy gate guarding a neglected garden. Branches tangled wildly, leaves decayed on the ground, and no smoke rose from the chimney. From outside, the whole place looked abandoned, yet faintly watchful.

The gate was unlocked. We pushed it open, its hinges groaning. We walked up the leaf-strewn path to the door. I knocked. Silence.
"Empty," Salah whispered, peering through a dusty pane. "Should we risk it?" "If Souad passed this way, I need to see inside."

The door yielded easily. We stepped into a circular hall with a marble floor and a high ceiling capped by a stained-glass dome. Colored light spilled through in fractured rays, painting the room in strange shifting hues.

The furniture was modest, faded with time—sofas with threadbare upholstery, a dining table with worn chairs. Ordinary enough. But the walls...

Every inch was covered with paintings.

"Whoever lived here was consumed by art," Salah murmured.
I gave a faint, uneasy smile. "By art… and by desire."

Nearly every canvas was erotic. Nude figures in languid repose, lovers entwined, women reading in the nude, dancers with bare breasts, and parted thighs. The work was exquisite, disturbingly vivid, as though the figures might at any moment breathe.

Salah froze before a painting—a semi-nude woman's face. "Oh my God."
"What?"
"It's Ahlam. That's Ahlam's face." And it was.

A voice rose behind us.
"Yes… That's the face you call Ahlam. But I prefer to call her Fawzia."

We turned.
A man stood in the doorway—average height, thinning hair, impeccably dressed. His gaze was sharp and unblinking.

Salah's voice trembled with shock. "You?" "You know him?" I asked.
"He's the one who detained me at the security center."

The stranger spoke with a cold, controlled edge.
"I told you to forget her. But you're stubborn. I even sent my daughter to

warn you." "Hala is your daughter? Are you Ahlam's husband?"

"Yes. I'm Riyad—Fawzia's husband, Hala's father. Why this persistence? Didn't Hala tell you she's dead? Why did you come here? Who led you to this place?"

"We're looking for my wife, Souad. I explained. Someone told us we might

find her here." "And why would she come here?"

"She was searching for Ahlam."

Riyad gave a short, bitter laugh. "She, too? What is it with all of you—men, women, everyone chasing her ghost?"

He gestured toward the paintings. "She painted them all. Every single one."

"But what is this place?"

"You could call it her refuge. She inherited the house from her first husband, Hajj Radwan, but kept it secret. I only discovered it by accident, going through her papers. This was her studio—her sanctuary."

"It feels like a hidden museum. Why keep it locked away?"

Riyad's eyes swept the walls. His voice hardened. "Because I want the world to forget her— and forget these paintings. More than once, I've thought of burning them. Sometimes I
believe she painted them to spite me." Salah whispered, "But she loved

you." "Loved me?" Riyad's lips twisted. "Yes. She told me herself."

Riyad chuckled bitterly. "How ironic." "Why?"

"She told you, her lover, that she loved me, her husband?" Silence. No one

dared answer.

"Yes... Perhaps she did, once. But it was never enough—for either of us. She wanted more than I could ever give, and I longed for something she could never offer. Her love exhausted me. Her exhibitions caused scandals, whispers of corruption, and immorality. Yet I stood by her, defended her, risked my career and reputation. And still she despised me—always smiling serenely, hiding a storm of anger inside. She was unreadable, unpredictable. In the end, I endured her illusions because she always returned."

Salah pressed, "But why did you abandon her when she came to you after Hajj Radwan's death?"

Riyad's voice broke, tinged with regret. "That was my greatest mistake. When she entered my office that day, I was overcome with fear. I didn't

recognize her—not because of the veil, but because she was lifeless, pale, drained of the fire I once knew. She wasn't the girl I had
dreamed of, the one I had desired. I felt only pity… and I sent her away. She never forgave me."

"But later, you did marry her."

"Yes, that was during the Israeli invasion in Beirut; our paths crossed unexpectedly. When I met her there, I realized how much I had messed up. It was shocking I never imagined seeing her behind a barricade in a Beirut suburb, armed and in a fighter's uniform. I was on a coordination mission with the Lebanese resistance, and she was there. She greeted me
warmly, and I could tell she was happy to see me. She looked more beautiful and energetic than I'd ever seen. My heart raced, and I immediately decided I had to bring her back. I asked her to return to me, apologized for my mistakes, and her response was extraordinary: she said if she survived the invasion, she would come back.

And she did.

"That means she forgave you."

"I don't think so. I don't think she ever forgot."

"But she came back to you. Doesn't that suggest she moved on?"

"Maybe. But she still didn't forgive me for my profession. She hated my security job. That was a red line I wouldn't let her cross."

"But you didn't leave her, though."

"I couldn't. The more she hated me, the more I loved her. We stayed like that for years. Being away from her may have been painful, but believe me, being close to her was even more painful. I had to forgive her recklessness and whims, and I couldn't abandon her."

"Then why did you divorce her?"

"I had no choice," Riyad approached one of the curtains covering a wall and forcefully pulled it aside. The curtain concealed a collection of photographs of a naked woman standing in a pool of water in a public park in a foreign country. The pictures showed people crowding around her, staring in astonishment, surrounded by photographers snapping away. The woman's features were blurred by colorful graffiti covering her face and entire body. The graffiti read: *Make love instead of war.*

"Oh my God, Salah said. I'd seen these photos dozens of times. Was it her—Ahlam?"

The whole world saw it. It was a stain on my party and diplomatic record—to imagine the wife of a diplomat in a foreign country walking like that. It made me suffer greatly. I endured ridicule, reprimands, and punishments from officials. The problem was they didn't
understand her. They didn't know that this was her naive way of rejecting the war. Some thought it was a ploy for fame. But they never understood it was childish behavior. They hurled every insult imaginable and called her the worst names—the mildest being that she was a whore. The authorities gave me one choice: Leave her

"Do you still love her, despite everything she's done to you?"

"Sometimes I think what she did was her only way to get rid of me." "I

believe she loved you in her own way."

Riyad laughed.

"Are you trying to make it easier for me? Do you think you're in a better position? At least I had her for years, while you couldn't keep her for more than a day. To love is one thing; to keep your beloved is another. She may have loved all her men, but she was mine, and despite everything, she always came back to me in the end."

"Her men? What do you mean?" Riyad laughed sarcastically.

"Do you really believe it's just you and me in her life? You're naive, so I don't blame you. I feel sorry for you and your miserable life. You should realize there are two kinds of women: the one man's women, and women like Ahlam."

He pointed at the paintings. "What do you see?"

Salah glanced over the paintings but didn't answer.

"I'll answer you, Riyad said men and women in scandalous sexual relationships. But if you look closely, you'll see that the women in all the paintings have one face the face of Ahlam. Did you notice that? As for the men, despite their large numbers, they don't have clear faces or defined features. Do you understand what I mean?"

Salah stood stunned amidst the nude photos and paintings of Ahlam. He turned away. "I'm confused. I'm not sure how I feel right now, and I don't know what to think."

"I told you to forget her and go your own way."

"But what about Souad? I said anxiously. Where could she be? The villagers saw her coming here."

"Maybe she went back where she came from."

Salah threw himself onto the couch in despair, his face reddening as he sank deep into thought. Riyad headed toward the exit, and before leaving, said:

"Close the door when you leave."

Salah stayed seated, gazing at the paintings. Then he asked me: "What do you think?"

"I think it's really over. You know everything about Ahlam. You have to move on with your life."

"Do you think he killed her?"

"What? What are you thinking? Don't forget he's her daughter's father.

And it's clear he loved her and still does."

He sighed in despair.

I can't forget her. The more I learn about her, the more mysterious she becomes.

"Don't make a goddess out of her. She's just an ordinary woman—an illusion. You have to forget her."

"I can still feel the softness of her skin under my fingers. I can feel her heartbeat in my chest."

"We have to go. The driver is waiting for us."

"Let me rest for a bit. I need to be with her for a while."

Salah closed his eyes. I let him doze off for a while and went out into the garden. The sun was nearly setting. I walked outside the wall and stood by the gate. The house overlooked both the village and the forest.

I could see the fog drifting down, penetrating the forest and hiding it from view. I stood there, watching the gradual arrival of night until only the lights of the village houses remained visible. The sounds of music and dabke drums began to reach me. I heard Salah calling me. He was standing in front of one of the walls, staring, transfixed, at a painting.

"Come quickly, have a look I can't believe what I'm seeing." "What is it?"

"Come quickly, I want to show you something."
He pointed at a painting. It was an oil portrait of Ahlam, reclining languidly on a couch. Her hair spilled over her chest, covering one bare breast. One leg stretched across the sofa, the other touched the floor. She rested one hand behind her head, gripping the armrest, while the other hung loose, holding an orchid that brushed the ground.

"Look closely. Do you see anything? Look at her hand." I leaned in but saw nothing unusual.
"The ring," he said, his voice trembling with excitement. "On her finger."

"So?"

"It's my ring the one I gave her, the one she gave back. She painted herself wearing it. Do you know what that means? It means she cared. That I wasn't just passing through her life, and she wasn't just a dream in mine. It proves we were real, not an illusion."

His words burned with longing:
I am the brush in your hand, painting nothing but my face. My smile covers all your canvases.
Whatever you paint an apple, a chair, a bird it will still be my shadow.
It will always be me.

I had no answer. Ahlam's story had drained me. I wanted only to find Souad. Exhausted, I lay down on the bed in the next room, and sleep claimed me as soon as my head touched the pillow.

I woke to the sound of rain tapping the window. The garden outside was slick and glistening, puddles pooling across the ground. From somewhere distant came the faint notes of wedding music. Salah was gone. I searched the house, but he was nowhere.

Where could he be in this storm?

I waited at the garden gate, in the pitch black. Dogs barked far off. A shape moved in the darkness Salah, rushing toward me, hair plastered with rain, clothes soaked and muddied. In his hands, he carried something.

"Where have you been?"

Panting, grinning with exhilaration, he held out a bundle. "I found them! We have to go— now!"

Orchids.

"Where did you get these? The forest?"

I took the flowers from him. He caught his breath, then whispered fiercely, "I found her. I found Ahlam."

I froze. "Ahlam is dead."

But he ignored me, too swept away. "And guess who was with her? Souad."

"Souad?" My voice cracked.

"Yes! They were together." "What? How?"

"I'm telling you, I saw them both. Ahlam is alive—alive like you and me."

"Where?"

"Come, I'll explain on the way."

He leaned close, his eyes blazing. "While you slept, I heard voices by the fence. I opened the door and saw her—Ahlam—trying to unbolt the gate. And Souad was with her."

"You're certain?"

"I swear it. There were other women too, probably leaving the wedding. But when they saw me, they panicked. They didn't recognize me. They didn't expect anyone inside. They turned back and ran. I chased them, calling Ahlam's name, but they slipped into the village. The rain was pouring. Chaos everywhere at the wedding. I searched the crowd until I saw them again running toward the forest. I followed. The trails were narrow and sick with mud, and the fog was swallowing everything. I kept going, and in the shadows, I could see them two women moving ahead, their laughter carried in whispers.

"And Souad?" I asked, almost breathless.

"They were whispering together. And yes—it was her. Souad."

"I hesitated to move forward—the ground was slippery. But then I smelled her perfume. I followed the scent, groping through the fog, pushing branches from my face. A silhouette appeared nearby. I called out for her to stop and reached out my hand. My fingers brushed against her shoulder, and I caught hold of the end of the scarf wrapped around her neck. She halted, panting, and turned toward me.

'Was it Ahlam?'

'Yes—Ahlam. She stood before me, breathless, then smiled, just as surprised as I was. Imagine that—after years of searching and despair, she was suddenly there. Despite the darkness, her eyes sparkled with happiness when they met mine. Then I heard the voice I had only dreamed of—the sweetest word, spoken with gentle surprise, a radiant smile on her lips: "Salah?"

She tried to say more, but the other woman seized her and pulled her away, vanishing into the mist among the trees. Their quick footsteps and faint laughter echoed as they retreated. Were they playing with me?

I stumbled after them, calling for her to wait. Branches lashed against me as I pressed forward until the fog lifted and I stumbled into a vast field of orchids. I searched desperately, but they were gone. Retracing my steps toward the forest, I lost my way, wandering blindly until the distant sound of wedding music guided me back toward the edge of the village."

'And Souad—was she with her?'

'I believe so. I'm almost sure the other woman was Souad. Look—these orchids are from that field.'

I eyed the flowers with hesitation, suspicion rising in me. He noticed and

asked anxiously, 'What's wrong? Why don't you look happy?'

'I am excited—but maybe that woman wasn't Ahlam. Perhaps it was someone else. Darkness and fog can play tricks on you.'

'I'm telling you—she spoke my name. She *was* Ahlam.'

Then he drew a scarf from his pocket and thrust it into my hands. 'Do

hallucinations wear French scarves?'

The fabric wasn't unfamiliar.

'Smell it—her perfume is still on it.' 'But this is Souad's scarf.'

'No, I took it from Ahlam's shoulder.' 'And Souad?'

'We'll find her too.'

By then, we had reached the forest entrance. Fog rolled heavily among the

trees. 'Do you think we can really find them?' I asked.

'If we don't find them, they'll find us. They must be searching for me as

well.' 'Wouldn't it be better to wait until morning?'

'Come. There's nothing to fear. Just follow me—and tread carefully.'

The forest began with towering oaks, their branches weaving a dense canopy that blotted out the sky. We pressed on, searching for a path through twisting, overgrown trails. The ground was slippery, thick with mud, leaves, and tangled plants. Dew and rain dripped from above, and the air was heavy with the scent of wet ground, herbs, and decay. A cold shiver ran through me. Fear lingered at the edges of every step."
Salah stopped and bent down, picking something from the ground. He turned and handed me a woman's shoe.

"Isn't this Souad's?" I stared, stunned.
"My God... yes. It's hers."

"You see now?" he said firmly. "I'm not hallucinating."

He pressed forward, clutching the shawl, while I followed, holding the shoe as if it were proof of everything we had just seen. The fog thickened as we went deeper into the forest. The branches above grew so dense that the sky vanished entirely. All I could see was Salah's shadow, a fleeting silhouette moving swiftly ahead of me.

The ground grew slicker, the mud clinging to my shoes. Branches tore at our clothes, scratching our faces and arms. Salah moved as though nothing could stop him, so quickly that I had to call out, begging him to slow down.

"We're almost there," he said, breathless with excitement. "How do you know? I can barely see anything."

"Can't you hear their voices?"

I strained my ears but caught only the rustle of leaves and the drip of water falling from above. Then—suddenly—he was gone. His shadow vanished into the fog. I called his name again and again, but silence pressed in around me, broken only by my own labored breath. Fear seized me, my body rigid, my voice trembling as I cried out for him.

Then, from behind me, his voice:
"I'm here. We're almost there. She's right in front of us. Follow me—hold

my hand." It felt like walking in a dream.

"Do you smell it?" he asked.

And yes—the air carried a faint perfume, drifting ahead of us. "They're

close. Just a few more steps."

Suddenly, a gunshot tore through the silence. The sound cracked against the trees, and I felt it whistle past me. From the distance, an all-too-familiar voice echoed, trembling with rage:

"Didn't I tell you to leave her alone?"
We ducked instinctively, pressing ourselves against the trunk of a tree. Salah gripped my hand tightly.

"It's Riyad," he whispered. "He's been following us." "Are you hurt?" I

asked.

"No. Stay quiet. He can't see us in this fog."

We crept forward carefully. Through the mist, a shadow flickered—close, too close. Then his voice again, lower this time, almost mournful:

"You should know—I am her first and greatest love."

A second shot rang out. Then the heavy thud of a body hitting the ground.
The silence that followed, was vast, suffocating, almost alive.

"My God," I whispered, shivering. "He… he shot himself." "Leave him,"

Salah said grimly. "We're almost there."

He pressed on with renewed urgency, dragging me with him. The fog began
to thin, and a warm breeze swept over us, heavy with the sweet fragrance
of orchids.

Then he stopped suddenly.
"Oh my God," he breathed, his voice breaking with joy. "We've arrived."

He threw his arms around me, trembling, almost laughing. "We've arrived."

"Where?" I asked, bewildered. "Come. Look."

The mist rolled back before us like a curtain being drawn. Below the slope lay
a vast plain, endless and green, blanketed with orchids that glistened in the
radiant sun. Warmth spread through my body, banishing the forest's chill.

In the distance, girls wandered among the flowers, filling their baskets,
their laughter rising like music. A small hut stood at the far edge of the
plain, a chair and a drawing board placed before it. And there—waving at
us stood Ahlam.

Salah turned to me, tears shining in his eyes. He cupped my face in his hands.
That's when I saw it is palms smeared with blood.

"My God," I whispered. "Where did this blood come from?"
I felt my body, but it wasn't mine. I looked at Salah blood poured from his
chest. "You're injured, Salah!"
"That's not important. We've finally reached our destination."

He smiled faintly and embraced me. "Thank you."
"For what?"
"If it weren't for you, I wouldn't have made it this far."

He gripped my hand tightly then collapsed. I tried to hold him, but my foot slipped at the edge of the slope. My balance gave way. I fell, tumbling down the grassy hillside, branches snapping beneath me as rocks and tree trunks battered my body. At last, I hit the ground.

Mud smeared my face, soaked my hair, clung to my torn clothes. Pain flared in my chest. I opened my eyes my cheek pressed to the ground, the smell of soil filling my nostrils.
Above me, I saw feet surrounding me. Girls' voices and whispers.

I had no strength left. My body felt numb. I tried to rise, but dizziness drowned me. Darkness swept in.

Chapter

Twenty-Seven

an you hear me? Do you remember what happened? I looked around in confusion. "What?"

"Thank God you're safe." The voice was calm, professional—a doctor's. He held my wrist, checking my pulse. "How are you feeling? Do you remember what happened?"

I tried to lift my head, but it felt heavy. My eyes roamed the room instead. A hospital. White walls. The smell of antiseptic.

"Yes," I said slowly. "I was in the forest. Where am I now?" "You're in the hospital."

Another voice asked, "Do you remember your name?" "My name is Ahmed. What happened?"
"You had an accident." "My ribs hurt."
"They're only bruised. You'll recover." I asked, "Who brought me here?"

From the corner, a familiar voice replied in accented Arabic: "The police and the ambulance."

"Ramesh? How did you get here?"

He chuckled. "Don't I have the right to check on your health? And make sure you'll still be able to pay my salary?"

I tried to laugh, but pain in my chest stopped me. The doctor left, and an Asian nurse entered. She checked my blood pressure, my temperature, and asked me in English about my condition. She asked me to move my fingers, reassured me, then left quietly.

I turned to Ramesh. "Where am I?" "I told you. In the hospital."
"No, I mean what brought you to Syria?"
"Syria?" He frowned. "What are you talking about? You're in Dubai. Rashid

Hospital." His words blurred in my mind. Dubai? But the forest, the mist,

Salah where was he?

I asked quickly, "And Salah? Is he alright?"
"Calm down. Don't talk too much. You'll be fine."

He didn't answer my question. Which meant Salah must be gravely injured or worse. I wanted to demand the truth, but exhaustion dragged me down.

"Close your eyes," Ramesh said gently. "Rest."

I obeyed. When I opened my eyes again, Nicole was standing beside him, smiling down at me.
"Nicole?"
She leaned close. "How are you feeling, dear?" "Fine."
"I was worried about you. I'll come tomorrow with some paperwork you need to sign." "What paperwork?"
"Don't worry now. Just rest."

She left. A nurse helped me out of bed and guided me to the bathroom. My chest ached with every step. I glanced at the mirror my beard had grown long. The reflection staring back at me looked like a stranger.

"Ramesh, why is my beard so long? How long have I been here?" "Since the accident—a week. You were unconscious."
"What accident?"
"The car, of course."
"What car?" I stared at him. "No, I fell down the hill."
He shook his head. "Fortunately, there wasn't a hill. The car lost control on Jebel Ali Road and flipped."

I pressed my hands against the sink, bewildered. My mind replayed only one memory: my body rolling down a forest slope, the ground, the mud, Salah's blood.

None of this made sense.

"I don't remember driving a car." "But that's what happened."

"On Jebel Ali Road?" "Yes."

"I wasn't even in Dubai. I was in Syria a week ago." "You've been in the

hospital for a week."

So I must have been in Syria a week ago.

"You haven't left Dubai for anywhere in a year."
"What's going on? Am I in another world, or am I under the influence of some drug?"

Ramesh kept looking puzzled

"And Souad? Where is she? Have they found her? Hasn't she called yet?

"Who is Souad?"

"My wife."

Ramesh didn't answer. He frowned, shrugged, and kept silent. He was hiding something. Dark thoughts pulled me in every direction. I grabbed his hand and squeezed it.

"What's wrong, Ramesh? Why won't you answer me? Where is Souad?"

"Calm down, Mr. Ahmed. You need to rest. Your mind is still clouded."

"What do you mean?"

"We'll talk later, when things have settled down."

I didn't let go of his hand. I held it tighter and pulled him closer.

"I want to talk now. Is she hurt, too? Where is she? Why hasn't she come

yet?" "Who are you talking about?"

"Souad—my wife."

"You're not married, Mr. Ahmed."

I stared at him in shock. His words didn't make sense. A wave of anger surged through me, especially when I saw the pity in his eyes—the look people give to someone they believe has lost his mind.

"Have I really gone mad? And what about Salah? He was with me. What happened to him? Was he shot?"

Ramesh smiled faintly. "There was no one else there. And there was no

shooting." "Strange... where did he disappear to?"

"There's no one named Salah," he said firmly.

"That's not true! You know him very well. Don't pretend you've forgotten." "Maybe," Ramesh muttered, shrugging, trying to stay polite to avoid my outburst.

"You *do* know him. Mr. Salah visited us at the office several times—you

even met him." Ramesh shook his head, lips pressed tight.

I grew impatient. "He asked you to write the 'Woman Wanted' ad for him. Don't you remember the ad?"

Ramesh smiled again. "Yes, I remember. But you were the one who wrote it, showed it to me, and asked me to post it online. We argued about it for a long time. I was against the idea, but you were so enthusiastic."

My voice trembled. "You're scaring me, Ramesh. What are you doing? Are you trying to drive me insane?"

Why was he denying everything? Why deny Souad? Why deny Salah? Could it be possible that they didn't exist at all? But if they didn't, then who had I been living with all this time?

"And Nicole? Is she an illusion too? She was here in the hospital, wasn't

she?" "Of course."

"She's French. She works for an insurance company. Isn't that right?"

"True."

"You see? My mind is sound. I'm not delusional. Nicole is Souad's friend— they traveled together to France."

"Nicole is your girlfriend," he said flatly. "You used to go out with her."

"Me? Nicole?"

Ramesh smiled knowingly. "Yes, Nicole. Don't you remember how she knocked on your door one evening, uninvited, and spent the night with you? Didn't you tell me afterward that her behavior was practically rape? You told me that yourself."

I shook my head violently. "That wasn't me—that happened to Salah! How could Nicole have stayed in my apartment when my wife was there?"

"You live alone in that apartment. Didn't I tell you? The shock is still clouding your memory."

"There's something wrong here. I was in Syria, in Tartous. I don't even know how I got here."

A sudden idea struck me. "Give me my phone. Is it here?" Ramesh opened the closet and handed it to me.

"I'll call Souad. I'll call Salah. You'll see I'm not crazy. I don't know why you're playing this game, but you'll see you're the wrong one."

I scrolled through my contacts—her name wasn't there. Neither was Salah's.

"Someone must have erased them—her name, his number... I don't understand. And what are these names? Selena, Mary Ann, Latifa? Who are these people? This isn't my phone. These aren't my contacts."

Ramesh laughed for a long time. "What's so funny?" I demanded.

"You really don't remember? You've forgotten Selena?" "Am I supposed to know them?"

"You knew them all. You went out with them. You took them to the Jebel Ali Hotel." "Me? That's impossible."

"You took all your girlfriends there." "No... you're talking about Salah, not me!"

That was as far as my mind could follow. I pressed my hands against my temples. "I have to get out of this hospital. I have to find out the truth myself."

"Tomorrow," Ramesh said calmly. "When Nicole comes to sign the insurance papers, you'll be free to leave."

"Then call her now. Tell her I'm fine and I want to go. Tell the doctor too."

"Why don't you stay one more day? I don't think you're ready. Wait until your mind clears…"
"I'd go crazy if I stayed here another day. I have to know what's going on with me."

About an hour later, the doctor and nurse came and ran the usual tests. I asked the doctor: "Is everything okay?"
"Yes."
"Then I want to get out of here."
"There are still some bruises, but you're free to leave tomorrow if you'd

like." "Yes, I want to".

I called Nicole to let her know that I planned to leave the hospital tomorrow. I asked her to bring the necessary paperwork for my discharge. Everything was arranged. After Ramesh left, I was alone again, replaying the events in the forest, scrutinizing every detail. Where had they taken Salah? Why was his existence being denied? And Souad had she only been a dream? Was I waking from a dream now, or still trapped inside one? Salah had been injured; he must be somewhere needing help. I touched the objects around me, running my fingers across their surfaces as if to test their reality. Were they real or would I wake to find them gone?

Nicole arrived after some time, accompanied by another employee from the insurance company. She sat in the chair opposite my bed. I studied her closely, trying to recall if what Ramesh claimed was true that I had slept with her. But no memory came. Nicole leaned forward, trying to kiss me on the lips. I gently pushed her back. She stepped away, embarrassed, a forced smile tugging at her mouth.

"How are you today?" she asked. "Fine."

She tilted her head, almost teasing. "Do you still remember who I am?"

"Nicole."

"That's good. So you've regained your memory. For a moment, I thought you didn't recognize me."

"Honestly, things are still confusing."

"As long as you remember me, you'll be fine."

She gestured toward the man beside her. "This is my colleague. He needs to ask you some questions about the accident."

"I don't remember anything about an accident," I said. "Don't you remember the car flipping over?"

"No."

"Don't you remember if someone was with you in the car?" "No… maybe my wife. I can't remember."

"Your wife?" Nicole laughed sharply. "But you're not married." "I am. Her name is Souad. We married last year."

At the sound of Souad's name, Nicole's expression shifted. She quickly masked it with another forced laugh, then leaned closer, whispering:

"Tell me honestly—was there a woman with you in the car?"

"I don't remember. I don't know. Your questions are driving me mad."

"There's no need to worry. It's just a routine procedure to close the case."

"Fine. What do you want to know?"

"The police report says that when they pulled you from the wreck, you were desperately asking about a woman, begging them to rescue her. But no one else was found in the car. You also asked for your bag."

"You're talking about Salah, not me."

"Who is Salah? Was someone named Salah with you?" "You know him. Don't deny it."

"No," Nicole said flatly. "I don't know anyone by that name. Should I?" "I don't know. I don't know anything anymore."

"Okay, okay—don't get upset."

She and her colleague whispered together. He clearly wasn't satisfied with my answers. After a short exchange, he left, leaving Nicole alone with me.

"Do you want me to help you leave the hospital tomorrow?" she asked.

"No need. Ramesh will take care of it."

"Fine," she said coolly. "I'll go then. It seems you can't wait to get rid of me. See you later." "Don't go, Miss Nicole."

"Miss Nicole? Why did you treat me like this?" "What do you mean?"

"As if I'm a stranger to you."

"Excuse me, but this is what I want to ask you about. Things are vague in my mind." "That's clear, but don't worry."

"I want to ask you, did we have a relationship?"

Nicole looked at me in surprise. "Do you really not remember anything?" I remember you perfectly, but I don't remember us having a relationship.

Nicole's face turned red, and her expression changed. I said to her, "Sorry if my question bothered you, but my memory isn't good enough."

"It's okay. What happened was that you invited me to spend a weekend at a hotel in Jebel Ali."

"Me and you?"

"Yes, anyway, that was several months ago."

"And Souad? You know her, right? She was your friend."

"I don't know anyone named Souad. May I ask who Souad is?" "She's my

wife. She's the girl I loved and married."

"If you married her, where is she now?"

"I don't know. The last thing I remember is that she traveled with you to

Grasse." "She traveled with me?"

"Yes, and then she disappeared."

"That never happened. I didn't travel with her. How could I have done that if I didn't know her? The events are jumbled up in your mind."

"If everything I remember didn't happen, where did the events and images in my mind come from? How can I remember events that didn't happen, and yet I don't remember spending a weekend with you at the hotel?"

"Your memory is confused, and you're imagining things hallucinations."
"They can't be hallucinations. The details are so precise they can't be hallucinations."

"I don't know what to tell you, but you need to relax a little. Don't push yourself too hard or be harsh on yourself. It's like when you wake up from a traumatic dream. The dream is so intense that it overshadows reality and takes over for a brief moment, but then it gradually fades away, and reality takes over again. You still haven't fully recovered from the shock.
Give yourself time to return to normal. To return to us—to the real world."

I had no choice but to force myself to accept what Nicole said, though every part of me resisted. I wandered the hospital corridors, weighed down by questions I couldn't answer. My thoughts kept circling back to Souad and Salah.

From my window, I could see the Maktoum Bridge stretching across Dubai Creek, the boats drifting along the water, the ferries gliding back and forth, and the towers glittering with lights that shimmered in the ripples below. I tried to stitch together the fragments of memory, but I no longer knew what belonged to reality and what belonged to a dream. The more I thought, the more I distrusted Nicole and Ramesh. They were hiding something and twisting something. But why? What interest did they have in deceiving me?

At dawn the nurse came in to check on me. I told her I was leaving today. When I opened the closet to gather my clothes, I froze. Inside were Salah's things—his white cotton pants and linen shirt, the outfit he wore the first time Souad and I met him at the mall, the same outfit he wore when he met Ahlam. His scent still clung to them, stirring something profound in me. Salah had been here. I was certain.

I asked the nurse whose clothes they were. She said they were mine—the clothes I had been wearing when I arrived at the hospital.
"That's impossible," I told her. "They're not mine." But she insisted.

To prove it, I put them on. They fit perfectly, as though tailored for me. I stared at my reflection in disbelief. Were they truly mine?

I pulled out my phone and scrolled through the contacts. No Souad. No Salah. Only Nicole, Ramesh, and a few old friends from Dubai, people I had known long before my marriage. My marriage was it just something my mind created? Still, Souad's face, her voice, the memory of Tartous and the forest in Sarstan—all of it stayed inside me, vivid and relentless. How can an illusion leave such strong traces?

I didn't wait for Ramesh to escort me. At 7:30 a.m. on September 16th just a week after the metro's grand opening I left on my own.

I took a taxi to City Center Mall and headed straight to the metro station. Souad and I had ridden this train so many times. As I stood on the platform, the announcement came. The train slid into the station, and the doors opened. For a moment, I hesitated, but the crowd pressed me forward until I was inside. Through the window, Dubai stretched out—its towers rising like challengers to the sky, the desert sun blazing, its rhythm utterly foreign to me. Yet in my chest lingered the smell of rain-soaked soil and the trees of the forest.

At every station stop, my heart skipped. Each time the doors opened, I half-expected Souad to step in, her short hair falling over her eyes.

At the Mall of the Emirates, I left the train and walked home. I slid my key into the lock, uncertain if the apartment was even mine. But the door opened. Inside, everything was as I remembered the living room, the bedroom, the wardrobe with only my clothes inside. No trace of Souad. No perfumes. No cosmetics.

But in the bathroom, I found it the sign that restored my faith in myself the mirror. The glass was gone, the frame still hanging on the wall, the floor scrubbed clean of shards. Souad had broken it. Proof she had been here.

I grabbed my phone and dialed Nicole.
"Souad is real," I told her. "She's been here. There are traces of her in the apartment." "What traces?" she asked.
"The mirror. The broken glass in the bathroom." "What about it?"
"Souad broke it."

Nicole fell silent.
"Did you hear me? This proves she's real, that she was here. Why don't you answer?"
"I never said Souad doesn't exist," Nicole replied at last. Her voice was calm, almost too calm. "She may exist somewhere. But she was never in your apartment. You live alone." "And the broken mirror?" I pressed. "I was with her when it shattered."

Another pause. Then Nicole asked quietly:
"Do you really not remember what happened?" I froze. "What happened?"

"I broke it." "What?"

"About two weeks ago, I came to your apartment unannounced. I was drunk and unbalanced.

How could you not remember that night? You jokingly told me repeatedly that I raped you that night. Excuse me, but that's the exact expression you used. It makes me laugh every time I remember it."

"And the broken mirror?"

You and I argued when I heard you mistaking me for Souad during the night. You kept saying her name instead of mine. This annoyed me, and I lost my temper. I went into the bathroom and hit the mirror with my hand. It broke, and I cut my hand. You personally took me to the hospital.

I was stunned when she told me this strange story. I angrily said,

"What is this fictional story? Souad was the one who broke the glass in the apartment. She was the one I took to the hospital."

Before she hung up, she said in a sad, reproachful voice, "The scars remain on my hand."

I stared into space for a while, the phone still pressed to my ear. Finally, I gave up and collapsed on the couch, exhausted by fatigue, anxiety, and confusion. I tried to calm my mind, but thoughts kept flooding in, throwing my nerves into chaos.

I left the apartment and decided to go to the office. There, many things might become clearer. I went down to the building's parking lot but couldn't find my car. Then I remembered they had said it was being repaired due to an accident. I walked to the Mall of the Emirates. On the way, I looked around at the buildings, streets, and cars nothing seemed out of the ordinary.

I entered the mall and wandered around before heading to the station, trying to relive some memories with Suad. It was still early in the morning; some shops hadn't opened yet. A few employees and workers were just arriving for work.

A woman walked past me, then overtook me quickly. She didn't look at me, yet I recognized her it was Maria. What brought her here? I followed her, trying to catch up. She must have sensed my presence because she quickened her pace. I continued after her, determined and stubborn. Each time she heard my footsteps drawing closer, she sped up until she reached a photography shop. She stopped, quickly opened the glass door, slipped inside, and closed it behind her.

I walked up to the door and tapped on the glass. She emerged from deeper inside the shop and stood far from the entrance. She looked angry, which surprised me.

"Hello, Maria." "What do you want?" she replied sharply.

"This is Ahmed. Do you remember me?" "I know who you are. What do you want? Didn't I tell you I don't want to see you??" I sent you a picture to your email."

I was relieved she recognized me "What picture?"

"The woman you asked me to draw."

 "I haven't checked my email; I was in the hospital "May I see the picture? I can't access my email now." She hesitated, then returned with a roll of photos behind glass, showing Ahlam—the same as Salah had shown me. "It's wonderful."

My compliment seemed to calm her. "Is it the same you sent to Salah?" I

asked. "Who is Salah?"

"How could you not know Salah? He gave you her description. Didn't we meet at the restaurant? Souad was with us—she's my wife."

"I don't know Salah or Souad. You gave me the details "How could I give

her description if I don't know her?"

"You said you lost track of her long ago and were searching for her. Now, please leave." She went inside again. I tapped the glass. "Why are you angry with me? I don't remember anything, and I had an accident."

"I told you I want nothing to do with you. Your attempts will fail. You're the last man I'd consider. Leave"

"I respect you and mean no harm. I'm sorry if I offended you. I truly don't remember anything."

"You're strange and persistent. What do you want now?" "I just want the original drawing." "I sold it to a perfume company for their ad campaign. It will be in the metro stations.
Goodbye, Mr. Ahmed."

I realized that my problem lay with people, not places. The places were sharp and undeniable in my memory, but the people were blurred, clouded by contradictions.

I boarded the train from the metro station and headed to Media City, where my office was located. Along the way, I deliberately scanned the station walls, searching for the advertisement, the perfume, and Suad—but found nothing.

I arrived at the office and found it closed; Ramesh hadn't arrived yet. The place immediately felt familiar, giving me a sense of belonging. I had expected to feel alienated, but instead, walking into the unchanged office restored some of my psychological balance.

I sat behind my desk. My papers, pens, and tools were all in their usual places. The computer was the same. I looked at it as though seeking help from an old friend one that knew me, kept my secrets, stored my data, and preserved fragments of my life in its memory. Here, I might find the key to my secrets, the light that could finally expose the shadows surrounding me.

I began checking the computer's contents the files and folders but there was nothing unusual, only projects and documents related to office work. I opened the browser and my email. There were many unopened messages. Then I noticed something strange: some were addressed to "Salah." That meant Salah was real, not a figment of my imagination as everyone claimed.

I searched for Souad's name but found no incoming or outgoing messages for her.

Ramesh entered carrying a bag. He was delighted to see me, set the bag on my desk, and hurried to the kitchen to make coffee, as usual.

From the kitchen, he called out,
"How's your memory? Still blurry? I was worried about you yesterday you were in terrible shape."

"I was, and still am, my friend. Many things remain vague and foggy. For example, why are some of these messages addressed to Salah, when he supposedly doesn't exist?"

Ramesh came over, glanced at the computer, then smiled.
"I never said he doesn't exist I just said I don't recognize him. As for your email, I don't read it, so I can't help you there. But it's a puzzling question why would his messages
come to your address? Couldn't it be that you're the one using that name in some of your correspondence?"

"I don't know."

I looked at the bag. "What is this?". He set the coffee cup in front of

me. "It's your bag." "My bag?" I examined it and immediately recognized it.

"No, it's Salah's bag."

Ramesh smiled. "They took it out of the car. It's locked. It has a three-digit lock. I hope you still remember it."

I looked at the lock. Only one number came to mind: three nines. I entered the three nines, and it opened.

"See? It is your bag." Ramesh said in a triumphant tone,

Inside were office papers and a gift box wrapped in a red ribbon. I took the box and turned it over.

"It's a gift."

"What's inside? Ramesh asked curiously.
"I don't know, but I can guess, it's a bottle of perfume."

I opened the box. Inside was a bottle of "Three Nines." I uncapped it, and the scent of orchids drifted out. It was the same perfume — Ahlam's. Tucked inside was a small card that read: *Our appointment is 9/9/9 at nine o'clock. The scent of the perfume will bring you to me. Ahlam.*

"Ahlam? Ramesh read the card. - It's the metro opening time. You must have been on your way to meet her when the accident happened."

I wondered in astonishment: "Ahlam and I? How could I date Ahlam?" I put

the bottle back and continued searching my computer.

"What about Souad? Is it possible that she's nowhere to be found on my

computer?" Did you check your incoming and outgoing messages?

"Yes. There's no sign of her."

"Look for her in the photo folders. You might find a picture of her, though I doubt it."

I opened the photo folder and began examining it. A folder named *Sarstan* contained photos of me with someone, holding an orchid. I found a special folder for *the Kama Sutra* — photos similar to the paintings Ahlam had.in Sarstan

"Look at the Kama Sutra photos."
Ramesh glanced at them. "You still keep these photos?"

"Yes, I still remember our discussion. I wonder what made us mention the subject?"

"It was Ahlam, the online friend you were corresponding with. She was interested in the subject and was thinking of going to India to study it more closely. Don't you remember that?

"Ahlam was my online friend? She sent me the perfume?"

I kept searching through different folders. Finally, I found a file named

"Private, Syria". I opened it, and there was the surprise.

"Ramesh, come and see. I told you I wasn't crazy. Here's Souad".

These were photos of me and Suad at my grandfather's house. She was in her school clothes
— in the garden, by the fireplace, under the trees, laughing and trying to walk straight. There weren't many pictures, but they were enough to restore my self-confidence and make my heart beat for Souad again.
"See, Ramesh? This is Souad."

Ramesh looked at the pictures carefully and meticulously. Then he shook his head and shoulders.

"I've never seen her in my life. Is she the girl you want to marry?"

"She's the girl I already married. You know her, you've met her many times, and she used to come here all the time."

"Sorry, Mr. Ahmed. But the truth is, I haven't seen her or met her." I looked

at him suspiciously. He spoke with confidence.
why would he deny it? He hadn't seen her or met her, and neither had Nicole.

I thought for a moment. A strange question crossed my mind — one that

made me shiver. Listen, Ramesh, is it possible that…?

"That what?

"That I haven't married Souad?

THE FINAL CHAPTER

I am a fragment of an immense riddle—a lone shard among countless, scattered, endless pieces. Together, we are meant to weave the breathtaking tapestry of existence. Yet I am the mischief-maker; that is my nature. Something in me is awry. My form does not fit, my pattern resists the whole. My very genes are strange, and the puzzle rejects me, casting me aside. So I wander, searching for a hidden crevice where I might belong. But existence itself grows restless, for it cannot be whole without me. And that, in itself, is yet another riddle.

I picked up my phone. I searched through the numbers and found "Farid France." What should I tell him? Is it reasonable to ask him if I married his sister? What if he asks me about Souad? Should I tell him that she disappeared? How should I explain that to him?

I hesitated, but finally, I dialed the number. I waited. His voice spoke in French. I said to him in Arabic:

"Hello, Farid. I'm Ahmed. How are you?"

"Ahmed? Hi, how are you? And how are you doing?" "I'm fine."

" I miss you very much. What reminded you of me? . Not long ago, I was in

Damascus, my sister Souad and I spoke of you. Do you remember Souad?"

"Of course, I remember her. That's why I'm calling you. It's a subject that concerns her and me. Can you manage to meet me in Damascus?"

The picture had not yet cleared completely in my mind. But what filled me with joy as I carried my bag was that I was going to Damascus to Souad. I did not want anyone to drive me to the airport. I took the metro to Dubai Airport.

Nicole asked me in a sad voice: "Where are you going?"
I replied joyfully,
"I've found her. I've found Souad. I'm going to her."
She did not comment, and a silence settled between us, broken only by the sound of her breathing. Then she hung up.

I drifted into my thoughts, watching people get on and off the train, stations passing one after another until the announcement came that we had reached the last stop, and the train began to slow down.

We arrived at the airport. The carriage door slid open, and I was taken aback by what I saw: a picture of Ahlam holding the perfume bottle, covered the wall opposite the train door.

The station was suddenly empty. I stepped out of the train and walked toward the passenger hall, dragging my suitcase behind me. I passed by the cafeteria it wasn't unfamiliar to me. Its tables and chairs felt known: a traveler dozing on one of the seats, a family chatting together, two men reading newspapers over their tea.

And there, in the corner I knew so well, sat a lone woman with her hair cascading down, wearing a white blouse and a tight skirt, her legs crossed gracefully like a princess. She held a coffee cup in one hand, and before her sat another cup. She looked at me and smiled. My heart skipped a beat at that smile it was Ahlam.

Ahlam, in all her beauty, femininity, and mystery, looked at me with the magic of her radiant, gleaming eyes.
She was only a few steps away, waiting for me.

A deep sadness welled up inside me. I wanted to ask her: *What is your secret? What are you made of?*

Her whisper came to me through the stillness of the station:
"I am made of almonds and honey, of the dreams of youth, of the beats of your heart and the threads of your desires."

I stopped, gazing at her my eyes locked on hers, her smile carving itself into my heart. In her gaze was a silent, insistent invitation.

The loudspeaker announced my flight. I stepped forward hesitantly, still staring at her… She remained in her seat, waiting.

A lump rose in my throat, and a tear slipped from my eye. I couldn't lift my gaze from her, but I kept moving forward without stopping. Her lips curved into a smile a farewell smile as she watched me walk away, her fingers playing with the other cup. My cup.

"I am the one you've been waiting for, the one you've been searching for. I possess the qualities you asked for. I am Ahlam."
I kept looking back until she disappeared.

You and I a drifting drop of the cosmos…
a rose petal wandering through space at dawn, Scattering longing, yearning, and a mysterious desire, An embrace that ignited the sun so the moon smiled.

Yes, we were there, you and I, far away in time, before humankind.

I stayed at my grandfather's house, the same house where I had once brought Souad on a cold winter's day. The garden was in a pitiful state, the ground strewn with dry branches and yellow leaves. I hadn't set foot inside since that day. Even the living room remained untouched, still bearing traces of us: blankets on the floor, the charcoal stove in the middle of the room, and beside the fireplace her drink, long dried, yet still in its place.

I headed straight to Souad's house. I knocked eagerly, heart racing, but it was Farid who opened the door. He greeted me warmly and told me she wasn't there.
"We'll have to surprise her in Tartous. She's with my mother." "Tartous?

What are they doing there?"
"After the exams, my mother always takes her to rest. Come with us—it's a beautiful, magical place. We'll have fun."

We set off for Tartous. I was amazed. I remembered making this very trip once with Salah and now here I was again, retracing the same road, this time with Farid.

"It's an old house in a small village called Sarstan," Farid explained. "A beautiful spot with an enchanting forest, almost untouched by sunlight because of how dense the trees are."

About ten kilometers before Tartous, the car veered onto a side road toward the village. The road twisted through mountains, valleys rising and falling on both sides, until we reached a narrow dirt path.
"That's as far as the car goes," Farid said. "We'll have to continue on foot."

Ahead lay a small village, its houses and people barely discernible. We walked through its streets, exchanged greetings with passersby, then followed a winding path up toward a secluded house. A chill of fear swept over me it was the same road I had walked before, in what had felt like a dream.

At last, we reached the house. My heart pounded as I stood beside Farid while he knocked and rang the bell at the same time. From within, we heard Umm Tawfiq's voice rushing toward the door. She opened it, her face alight with joy.

"Farid? What a surprise!" She embraced him tightly, then noticed me.
"I brought a dear guest," Farid said.

"Ahmed? How wonderful. What a surprise! Come in."

Farid carried his bag inside and asked, "Where's Souad?" "In her room."

She turned quickly to fetch her.

We stepped into the living room a wide, circular hall beneath a stained-glass ceiling. Then Souad came running.

I looked at her with all the longing of the years behind me. Yes, it was her the girl I had waited for outside the school gates.

She froze in disbelief.

"Aren't you going to greet your brother?" Farid teased, laughing. He pulled her into his arms, but her eyes stayed locked on me, stunned, over his shoulder.

Farid picked up his bag, took his mother's hand, and said, "Come on, let's put this in my
room. There's something important I want to tell you." They disappeared, leaving us alone.

Souad stood before me, a tear trembling in her eye but refusing to fall. I drew her gently into my arms, pressing her against my chest.

"I missed you."

She said nothing, only laid her head on my shoulder and wrapped her arms around my neck.

"I can't believe you're here," she whispered. "I thought I'd never see you again. Where were you? Where did you vanish to?"

"I was on a long journey. A hard one. But I'm back. I know you must hate

me." Her voice broke. "I can't hate you. I never could."

I searched her eyes. "Did you wait for me at the school gate that day?"

"That day, and every day."

"And will you wait for me tomorrow?"

She nodded. "Tomorrow and every day." My eyes burned. "Will your

clothes be wet?"

A faint smile touched her trembling lips as she wiped her nose with the back of her hand. "Yes. And you'll have to chase away the fly from my chest."

"If you only knew how much I've searched for you." "I searched for you too.

It's been hard."

"What have you been doing all this time?" "I was drawing."

I looked at her in surprise. "You draw?" "Yes."

"What did you draw?" "Come and see."

She took my hand and led me to her room, pushing the door wide open.

"Look."

I froze in a mixture of wonder and dread at the sight before me. On the wall hung a large oil painting Souad herself, lying languidly on a couch. Her hair cascaded over her chest, veiling one bare breast. One leg stretched across the sofa, the other draped down to the floor. One hand gripped the armrest, while the other holding an orchid dangled limply until it touched the ground.

The End
Mahmoud Farra

www.ingramcontent.com/pod-product-compliance
Lightning Source LLC
Chambersburg PA
CBHW070438300726
48975CB00007B/1970